THE SURVIVORS BOOK TWO
NEW THREAT

BY

NATHAN HYSTAD

Cover art: Tom Edwards Design

Edited by: Scarlett R Algee

ISBN-13: 978-1986866743

ISBN-10: 1986866742

Also By Nathan Hystad

The Survivors Series

The Event

New Threat

New World

The Ancients

The Theos

Red Creek

ONE

I could hear him coming from the main level, his nails click-clacking on the hardwood floors. It was his morning routine: step on my chest, lick my face, sniff Mary, and then hop down off the bed. I think he checked the back door, then the front, then a quick peek through the window. He was seeing if his previous owner, Susan, was there. She wasn't.

I felt his pain. It was the same pain most of the world was feeling, after half of us hadn't survived the *Event*. We all opened doors expecting to see someone we knew, only to see their bedroom empty. I had to stop myself at least twice a week from dialing my mom's phone number, and that wasn't an easy revelation to live with. The pain of loss was widespread, but the whole thing had left humanity stronger than they'd been in a long time; maybe ever.

Mary rolled over and rested her head on my chest. "You know we don't have to go today," she said, nuzzling in closer.

"I think we should. Plus, it'll be good to see Magnus and Natalia again." I stopped, and Mary turned and looked me in the eyes.

"What is it?" she asked.

"I actually think it's time to move on. I can't live here anymore. Not after all that's happened, and I know it

1

must be a little weird for you to be here too." Even though I'd changed the furniture when Janine had died, I knew deep down the whole scenario wasn't ideal for either of us.

"Dean, it's okay. It's not like we've lived permanently in any of these places over the last year. At least the house has more room than my condo in Washington, and Carey seems to be happier here. But I think he'd be happy wherever we take him," she said with a smile. On cue, the spaniel hopped on the stool at the end of the bed and catapulted onto my stomach.

"Okay, Carey, what do you say? Want to come to New York with us today?" I asked the now-rolling-around dog.

"I think that means yes," she answered for him.

Less than two hours later, we were loading the truck with our bags, for the second time in a month. It would be nice to settle in somewhere, but we had to figure out just what we wanted to do. The economy still didn't know what it was doing, and the world powers were contemplating a global currency. There were so many empty properties now, and some estates had nowhere to go, whole families gone at the same time.

Looking around the living room, I slowly closed the door, breathing out, somehow feeling like this was the last time I'd see my house. If I'd learned anything over the past twelve months, it was to trust my gut. I locked up and glanced toward the truck. Mary was in the passenger seat with Carey sitting beside her. They were both looking at me, and Mary gave me a soft smile. Her smile managed to make me feel like a teenager again. There was a warmness I'd never known from a woman before, and I couldn't help but feel like we were meant to meet and stop the invasion. It made us strong. It connected us forever.

Soon we were heading down the road, passing the church down the street, driving down the road I'd seen James getting almost beat up on, the day *they* arrived. It felt like yesterday at times, and like a decade ago at other times.

Stories had come out of the horrors from the cube ships. At the time, we hadn't given it a lot of thought, but it made sense later. Once everyone realised they were on ships going God knew where, the trouble began. There were stories of fights, murder, riots, and rape. No one was safe from the events, and it made humanity take a good look in the mirror. There were countless survivors with stories to tell, and thousands of people were arrested afterwards. It was another gray area with no proof and no trials. There were a lot of lawyers and people smelling profit, but the government didn't allow this.

Their process seemed to have worked, and the arrested were left on an island, fenced off from the world. It was either that or shoot them back into space, all in a transport vessel like they'd done their atrocities on. Everyone knew there must be some innocents among them, and guilty among us, but it was the best they could do at the time.

Safety was imperative after the hell everyone had been through.

My hometown was almost a ghost town. Most people had left for the big city, and over half of the town had died up *there*. Being a bedroom community, we had a lot of elderly; they were the first people to go, with no water, and as the illnesses spread like wildfire, only twenty percent of people over seventy survived the journey. Things had changed on Earth.

We cruised down the highway, and for a moment, it

felt like a weekend drive to the city. But it seemed, nowadays, it was never just a drive to somewhere. There was always an underlying tension to life. While I was thankful to be alive and have people around me again, we all knew there was life out *there*, and *they* weren't our friends. It was like a constant buzz in your ear... knowing. We knew a lot more about them, thanks to Mae. Half human, half Kraski. We just called them hybrids, which Mae claimed to not find offensive.

"Honey, what do you think they want to see us for?" I asked for at least the third time since they'd called Mary.

"Still not sure. But I'm hoping it's to give us a mansion on an island to retire to," she quipped.

"Well, if we're going there with Magnus and Nat, I hope we don't have to share a house with them too."

We neared the city, and I saw the large area of fields filled with cars. All around the world, there were similar areas. Once everything had settled, the cleanup began. One of the most trying things had been clearing the empty cars off the roadways. If they weren't claimed, they were towed into fields, where mobile crushers would eventually come and recycle the materials. The world was in a state of flux, and it was doubtful everything would be straightened out for years to come.

"It'll be good to see Mae too. I hear they're doing some amazing things, tech-wise. I guess there have been some dramatic medical advances just from the computers on the ships." I could see Mary look at me from my peripheral vision. I still had this nagging suspicion she was a little jealous of the fact that Mae was the spitting image of my dead wife, but she had never acted strange about it, and she and Mae had become fast friends.

"I heard, and I doubt they're even leaking half of what's really going on. Top secret. But I have a feeling your charm can get us the inside scoop when we get to D.C.," I said with a wink.

"We'll see. If I can be honest, I want to see what kind of reverse engineering they've done with the Kraski ships we have. I mean, this could really shrink our universe," Mary said, a twinkle in her eye.

"I'm happy with a small universe… a tiny one, in fact. One that just involves the east coast: you, me, and this pup here."

In a quick thirty minutes, we arrived in the Upper West Side. As we passed the museum, I thought back to the moment I saw the ship above the truck, and Ray running at me. I'd forgiven him a long time ago for what he did. Vanessa had convinced him to turn the Shield off, and he thought he could save his family for it. We were no worse for wear, but Ray was dead, and his family would never see him again. We never told anyone what happened that day. It was thought he was killed by the Kraski, and I intended it to stay that way.

Even though it was New York on a weekend, I still found a parking spot on West Central Park. It would have blown my mind a year ago. Now the vacant streets just made me remember all we'd been through. We got out of the truck and soon we were taking a nice walk through the park, and it felt great. Carey pulled at his leash, sniffing everything he could along the way.

"What if we just got a place here? A condo on the park?" I gazed back at the beautiful buildings to the west of us, peeking at us from above the trees. "We can walk Carey, go for runs in the park… see a show every now and then." I tried hard to sell it.

I wasn't sure what Mary would say, but she just smiled at me and held my hand. "I think that's the perfect idea."

"So do I," I said, and we walked the rest of the way in near silence, just enjoying ourselves.

The Boathouse was coming up quickly, and I could spot Magnus' red hair from a way away. He came trotting toward us, and Carey growled a bit as he saw a shape rushing at us. When he saw who it was, he turned into a wiggling mess.

"Dean! Mary!" He grabbed Mary and squeezed her, spinning around. "How have you two been?"

"Buddy. We talk every couple days," I said, laughing at his excitement.

"I know, but we haven't seen you guys in weeks," he said, motioning to Natalia coming down the sidewalk toward us.

Mary waved to her, and I saw Nat's eyes light up just a little bit. She was a closed-off person, and even though she had started to talk again during the events of last year, she still said few words, at least in public.

"Hi, Nat," I said, and gave her a light hug. She smiled and hugged Mary. Before we knew it, we were sitting on the patio by the little lake by the Boathouse, watching a few couples idly paddle by in rented canoes.

Mae walked in as we were finishing our meals. I had a flashback to the night I'd seen Janine here for the first time, eight years earlier. My throat closed up a bit, and I pushed aside the feelings and memory. So much had changed since then.

"Sorry I'm late. We had something come up last night," she said, sitting down at the table. We cleared a spot for her, and after waving the waiter over, she ordered a latte. "I can't get over the luxuries of Earth. We were used to protein slop up there." She pointed to the sky and my stomach tightened.

"What happened?" Mary asked.

"You know how our group is still under surveillance, right? Well, a couple of the ones I had marked as potential dissidents have been meeting secretly. Of course, they have no idea the government is watching them. They're tired of being confined out on Long Island, but most of us understand the concern. We were piloting your people to their deaths."

"Most of us know you guys were doing what you thought was best. And almost all of you have been more than amiable since arriving on Earth. Sharing knowledge and being productive members of New Earth." Magnus said this, and the name some people had been giving our planet sent shivers down my spine. If anything, this was still old Earth. Perhaps half-Earth. That might have been more fitting. The planet was still the same; it was the people that had changed.

"Well, we've been keeping an eye on them, and last night the mics picked up a name. Not one anyone on this planet wants to hear about. The *Bhlat*." She said the last in a hushed tone, and we were all leaning in around the table. Damn. We'd learned a lot about the race from Mae and the other hybrids, but it still seemed like only a little.

"The Bhlat? Why would they be sneaking around discussing that?" I blurted, and the answer came to me before the words were out of my mouth.

"It seems to be the game these days. The Deltra infiltrated the Kraski, and the Kraski hybrids like us. It seems only fitting that somehow the Bhlat had gotten to someone on the Kraski before they evacuated their planet." Mae stopped and looked at each of us before continuing. "If you thought the Kraski were bad news, you were wrong. They were just low-level compared to these guys. Sure, they took the Deltra and treated them like slaves, but they kept most of them alive. The Kraski only decided to kill all of humanity near the end. Those transport vessels were supposed to bring their people with them. That was, until the Bhlat came and destroyed them."

We knew this story, but it still drew us in: a huge intergalactic war we were now a part of.

"If these guys find out where Earth is, it's only a matter of time," Mae said.

"Do you think there's any way to prevent it?" Magnus asked, chest puffing out a bit.

"I hope so. I'm starting to like this world."

TWO

The trip to Washington went by fast. Mae rode with us, and Carey sat in the back with her. She had started off cautious of the animal, but had quickly warmed to him, and now they were old friends. Carey rested his head on her lap as we raced down the interstate to the capital city.

I drove to the Capitol building. The sun shone bright in the sky, and for a moment, I thought I saw something. Was it a ship? Then my panic subsided as I recognized the shape. It was an airplane. Flights had begun six months after the Event, and though most of them were still commissioned flights by world powers, they were becoming more and more common to see.

As we approached the Capitol, I was in awe of the beauty of it. There was something about classic architecture that appealed to me. Domes and pillars. They were a sign of strength.

We stopped at a security booth and we all showed our passes to the guard at the gate. He frowned the whole time and gave me a double look before heading into his little booth. He made us wait good five or so minutes, before grunting that we could go on through.

"Nice guy," I said sarcastically.

"We've all been through a lot. Try to not judge anyone too harshly," Mary said, setting her hand on top of my right thigh. For a tough Air Force vet, she had a heart of gold and an awareness of other people that continued to inspire me to be better.

"Sorry, honey. You're right."

Standing by the front doors, we waited for Magnus and Natalia, who appeared to be having an argument with the same security guard in the parking lot.

When they got to the entrance, Magnus was still red, and Natalia was laughing at him.

"Don't ask," he muttered, and we entered. I'd been there many times, but the sight of the work put into it blew me away each time. A quiet, spectacled man greeted us and led us through the rotunda, and instead of making our way to one of the massive halls, we headed back into the library. The smell of old books, leather, and wood wafted to me and I wanted to stop and sit on one of the chairs, to relax with one of the ancient bound history volumes.

Instead, we were guided to a back door; the man guiding us unlocked it. Armed guards were at either side of the room, and they watched us with either interest or duty. Through it we went down a spiral staircase that was dimly lit by some ancient-looking wall sconces. I had a feeling we were heading somewhere few were allowed to see. Mary was behind me and she put a hand on my shoulder, giving me what felt like a reassuring squeeze. I turned back to her and lifted my eyebrow: a "what is going on here?" look.

"Dean, maybe we finally got invited to the Senate's cigar club." Magnus gave me a nudge with his elbow as we reached the basement level.

"This way," the guide said, leading us down a long hall lit by the same sconces. It gave the hallway an ominous feel, and I felt like this was going to be more than a casual "thanks again for saving the world" meeting.

"I have a bad feeling about this," Natalia said quietly.

"Yeah, me too," Mary replied, holding Carey's leash as he looked around, sniffing everything he could get his nose on.

We were led through a mahogany double door and entered a room with a few people milling around a large table. I spotted the interim president, Patrice Dalhousie. Since the previous one hadn't made it, nor had the vice president, someone had to fill the spot. There was talk of another election, but the polls showed everyone was happy with the way she was running things. A proper balance of philanthropy and economic stimulus, at least in my eyes.

The president noticed us and waved us over to the large table. She was a striking woman of middle years, jet-black hair in a conservative ponytail for the meeting.

"Welcome." She smiled widely, and if I didn't know better, she was genuinely happy to see us. She gestured to the empty chairs. "Please, have a seat."

The other people around the room stopped their conversations and came, taking seats on the far side of the table.

"Would anyone care for refreshments? Coffee, tea?" she asked. I found myself taking an early liking to her. Where someone else might expect someone to do their simple tasks for them, she started pouring us coffees and passed the cream and sugar over to Magnus.

I sat down, sandwiched between Mary and Natalia. Magnus and Mae finished the group off to our right. I held my cup of coffee in my hand, waiting to see why we were here. I glanced at the rest of the group and thought some of them might be familiar, but I wasn't sure. There was a man in uniform; a lot of medals hung from his breast. Before I could guess who they all were, Dalhousie stood up. The room was silent as she took in a breath.

"We have to talk about the threat at hand. We asked you five to come for your insight. You are the saviors of our race. We owe you so much. Everything. It's because of your efforts that we're here today. First off, we want to make sure you have everything you need. If there is something you're lacking, let me know and I'll personally take care of it if I have to."

"One of the others left behind might have saved you," I said, unsure why I felt the urge to say anything.

She shook her head, and a few others did as well. "I don't think so. We were hours at most from driving into the sun. It was all on you."

Over the course of the year, we'd found out there were eleven others left on Earth. Their stories were close to the same as ours, and they were from all over the world. Clusters from Africa, Australia, and even two from Canada. The closer the hybrid to the Shield, the more effect it would have on their health. The ones who tried to land in the southern US, or South America, died in weeks, sometimes. Turned out the ones from Canada were only a day and a half behind us. They arrived to find the Shield gone, and a few alien corpses. I tried to imagine how crazy that must have felt, and how gut-wrenching. They wouldn't have known what happened or if anyone had succeeded. They found out a week later as the massive black vessels broke atmosphere and lowered to the Earth once again.

"Thank you for your generosity, Madame President," Mary said.

"Please, call me Patty," she replied. "Allow me to introduce everyone. On my left is General Joshua Heart. Beside him we have Jeff Dinkle, our head of White House Communications, a position formerly know as

Press Secretary." The man nodded at us, and I realized where I knew him. He had a talk show on one of the major news networks, where it wasn't unheard of for him to discuss extra-terrestrials, or outer space in general. Not the farmers' fields and drunken farmer interviews, but more of an intellectual, theoretical discussion-type show. There were a few sleepless nights a few years ago where I could recall being bleary-eyed and watching his show, thinking it unlikely we weren't alone. Boy, was I wrong.

"Across from you is Allana Lockley, and her partner in crime, Harry Middleton. I'll spare you the old-world titles they would have had within the government. They are our resident physics wizards, and finally, we have Clare LeBlanc and Trent Breton, engineers like none other," Patty said, smiling wide.

It was an odd mix of people for us to be meeting with.

"You're probably wishing I'd just get on with it." She waited, and when no one replied, she continued. "We're creating something of an Earth Defense Unit. We have delegates from around the world coming this week to convene and figure out a plan. The world will soon have a unified government. The one thing this *Event* has done is take down borders. Crime is down, we have space for everyone, war is almost non-existent, and we're going to work as one to build a stronger world. One we're going to protect with our lives."

Magnus and Natalia were nodding, being sucked in by her words. I was getting a small knot in my stomach as she spoke, and Mary squeezed my hand.

"What does this have to do with us?" Mary asked.

"We need your help." There it was, the favor, as if we hadn't done enough for them yet.

"What exactly do you need from us?" I asked.

"We just want you to be on the team. The defense team. You four did something so amazing, and it showed strength, resolve, tenacity, and intelligence. Mae, you helped convince the others to save us, and continue to lead your kind. Perhaps sooner rather than later, we can have them intermingling with the rest of the world, rather than caged like they are. We're sorry for the way it has to be now." Patty looked sympathetic as she spoke.

Mae's eyes glistened a little as she took it all in and responded. "We actually understand, and if I can be honest, appreciate the treatment. Most of us were ready to die and kill your kind just because we were trained to do it. We may not have thought it was right, but most of them are good people, and do want to be members of society. I can't say that all of them are cooperating, but we're keeping tabs on them."

I drained the rest of my now-cooling coffee and set the cup down, the noise a little jarring in the pin-drop quiet room.

The man who'd guided us down here walked over from his spot by the door, and slid a panel on the wall, revealing a large flat screen. He touched it on the lower left side and a video loaded.

"What you're about to see is what we've been working on for the last year. If we're going to have a shot at defending ourselves, we have to be prepared," Patty said, voice climbing as she spoke.

The video started playing and the camera showed a shot from the ground, probably filmed with a military vehicle driving. It was of a massive desert landscape, possibly in Arizona or New Mexico, or maybe even somewhere else in the world. As they moved along, we got sight of a huge building. It was hard to tell the actual size of it from this perspective, but I was guessing at least five hundred thousand square feet. Beside it was one of the gargantuan transport vessels. It sat on the ground, juxtaposition to the light sand, a black monolith looking out of place on our world. I thought back to the first time we'd encountered one of them in space, some way away from the sun. That's where we met Mae… after killing all her counterparts. I had a lot of blood on my hands and wondered if there was any way I could decline whatever position they were going to ask me to fill. I knew I could never go back to being an accountant after all of this, but… I could be something else. I'd had enough of killing, that much I knew.

They got closer, and as they stopped, a vehicle akin to a large golf cart came to greet them. The camera showed the president and General Heart getting off the Humvee, with Harry and Clare in the cart. They loaded up into the unit and large bay doors slid open. Inside the building hovered one of the gray ships we'd flown in. The Kraski ships were there. Beside them were some black ships, similar in design.

"It turns out there were a dozen of these vessels in all the transport units," she said, the camera showing them all lined up inside the huge open room.

"What are those?" Magnus asked, pointing at the black ships on the right side of the screen.

Patty smiled. "Those are prototypes. You see, the team here has reverse engineered some of the technology we found. It was quite amazing. I'll let Clare describe it a little better."

Clare stood up, her face turning a light shade of red before she started speaking. I wasn't sure if she was nervous or just excited. "The things we found were quite remarkable. First off, you flew these ships." She nodded to Mary and Natalia. "You know how amazing it was to fly something that doesn't lurch or toss you around as it speeds up or slows down. These inertial dampeners, as we call them for a lack of a better term, are quite impressive. We learned how to simulate it and have tested it in our own units. After a few faulty runs, and a couple banged-up test pilots, we have it down to a tee.

"We've added tracking into each new ship, and" – the screen shot switched to a man putting on a suit, much like the ones I'd worn into space, only it appeared these fit humans — "the suits have been perfected. They have built-in communicators, and with the data from the ships' computers we found, built-in translators too. We've tested them with the Kraski records, and the Deltra we had, and they work like a charm." Clare smiled widely, proud of everything they'd accomplished.

"That's pretty cool," I said quietly. I, along with a couple others at that table, had experience with those Kraski suits, and imagined they would be much better-fitted to our bodies. I still didn't want to be one of the people testing an air-tight suit in space for the first time. It was scary enough using one of them when I'd had no choice at all.

"To what end?" Mary asked. "Why are we doing all of this?"

The president turned to her. "They'll be coming for us. We know that. We have to be ready for it. We'll need ships, suits, communication…" She paused. "We'll need weapons."

My skin crawled and, for a moment, I thought I could feel the hybrid blood pulse through my veins, the transfusion they gave me to save my life still reminding me it happened. My back tensed then too; I tried to calm down and loosen my tight spine. Ever since that day, getting shot up by a hybrid that looked just like Mary's dead husband, I got daily reminders of that moment. I always seemed to notice my back was just a little off when I thought about the *Event*; otherwise, I usually felt normal. Unfortunately for me, I thought about it a lot.

The video switched scenes, and it cut to large metallic gun-shaped devices in the field near the base. Large targets were on display in the distance. Had to be a few hundred feet away. The sound was silent; then we could hear a light whine. Before we knew it, the noise was constant and a red light widened like a sphere around the weapon shaft. One instant, it was there humming; the next, the shaft was gray again and a target far in the distance exploded.

"So, we have some badass guns. Good." This from Magnus, my large red-haired friend. A smile crossed his face, and I couldn't help but smile back at him being excited by this. The ex-mercenary was always hoping to blow stuff up.

"We have other things in the works too. Things the Bhlat can't know about. My apologies about not showing them to you now." She looked around the room, catching everyone in the eyes. "We have to be one hundred percent sure word won't reach them. Sure, we're in a safe room, but we can't show all our cards quite yet."

Mae's upper lip twitched a tiny bit, probably indiscernible to anyone else. I knew she wouldn't hold it against the president, but she was still probably assuming the mole threat was her, since she was the only off-Earther there.

"Mae," the president said, turning her attention to her, "we need you out in Long Island. We think there are some bad apples out there, and we can't have that. The Bhlat name has been uttered on our surveillance a few times, and we need to know who's saying that name, and who they're saying it to. We also detected a couple odd transmissions leave the area, and we have no idea where they came from or what kind of message was sent. I know most of them trust you. It might be tough to track down, but can you do this as your first task as a member of the Earth Defense?" She said it in an odd mixture of authority and hopefulness. I knew what Mae would say.

"Of course," she said.

"We can go with you, Mae," Mary said, reaching over and squeezing my hand.

THREE

The bar was my favorite kind. Lots of wood everywhere, and cold micro-brewed beer on tap. Carey joined us and the bartender almost told us "no pets," until he recognized who we were. He didn't say anything about it, just brought over a bowl with fresh water in it, and a piece of sausage. He quickly became Carey's best friend. I looked around and thought about how much Ray would have probably loved it here too. My heart twinged at the memory of him.

"Earth Defense Unit. Who comes up with these names?" Magnus took a pull from his beer, spilling a little bit as he set the pint glass down with a fling of his arm. "It just sounds so ridiculous."

Mary nodded but didn't say anything, and I could tell she was deep in thought about the whole thing. She was probably leaning toward telling them no to the position, and I was leaning so far over, I almost tipped on my face.

"I don't know, I think it's fitting." This from Mae.

"That's because you aren't from around these parts, m'lady. On Earth, it sounds like something out of a bad video game," Magnus quipped.

"It doesn't really matter what they call it. It's probably necessary to have. But if they really want to honor us for saving the world, they might want to do it another way than shoving ships and guns in our hands," I said, hoping

I was on the same page as the rest of them.

Everyone was quiet for a moment, until Magnus barked out a laugh. "Dean, you're something else. I'm with you one hundred percent. But what if? 'What if' has been playing an earworm in my head for weeks now. What if they're right? What if these alien bastards are making their way here? The Kraski did it. Hell, the Deltra led them here in a centuries-long game. That means for hundreds of years, they've known about our world. That doesn't bode well for us, my compadre."

"So what would you have us do, Mag?" Mary asked, speaking for the first time since we'd left the Capitol building.

"I say we suit up, join this EDU, stop Earth from being invaded, and then kick back and retire on a beach with a stockpile of cigars and Canadian whisky." He smiled widely, and I couldn't help but get swept up in his enthusiasm.

"I'm in." This from Natalia. Her eyes shone bright and she smiled at Magnus.

"I have nowhere else to go. We have a job to do," Mae said. I knew she was probably hesitant to become a spy on her own for the humans, but she did seem to want to be helpful, and not only that, we all liked her a lot.

That was three in. I looked to Mary, who grabbed her beer, held it high and said, "Why the hell not? I'm in if you are, Dean."

How could I say no, then? It was determined for me right at that moment. I was going to stay in the fight, be a part of the Earth Defense.

"I'm a little young for retirement. I'm in." We all clinked glasses and drank deeply.

We had more than a few beers, followed by some food and a few more, knowing that the next day reality would sink in once again. We let loose, hit a dingy karaoke bar, and sang bad songs until way too early in the morning.

My head swam from the alcohol as we lay on the hotel bed, the three of us exhausted from a long day and an even longer night. I couldn't help but feel like we were making the wrong choice.

"*D*ean, we'd better get up. We have to catch the train to New York in a few hours." I heard Mary talking, but my head pounded and I couldn't see her, considering my eyes were closed and I had half the bed's blankets over my face. I pulled them down, squinting against the sunlight creeping through the blinds. The clock at the nightstand read nine AM.

Carey stretched at the foot of the bed, making a grumpy noise. He would be tired after all the beer-spilled floors he'd had to trudge through. I suddenly felt like a horrible pet owner. I'd make it up to him with a nice walk before the train ride.

"Long Island by this evening, then we go out to this secret area where the ships are being held," I said, and Mary nodded. She looked no worse for the wear, and though she must have felt as bad as I did, she didn't show it. I could tell she'd already showered and was surprised that I hadn't even noticed her getting out of bed.

"I wonder how they keep that place a secret. I mean, did you see the size of that building, and the black transport vessels? They must have a no-fly zone or something over it." Mary was packing her things up, and I knew it was time for me to get my slow-moving body out of bed.

I thought of the black cubes that had come down that ominous day. An omen of a new era for Earth. Then I could see them in space, some turning around, some burning up in the sun's intense heat. Millions of lives snuffed out in an instant. Just like the Kraskis' lives. They had come to our planet to rid themselves of us first, but it was a weight Magnus, Mary, and I would have to live with forever. The genocide of a race. I could feel my pulse racing and my head spinning. Over the past year, I'd thought about it many times, but never let myself dwell on it. There was too much going on, and I knew nothing could change what we'd done. I also knew that none of us would change bringing that Shield onto their ship. We'd done what we had to do.

Part of me still wondered if diplomacy could have worked. Was there any way we could have had a parlay with their leaders and made some sort of arrangement? Could we have all lived in peace: the Kraski, Deltra, and humans? Judging by the fact that they were all so eager to destroy each other, I doubted it. Still… the chance that it might have worked still lingered in the back of my mind, and it might always linger there.

I looked over at Mary after a too-long moment of silence and could tell she'd been thinking about the cubes as well. About the Kraski and the Deltra.

"We still have the hybrids. We can still try to stop these Bhlat from destroying us." The idea of us having to help save the world again seemed ridiculous to me. Weren't there more qualified people out there than a widow, widower, bodybuilder turned mercenary, and a former kidnapped mute woman?

She just smiled at me, a smile that crinkled her eyes just the right amount to feel the love emanating from her face. My heart melted, and the hangover suddenly felt less oppressive.

"Dean, meet Carey and me at the café down the street in twenty," she said, reaching for his leash. Carey hopped off the bed and rolled around on the carpet.

A half-hour later, I rolled my luggage into the elevator and held the door as I heard someone call out. A prim middle-aged woman entered, bringing a waft of expensive perfume with her. She passed me without a glance.

"Lobby?" I asked, and she turned to me. A moment later, her jaw fell, and she blinked a couple times.

"Dean Parker?" she asked, her voice a squeak. I didn't have any idea who she was.

"That's me. I'm sorry, I don't think we've met."

"Of course we haven't, but I know you. Everyone does. I was on thirteen." She meant the number that later had been assigned to every transport vessel. There were books being written about each of the vessels, and what they'd endured. I wasn't sure I could ever read them, knowing every delay I'd had on my journey had amounted to more deaths out there in space.

Something clicked in my head as I looked at her. "Wait. You're Katherine Adams. I've heard the stories."

She had the decency to blush, and that was something I didn't expect from this woman.

"Yes. I'm tickled pink that you of all people would have an inkling of who I am. I just want to thank you for everything you did."

"The way I hear it, you deserve a lot of accolades. You saved lives up there. You created a medical center and a police force, and helped so many people." I wasn't exaggerating. She was the real deal. Thirteen was a real inspiration, and once all the vessels had turned around and headed back for Earth, a lot of her ideas were implemented on the other ships. She was a hero.

The elevator chimed and the doors opened to the lobby. I once again stuck my arm out to hold the door as she went by, purse slung over her shoulder. She looked just like a woman on the way to a club in the Hamptons, and I couldn't help but feel inferior for a moment.

"None of it would have meant anything if you and your friends hadn't saved us all. We are forever in your debt." She stepped in and gave me a hug. Not one I would have expected, rather a close, firm hug that you'd save for a loved one you hadn't seen in a long time. I returned it with the same vigor, and I realized we had all been through so much. We each had a story now, one that we all shared, and this made us all closer.

We stood there in lobby, embracing like old friends for what probably was too long, and when we separated, she wiped a tear away with her hand. My heavy heart lifted at that moment. I knew we could rise above everything that had happened, and anything that would come against us.

She moved back as if noticing she might have overstepped some social boundary, but I put her at ease with a gentle smile that meant it was as much my hug as hers. "I'm really glad we got to meet," I said, reaching for my luggage.

"Dean, if you're ever in the area or just want to talk about anything, get in touch." She pulled a business card out of her purse, and I flipped it in my fingers, rotating it to read the text. *Survivor Support Family*, it said in blue lettering across the white backdrop. Her name, email, and cell phone number were on there. It said "Founder" under her name. As if this woman hadn't done enough, she was behind an international support group for anyone who needed it after all that had happened. I wanted to hug her again. At the same time, I felt shame for my own lack of effort over the past year. Just because I'd helped then didn't mean I shouldn't help what we'd salvaged.

"I will. I just know Mary would love to talk to you," I said, meaning it, and she lit up. We parted ways, and I couldn't help but feel an extra motivation for the next few days.

The walk was brief; only a few people walked around the streets that would once have been as busy as any in North America. Now it was almost empty, a shell of what it used to be. Things like corporations looking to appease shareholders almost ceased to exist, as did the stock exchange, but I knew it was only a matter of time before corporate greed and selfishness once again took hold, choking out the needy and separating the classes as always. If I was going to protect this world, I wanted to make sure the president was going to keep the world on track. I had never considered myself anything but a capitalist, but things had changed, and we needed to adapt.

I heard a bark, and right away knew it was my little buddy Carey. I used my free hand to wave to Mary, and she gave me the sweetest smile in return. I really loved that woman. Going through what we had together not only made us stronger as people, but we were so tightly bonded I worried what would happen to either of us if…something happened to the other.

I couldn't go through it again.

"Hey, bud." I heard Magnus' voice boom at me from across the street, and Natalia waved over at us. They looked around and started to cross the street toward me when a police cruiser raced down the street, sirens blaring and cherries flashing. He pulled Natalia back just in time, as another car sped down the otherwise quiet road. Her luggage wasn't as lucky. It lay flattened as another half dozen police cars passed over it, soon followed by a couple of ambulances.

When the commotion was over, I turned to see Carey and Mary beside me.

"What's their rush?" she asked.

Magnus was now in the middle of the street yelling at the convoy of emergency vehicles, and Nat was dragging her bag to us on the sidewalk.

"Good thing I didn't pack my favorite pants," she joked, eyes conveying her humor. It was so nice to see her making wisecracks, considering the first few days I'd known her, she was hard and mute.

"The sirens are still loud, so they can't be far from here. Let's check it out, it might be coming from the White House," I said, looking down the way and almost seeing the White House grounds. I'd almost forgotten we were only a half-mile from there.

We made our way down the road, the street getting busier with people as we approached the gated greenspace. There was a large group at the front gates, a man talking passionately into a bullhorn. Carey sidled up to my feet as we stopped, not liking the noise or the crowds. I knelt and petted him, scratching him on the ear, and assured him everything was okay.

"What do you think this is all about?" Mary asked our group.

Magnus shrugged. "Since the beginning of time, people have been gathering in town squares to complain about things. Why should that change now?"

We moved a little closer and could see the gates were closed. I tried to guess at the ever-growing crowd, and put it at around a thousand, but more were streaming in all the time. Someone had let the people of the city know there was something of interest going on, and I didn't like the feeling the crowd was giving me. Finally, I saw some signs being thrust into the sky with angry vigor. *Don't forget the Event! Down with Dalhousie! Genocide is never okay!* That last one stung me, and my breathing picked up. It was public knowledge that the Kraski had been destroyed, though the details of exactly how remained blurry. My name had been tossed around, of course, and I'd been asked for months by reporters and people on the street about my take on it. I refused to comment. Not because I felt regret for doing it, but because they would never understand that I had to do it. I didn't have a choice. It was humans or Kraski. I chose my people, and it was something I would have to live with for the rest of my life. I was at peace with it.

Mary must have seen it too, because she reached over and touched my arm. I smiled at her briefly and tossed a look at Magnus. He was there with me. We turned the Shield on together, killing the last of a race. A bond from something so big, we would always be connected by it. He looked back, his lips pressed tightly together. He gave me a quick wink, like it was no big deal, and I really liked that about him.

"Hey, guys, check out that one," Magnus said, pointing at a large green sign. *Uranus or bust.* At least some people still had a sense of humor.

As we moved through the people, I finally saw the man speaking into the horn. He was on a homemade wooden pedestal so everyone could see him. He wore his hair in a man-bun, and I could see the passion for what he was saying burn out through his eyes. He was an intense man.

"...Dalhousie is just like the rest of them, and maybe even worse. She brings with her the open air of concern and caring, but then gives preferential treatment to the elite, and if you break down her platform, she's bringing the USA into a communist state!" he yelled into the speaker, and was cheered on by most of those around him.

I nudged up to Magnus and spoke just loud enough for him to hear through the crowd noise. "I don't like the feel of this. Keep an eye out for a weapon. Our people are on edge these days, and this is just the kind of scene where someone will be pushed to do something they normally wouldn't. And if they have the crowd behind them, it could get ugly."

"I hear you, brother." He gestured to his ankle, and I saw his pant leg was just a little more pushed out on that side. He was carrying. Probably not technically legal in the new D.C., but he was, after all, appointed to the Earth Defense Unit by the president herself. It made me wish I was carrying something too, all of a sudden. If he was, that guaranteed Natalia was too.

Mary pointed past the people. An entourage was coming from the White House. Soon I made out the dark hair of the president as she was flanked by numerous Secret Service agents. We were about thirty feet from her, but I could see her unease at having to deal with this. If I had to guess, she was advised to let them be and ignore the protesters. From my short interactions with her, I could tell she was passionate and thought her cause was just. She would do anything to have buy-in from the masses, and probably thought talking to them here would help do that. Looking around at the angry people, I wasn't so sure.

She stopped and a podium was dropped off by a van, with a built-in microphone and speaker. Her voice came through crisp and clear in opposition to the guy's cheap hand-held horn.

"Good morning, everyone. Times are changed now, and I'm not one of your old leaders. I want this to be a time of peace among all of us. We have to work together to accomplish this. The reality is, we have more to worry about than squabbles amongst ourselves. We must look to the skies and defend our home. To do this, we need to be a solid, cohesive planet," she said, pausing as everyone had turned their attention to her.

"Then why is my brother locked up? He didn't do anything up there. I know it." The man turned to her as he spoke. Now his anger was coming a little clearer.

"We have dealt with the crimes during the days of the Event the best we could. Many people were hurt, raped, killed… I don't know what you brother did, but we're confident in our system. While it wasn't one hundred percent effective, we had no choice but to punish those who harmed others during that strenuous time. What happened to us all gave no one the right to hurt another person. If anything, it gave the world an opportunity to help those in need, and many people did rise to the occasion." Dalhousie was nailing it.

The man fidgeted from side to side, and he got closer to the gate, moving off his box. "You're wrong. You're wrong about everything." He was only about fifteen feet from her now, and I could see the Secret Service guys tensing. Magnus had moved around and reached for his ankle. With no one else noticing, he'd slid his gun from his ankle to his belt on his back. Nat moved the other way, and they were on opposite sides of the guy. A shot fired, only it came from behind us, not from the bullhorn guy. Dalhousie was being brought down by her guards, and Magnus tackled the man at the gate. Another shot rang out, and Mary took off, leaving me with Carey. The crowd was on the ground very quickly, Mae and I among them. Twenty yards away, on top of a black van, was the shooter. I saw a pylon go flying toward him, and then Mary was climbing the hood of the van, rushing at him like a bull at a red cape.

Finally, I shook off the shock and passed Carey's leash to Mae, running to the back of the van. He landed hard on the ground, and his rifle went flying. The van started to move, the driver evidently not wanting to get caught alongside the shooter. I was on the gun in a heartbeat, and Mary was jumping off the speeding van, rolling as she hit the ground. Holding the rifle at the man's chest, I walked backward to make sure Mary was okay.

She was on her feet in moments, rubbing dust off her pants. "Thanks for the backup, Dean." She smiled hard at me. By then, the Secret Service were all around us, one holding a gun at the two of us. I turned the rifle around and held it out butt first.

"I'll be your backup anytime, if you want to take the climbing and jumping role," I said, suddenly wishing we'd never made the trip to D.C.

FOUR

Dalhousie looked frazzled. The crowd had dispersed, rather than cause any problems. They had all been through a lot, and maybe the gunshots had been a reminder of their mortality. They'd all seen enough death. We stood in a quiet part of the White House not ever open to the public.

The bullhorn guy had been shot. The van had gotten away, but the surveillance cameras should have picked up some details. The shooter was in the next room, and so far, hadn't said anything to the Secret Service agents.

"So why the hell did they shoot him? Were they just that bad at aiming?" the president asked.

I'd thought about it, and since we didn't know anything about the shooter, or really the victim, we could only speculate.

"It could be they were trying to pin it on you guys. Someone spoke out, and the government swept in and shot them. Could be just enough of a spark to create a fire in the world today. I have to think there are groups out there who want trouble, so they can profit from chaos," I said, probably on the right path with my thought pattern.

Magnus puffed up, looking angry. "I saw the same kind of thing a lot in eastern Europe. A lot of times, a group would try to get the people riled up about another group, typically government, and then while all the shit was going down, they'd fly under the radar. Weapons trading, financial scams, drugs… whatever makes money."

Dalhousie nodded. "Magnus. Can you go in there and interrogate that bastard? I wouldn't hold it against you if you let the perp think he killed that kid out there. I know he only grazed his arm, but let's make him think there's something terrible waiting for him after he's out of here, unless he cooperates."

"You got it, ma'am. Though I've only been on the receiving end of those things," he said, watching me raise an eyebrow to his statement. "Nothing like that. It was just a misunderstanding," he assured me. I couldn't help but snicker and held it back after Mary frowned at me.

"Don't we need a good cop for the game?" I asked.

"Are you volunteering, Dean?" the president asked.

I wasn't but didn't know if I could get out of it. I had no idea what to say or do in this situation.

"I'm not sure I'm the man for the job." I could already feel the sweat dripping down my back.

"Sure you are, buddy." Magnus clapped me on the back. "Nothing to it. Follow my lead."

And just like that, I was heading for my first interrogation as an Earth Defense officer. I still hadn't had my coffee yet. As if someone read my mind, a page brought in a carafe and a pile of paper cups. Just in time.

With a fresh cup of steaming Joe, I followed Magnus into the small office off the board room. The shooter was sitting on a chair, hands cuffed behind his back, his jaw resting on his chest. His head lay still, and I worried he might not be breathing, but when Magnus cleared his throat, the man's mouth twitched.

"What's your name?" Magnus asked gruffly. The man

lifted his head but kept his mouth shut, glaring back at the unlikely pair before him.

"I said, what's your name, soldier?" Magnus asked again.

The shooter's eye spasmed at the word *soldier*, and I knew Magnus had struck a nerve.

Waiting a few moments for a reply that wasn't coming, Magnus continued. "Army?"

Still no reply, but I could tell Magnus was on the right track. The man's posture went from deflated to rigid and proud in less than a minute.

"Listen, the guy you shot is going to be okay. The president also doesn't think you're the brains of this operation, so just play along, and you might just get a slap on the wrist." Magnus leaned over the small table, half covering it with his wide girth.

I doubted this guy was getting just a slap on anything, and we actually hadn't heard back on the health of the gunshot victim, but since it was just a flesh wound, the odds were he was going home tonight.

Magnus was getting annoyed, and I could see a little vein start to pulse in his forehead. "Who. Sent. You?" he asked through his teeth.

The man averted his eyes again, and I knew it was time to change gears. I sat down on the plastic flip chair in front of him and quietly spoke. "What number were you on?"

Everyone left on Earth had been on a transport vessel just a year ago. The horrors they went through, and the pain of the losses, were still fresh in our minds. It was a simple question, seemingly harmless, but it would invoke a lot of memories, undoubtedly bad ones.

"Twenty-three. I was on twenty-three." He made eye contact with me for the first time.

I scanned my memory of the records. I didn't know all of them, but the American ones had more exposure here, so I'd heard tales.

"I'm sorry," I said, putting my coffee down on the table. "You want a coffee?"

He looked up at Magnus and then back to me. His eyes then lowered to his hands, which were cuffed behind him, and he shrugged.

"Just give me a second," I said, and left the room. I returned in a moment with the keys and a black coffee. They had given me a little grief about the tactics but were happy to see he was finally responding to something. They didn't want to slow down any momentum I'd gained. Magnus just hung back as I undid the cuffs, happy to let me take the lead for now, but I knew he was ready for action should he be needed.

The man rubbed his wrists, just like they always did in every cop show I'd ever seen. For a second, I felt like I was behind the camera of one of those nineties shows where a bald cop with a moustache always caught the bad guys, and then slept with a woman way out of his league.

"Twenty-three was a tough run. Only something like thirty percent made it, I think?" I asked softly.

A shaky hand reached for the steaming black coffee and he took a tentative sip. "Thirty-four," he corrected. "The third worst out of all of them."

"Want to tell us about it?"

He looked like he was about to shut me down, but then something changed. His eyes softened, and I saw his shoulders slump ever so slightly. I knew we were all carrying around so much weight from the Event, and not everyone had an avenue to release the pain. Sometimes all someone needed to do was talk about it, and they could move on with their lives. Suddenly, I felt bad for the guy.

"I got back from the Middle East six months be-fore…well…before *they* came. Wasn't doing so hot. I tried to get a job, and all I could get was pushing a broom on a crappy strip mall construction gig. My wife was riding me to do better, like her being a hairdresser was this glorious crown-worthy enterprise." He stopped, and I could see his eyes were getting wet. I assumed his wife wasn't one of the lucky ones returning to Earth. "Anyway, things weren't good between us, and when those ships came, I almost wished they would just end it. Blow us up. Make my memories mean nothing." He took another sip of cof-fee.

Magnus was leaning in, listening intently to the truth we were witnessing.

"When they didn't, we ended up being brought to twenty-three. Only then, we didn't know where the hell we were, or what we were doing. I was in one of those rooms, and some people were in like some kind of coma or something. Stasis, I heard them call it after. Most of us weren't. In there, we were piled up like livestock, people of every color, religion, and sex. The sick lay among the healthy. Someone gave birth the first day. I heard the ba-by girl is still alive and healthy. The small miracles." He looked at me, seemingly embarrassed at showing vulnera-bility.

"Anyway. Sick people died, we had no food or water, and once we realized there were floor after floor of these cages, some of us explored and tried to find where we were. It was like a sick game. Metal grate floors, sliding hydraulic doors, and no aliens. No threats we could see. Just time. People were fighting, some loved ones found each other, and we tried to have a system where we sepa-rated people. The sick ended up on one floor, and as oth-ers weakened, they were moved there. Doctors and others tried to help, but there wasn't much they could do with no supplies. It was terrible." He took another pause, and I leaned back, taking a sip of my now tepid coffee.

His posture changed. "Then I saw them. The hybrids, as we call them now. A bunch of men and women who looked alike. They had weapons. A lot of us died trying to attack them. I didn't bother. I knew they would mow us down like ducks at the firing range, so I hung back. Later, I followed them a ways and learned what floor they were on. The next day, I headed there, and one of them approached me from behind. I almost crapped myself."

The stories of the vessels were hard to hear, especially since the few of us who didn't get taken never had to witness it. We'd just seen the aftermath, and that was hard enough. I thought back to the first vessel we'd come upon on our way to the sun. The one where we'd found Mae… and killed the rest of the hybrids. Guilt rose from my gut and threatened to make me gag, and I pushed it back down. I had to do it. There was no choice.

The guy must have noticed me pale, and he raised an eyebrow to me. "Then what?" I asked, hoping to just move on.

"They brought me to a room, an off-limits area only they could get into. I thought for sure they were going to kill me. I mean, why wouldn't they? I was spying on them. Instead, he offered me a seat and gave me a glass of water. I mean, at first, I expected it to be poisoned or something, but figured it would have just been easier to shoot me, so I drank it. Next, he plopped a bar of food in front of me. He didn't talk, just set it down." He looked at me guiltily. "I ate it. As soon as I took that bite and felt my stomach churn from finally having something inside 'it, I knew I was theirs. I felt guilty but didn't care. The way I figured it, we were all dead anyway."

I wondered what endgame the hybrids on that ship had. If they knew they were just crashing into the fiery depths of the sun in a few days, what use did they have for someone on the inside?

Before I could ask, he continued. "At first, they just asked me to keep an ear out for anything out of place. Revolts, that kind of thing. I did. A couple times, I overheard plans from the captives to attempt a coup d'état, and before they could, the alien hybrids always found out. No one had any inkling it was me."

I noted how he called the people *captives* and didn't seem to include himself among their ranks during this conversation. Magnus probably noticed too, judging by the frown he was wearing.

"More people died, and by the time I realized I should have been using my time thinking of ways to get one of their weapons to turn the tables, it was too late. The heroes of Earth showed up and stopped them from destroying us all. I lie awake at night telling myself that had they not come to save us, I would have found a way to at least stop our vessel. I know that I'm kidding myself, but it's all I can do to sleep some nights." He took another sip of his coffee and set the cup down with a shaky hand.

Heroes of Earth. The name had a silly ring to it, but it was one of the many things we were hailed as after the return. We were all quiet a moment, and the guy squinted as he looked from Magnus back to me. Recognition sank in, and he paled even more.

"It's you." His hands went to his face, covering it as he blew a deep breath out. "All this time, I'm spilling my guts about working for the enemy, and who am I telling it to? Two of the damn people who actually stopped them from killing us all. Listen, I know you're going to judge me, but if I'd been on the outside, maybe I would have done like you too."

"I believe you would have. What choice did you have?" I asked him, and I told myself I would never have done what he'd done if I were in his shoes. It was hard to convince my brain one hundred percent. I was worried he might clam up now, so I had to stay on his side. "We need to know about today. Why did you shoot that man?"

I was jumping ahead, but if I was going to lose him, I needed to hit the gas quickly.

"I'm sorry. They had me. In those few days, they made me one of theirs. I felt more at home with them, sneaking around infiltrating my own people, than I did pushing sawdust around for a living. I get it. Transference, or whatever the hell you want to call it. I was converted to some sort of new ideas, and at this moment, I finally see it for what it was. I'm ashamed," he said quietly.

"So you were theirs, but after we got home, what happened? I'm missing something." Magnus stood up, and I wished he would shrink back down to be less intimidating.

"Once you showed up, a couple of them were convinced of your story. They fought about it, I was told, but they all ended up going along with it. I think the hardcore Kraski fanatics had a hard time agreeing, but they saw an opportunity for something. They were the ones who kept me on their side. They played nice with everyone, and we've all heard the remorse from the interviews, and the hybrids over the last year, but if you think they all rolled over and forgot their roots, you're kidding yourselves," Clayton said.

Dalhousie had been right to keep them all isolated in their POW camp out on Long Island. The Russians had wanted them, but the world had voted on the US. Likely they would all have wound up dead by some accidental explosion, but if what I was hearing went where I feared, maybe that would have been the best alternative.

"I doubt anyone thinks they're toothless," Magnus said. "Can we get back to the shooting today?"

"Before we landed back on Earth, two of them told me they would be in touch. They gave me some sort of tracking device or something." He pointed to the back of his neck. "Injected it in me. Didn't hurt."

Magnus stood tall again. "Is it still in there?" he barked.

The guy nodded. "Yeah, they contacted me a couple times, but not directly. Through a human, I think."

That had to mean they had a whole damned network here. Dalhousie and the rest had every reason to be cautious around the hybrids. Mae was on our side, though, this I was sure of. Well, mostly sure of. But then again, I'd been sure Ray was with me too, until he'd tried to stop me at Machu Picchu.

"You've never met them or spoken directly with them since you've been back?" Magnus asked.

He shook his head slowly. "They're all contained, as far as I know, so they can't leave. All I know is I was told to meet another guy. He had a van and some guns. We were given a place and date and instructions. That was today. I was told to shoot the guy with the megaphone, then leave. Of course, you know how that went."

"Ready to give us your name yet?" I asked.

"Clayton. Clayton Belding," he said.

"I'm not sure what'll happen to you, Clayton, but we do appreciate you being forthright with us. One last thing before we leave the room. What are the names of your hybrid contacts? The ones who kept at you after we arrived to bring you all home?" I reminded him about the saving part again.

He looked like he was scared or worried to tell me, but he gave in. I think he was just happy to be done being a traitor to his country, to his planet. "Terrance was the guy, and Leslie was the woman. I still don't understand why they have our names, but I guess if you're putting on someone's mask, you may as well take their name too."

Our trip to Long Island had just gotten more pressing.

FIVE

"*W*e've alerted the guards at the Long Island facility, and they're going to try to identify those two particular hybrids." The president looked tired; black bags sat under her usually youthful eyes.

Mae sat at the table, looking worried. Everyone had been watching the video as we spoke with Clayton, and the only consensus was we needed to follow and learn about the network being run by Leslie and Terrance.

"We can only expect there are many more moving pieces, and way more involved in this than just those two." Mary looked at Mae while she spoke, an apologetic air floating with her voice.

"I've got a chopper waiting for you guys. This isn't a time for you all to be taking leisurely trains around the coast. Magnus and Natalia, I'm hoping you'll come to the base, and the others can meet up with you there in a couple days if all goes well." Dalhousie was asking as a courtesy, I was sure.

Magnus and Nat looked at each other and shrugged their shoulders at the same time.

We spent the next hour or so discussing how we could get more information about the hybrid network, and by the time we were about to go our own ways, my head was pounding and it was dark outside.

"Do you guys mind taking Carey with you?" I asked,

knowing he would be much happier going with them than on a stressful trip in a helicopter to a POW camp. Carey barked when I said his name and sat beside my feet. Kneeling down, I petted him softly, telling him we'd see him soon.

"Of course not," Natalia said, calling him over. He did so hesitantly, and Mary crossed the room, grabbing the dog's leash and other essentials from her luggage. I wasn't looking forward to being separated from the guy, and I doubted he was either. At least he'd be going with people he loved being around: pseudo-uncle and aunt.

Carey accepted our goodbye without too much pre-amble, and soon we were being whisked away to Long Island.

*T*he military-grade helicopter lowered Mae, Mary, and me down to the school's football field. The camp, or residence as we were told to call it, was located at the local university grounds. With the turmoil of the world, most post-secondary schools had been on hiatus, with some trade schools and other specialized ones still running to make sure the world could still spin every day and night. This particular university was one that got swiped off the list of funding, and they were going to merge with a few other New York schools in the next year.

It worked out well because it had everything the hybrids could need while they were under our protection... or watchful eyes. They housed in the on-campus residence, and they had classrooms for learning about Earth and our customs and traditions, even though most had a basic understanding already since they'd been trained for coming here, as Janine and Bob had been. Mae told me that while they'd been taught a lot about humans, there were many missing things, like our sense of humor and obsession with sports. I'd laughed but was still scared at the implications that the Kraski had possibly known as much about us as they did. What did that tell us? That someone was feeding them information. Mae was under the theory it was from all the crap Earth was shooting around the universe in the form of radio waves, and other things I didn't quite understand. Maybe they learned what they did from watching the Cooking Channel.

Either way, the hybrids were here. We had them tucked away into a comfortable area, with food and activities… and a big fence around the perimeter. It was fully dark by the time we landed in the field, right smack dab on the fifty-yard line. The fence was lit up every fifty yards or so, and there were a few towers with spotlights roaming the grounds. There was a curfew, and armed guards in the towers. So far there hadn't been any incidents of trouble, at least none that the public had been made aware of. I realized that meant nothing, so I'd ask Mae to check into it later.

"Looks like we get an escort," Mary said, nodding toward the armed guards coming our way.

"They check everyone's blood. They want to know if any hybrids come or go." Mae had a distant look on her face.

"You okay?" Mary asked her.

She nodded slowly. "Yeah. I know this is better than most of us deserve, but it's still a life behind bars. Considering the alternative, I'd say I'm great, though." She turned her somber face into a forced smile and grabbed her bags.

The copter was loud, and Mary's hair blew in my face

as we set foot on the grass.

"Mr. Parker, Ms. Lafontaine, and Mae, right this way, please," a fresh-faced guard said, waving his hand. He sounded friendly, but he still held a gun in the crook of his arm.

They followed us to a building near the field, which turned out to be the old locker room. Weight sets still lined the wall, and near the door stood a device that looked much like a free-standing doorway. It reminded me of a high-tech airport metal scanner, only this one whirred as we approached, and was lit with soft blue LEDs.

"Please walk through, Ms. Lafontaine," Junior said.

"Call me Mary," she replied, walking through. The blue lights turned yellow for a moment.

Mae went next and the lights turned green, which I guess was to be expected. I walked through last, and expected to be yellow, so we could just go drop our bags off and get some food and shut-eye. It had been an extremely long day, and a bite followed by a pillow was just what I needed. The light turned green.

The guards raised their guns at me. "Why are you undocumented? You don't look like the rest of them."

Baffled, I shrugged. "Look, I think your machine is broken." Then it dawned on me, being shot by a hybrid that looked just like Mary's dead husband on that vessel, then the transfusion from Mae that would help me heal. I had hybrid blood coursing through my body still.

Mae seemed to know this was a possibility but must have forgotten, because I was sure she would have warned me of it.

"You guys know who I am? Dean Parker. The man who was shot trying to stop the entire population from becoming charcoal on the surface of the sun." I was tired, and wanted to contain my annoyance, but was having a hard time of it. I nodded toward Mae. "She was nice enough to help me out with some super-healing blood, and voila, a year later, I set off your little sensor. Can we just go on through and get some sleep before all hell breaks loose here tomorrow?" I was hoping there would be no breaking loose of hell the next day, but I pushed the theatrics a little far.

They conferred for a moment, but the gun that had been pointing at me a minute ago was down on the guard's side. That was a good sign.

"Roberts here will lead you to your bunks. No offense was meant, Mr. Parker. We thank you for what you've done. All of you." The fresh-faced guard tried to give us a weak smile, but it came out a pained look.

"Thank you. Have a good night," Mary said, grabbing her luggage handle.

We made our way through the locker room building and out into the fresh night air once again. It was quiet there, with no sign of anyone other than guards walking in pairs down the dimly lit sidewalks. Large black lantern posts stood every twenty yards or so, casting ominous shadows among the well-manicured lawns and hedges. I had a sinking feeling in my stomach as we made our way through the university grounds. We had the hybrids in prison but tried to make sure it looked like they were living in a wonderful place. I could smell flowers as we neared a garden to the side of us and wondered if we had human staff tending to these things or if the hybrids took care of the chores themselves.

Mary must have been feeling something was off too, because as we walked, she put a hand on Mae's shoulder for a shared moment that neither of them needed to speak for. As we walked by the next lamppost, I saw

Mae's eyes were wet. We were ushered into a beautiful brick building, archways over us as we walked into the large wooden doorway.

"We have you two in these rooms," the guard said, pointing at two doors in the residence, across the hall from one another.

I almost laughed at them giving us separate rooms, but they wouldn't know we were together. Neither of us said anything, but Mary did throw me a quick wink.

"Is anyone else on this wing?" I asked.

"Nope. Just you two. Mae, come with us, please." The guard waved her forward.

"Wait," Mary said. "Where are you taking her?"

The guard looked impatient, tapping his foot while keeping his face impassive. "She'll stay with the other hybrids, like she always does when she's here."

"No, she can have this room. I want her to stay near us." Mary stepped closer to Mae.

"Really, it's okay, Mary." Mae looked happy to see her friend stand up to the guards, but I wondered if it wouldn't be better for her to be near her people for information. Seeing the determined look in Mary's eyes, I didn't dare suggest this at that moment.

"No, it's not. You've proven yourself to us all. Stay near us. We still have to discuss a plan for tomorrow," Mary said.

The guard deflated a bit and nodded. "Fine, you stay here tonight. The dean expects to see you for breakfast at eight in the morning. We'll send someone for you."

"Can you just tell us where to find him? I'd prefer not to feel like a prisoner here too," I said. He opened my room door and pointed to a campus map on a small desk near the window.

"Right there," he said, pointing to a building near the

middle of the campus.

"Got it. Thanks, Roberts." I smiled at him. He quickly turned without looking back, leaving all three of us in the small dorm room.

"That went well, I think," Mary said, laugh lines crinkling around her eyes. I had the urge to boot Mae out and take Mary into my arms.

"It's late. How about we sleep, then regroup early in the morning?" This from Mae. Maybe she saw the look in my eyes. "And thanks for treating me like one of you. I'll never forget it." The words were touching, but ominous at the same time. I could feel goosebumps rise on my arms, and I wasn't sure why.

"Goodnight, Mae," I said, and closed the door behind her. "Good thing the room is all the way across the hall," I said, smirking at the woman I loved.

She sniffed the air and took her shirt off. "I agree. How about a shower first?"

Looking around, I realized dorm rooms didn't have their own bathrooms. They had shared toilets and showers on each wing. At least that was how my old school was.

"I know, I saw the sign down the hall." She opened the door, and I chased after her down the corridor. The hall was dim, and we soon found ourselves interlocked under a weak showerhead. We had plenty of time for saving the world later. That night we took for ourselves.

*T*here was a tentative knock on the door, followed by a harder one seconds later. I rolled over and checked the time. Seven on the nose.

"I think it's for you," Mary said weakly.

"You always say that. Oddly, it never is." I rolled out of the small twin bed, realizing I was naked.

"Good morning, sleepyheads," Mae said from the hall.

After sliding into some pants, I opened the door. She held a tray with three coffees in it, each marked with our names. Here we were sleeping, and Mae was thinking of us. She truly was a great friend.

Smiling and saying thank you, I ushered her into the small room. Mary had pulled some clothes from the chair beside the bed, and magically got dressed in moments under the blanket.

"How about we take these to go? I have some news. Take a few to get ready. Leave through the entrance, and head left. About a hundred yards down is a park. I'll be at a bench." She looked at me and laughed, then took her coffee and left.

"What's so funny?" I asked Mary.

She looked down, and I followed her gaze. My pants were on inside out. I burst out laughing, almost spilling my hot coffee.

A few minutes later, after we'd bird-bathed in the bathroom sink, we made our way over to Mae. The morning was beautiful, a single wispy white cloud slowly trailing through the otherwise clear blue sky. It was going to be a hot day.

Mae was sitting on the bench, legs extended and feet crossed. She held her coffee in her hand on her lap, and I was shocked to see how much she looked like Janine right then. That was exactly how she sat when she was in a contemplative mood. My heart suddenly ached, and surprisingly, I didn't push it away, I embraced it. I felt the love I'd had for Janine fill me. The tender moments, the tough ones, the end of her life, the betrayal I'd felt at learning the truth; they all filled me, and for the first time in years, I felt true. True to myself, and true to Janine.

"Are you okay, Dean?" Mary asked.

"I am," I answered, and I was. I felt her fingers slide through mine and squeeze my hand slightly.

"What did you find out, Mae?" Mary asked, letting go of my hand and sitting down on the bench beside her friend. We knew Mae would have gotten up early to poke around the other hybrids and hear the latest gossip and news.

"They were a little tight-lipped around me, at least the few I spoke with. Remember, to some of them, I'm the turncoat. Even to the ones that are happy to be here rather than dead, I still did something I wasn't supposed to. But a lot of them are happy. It just goes against their indoctrination, which is weakening all the time. I do think there's a larger group of dissidents than we originally guessed. I don't have anything to back this up, but the averted eyes and nervous toe-tapping I got this morning told me enough." Mae took a sip from her coffee and kept staring forward at the dew-covered grass in the park.

"Did you ask about Leslie and Terrance, the two names Clayton the shooter had for us?" I asked.

"I mentioned Leslie in passing to someone I didn't know well. Asking after her like we were old friends or something. Jarvis paled and told me he hadn't seen her in some time. That she must be busy with a project for the humans or something. A bunch of BS, if you ask me."

It didn't seem like we were going to be able to get far on Mae's previous relationships. We were going to have to rely on the intel of the guards, and the so-called "dean." What a presumptuous name to give the head of the camp. It was softer than calling him what he really was: a warden.

"I'm sorry, guys. I wish I could have done more," Mae said.

"I have an idea." Mary smiled widely and took a drink of her coffee.

SIX

The dean's office was my kind of place. Mahogany wood desk, floor-to-ceiling bookcases, not just filled with pretentious unread textbooks and encyclopaedias. I saw some King and Child in there too, along with a few of my favorite sci-fi authors. I wouldn't mind getting locked in there for a few weeks. He even had a connected wash-room and a small wet bar, with what appeared to be Scotch in a decanter and one of those fancy digital single-serve coffee makers.

We sat crunched together in front of his large desk, our chairs nowhere near as comfortable and leather-clad as his. When we'd arrived, we were ushered in; I vaguely remembered the guard last night mentioning breakfast with the dean, and my stomach growled at the notion. Maybe he was too busy to eat with the likes of us.

After ten minutes of sitting there, I got up and started flipping through an old Clarke paperback, admiring the classic cover. I'd been lucky enough over the last year to have more free time than I'd had in years, since I hadn't gone back to working as an accountant. One thing I had missed was reading. Somehow reading about alien civilizations, when I knew it was real, took some of the fun out of it.

The door opened, and a tall man stepped through. I'm not ashamed to say he was very handsome, his light hair neatly combed in a look I didn't understand how to accomplish. I felt inadequate, with my sink-rinsed hair and wrinkled plaid shirt.

"Good morning," he said. "I'm so sorry to keep you waiting. I'm Skip Anderson, otherwise known as the dean." He spoke with a prim accent. Not one I could place within a region, but more one acquired through an upbringing in private schools and Harvard education.

I was still holding the book, and when I saw his eyes scan to it, I set it down. "You a fan of Clarke?" he asked.

"Sure. Who isn't? He revolutionized science fiction. But I'm not sure I have a stomach for any of it anymore," I answered.

"I always liked Asimov better. Robots always interested me as a teenager. Back to business. You really believe this guy from D.C.? There's no way our hybrids could have contacted him," Skip said smugly.

Mary rolled her eyes. "I highly doubt that. We learned that there's an intricate hybrid network of terrorists, recruited even in space. They had a long game, that's for sure."

Skip leaned forward, frowning. "That's impossible," he said, voice raised. "They have no way to communicate, and no way out. We have things under control here."

"We were told your surveillance heard some keywords. What can you tell us about that?" I asked, wondering if he would lay his cards out on the table or hold them close to his chest.

"Yes, we have, but those *people* are under our care now." Skip spat the word "people," and Mae tensed as he spoke.

"Which people?" I asked.

"The ones causing the stir at the Oval Office, and evidently around the world. They sent another group of guards when they heard the word *Bhlat* come through the speakers. As if one of them saying the name of a race will actually make them appear and destroy us." Skip looked like he was about to stand up, and the handsome man took on a dark, unpleasant face.

"You do remember what happened under a year ago, right? Where were you that day?" Mary asked, probably thinking it would diffuse his undeserved anger.

Skip slid back in his chair; her question seemed to have the desired effect. He looked much younger than his forty-something years as he began to quietly speak. "I hate those bastards." He looked at Mae for a brief second and averted his eyes back to his desk. "I lived in D.C., well, Arlington. The ships came and I still went to work at the senator's office. I remember being so mad that no one else showed up. Can you imagine me at work, trying to email files and work on a presentation while we had these gray ships over us, and a bunch of those behemoth vessels looming over the world? What an idiot I was." He stopped, getting up to cross over to his wet bar. His hand moved to the Scotch, lingering for a few quiet moments before continuing to the single-serve coffee maker. "Coffee, anyone?" he asked, trying to put on an affable voice.

We all shook our heads silently, me wanting him to continue his tale.

"Very well." He made a cup of coffee, and took it black back to his desk, sitting up a little straighter. "Sorry about that. It's hard going back to that day, I'm sure for all of us. There I was like a crazy man, working as we were invaded, and my wife was trying to get me to come to her. Well, my ex-wife. She called me first thing and I told her I couldn't see her. I was still angry with her for leaving me. She'd left a few months earlier, telling me all I cared about was work, and never had time for her.

"She wanted a family. Kids, white picket fence…I thought I did too, when we first met. Only the older I got, the less I wanted that, and the more I wanted a career in politics. We were drifting, but… I didn't want to admit it." He was taking us on an extended journey through his time of the Event, but I assumed this path was relevant to the big picture. "She decided to head out of town, I guess. She made a break for it, but no one escaped, as we all know. Well, except you two and your friends." He said the words with a drip of envy. "I was just leaving the office when the sun had set. I still can't believe I stayed there all day. No wonder she left me." He took a drink of his coffee and stared blankly past us toward the door.

"Hey, life is full of growth moments. None of us were or are perfect. It's what we do with our teachable moments that define us and change us," Mary said, again impressing me with her ability to spout out positive messages.

He looked at her and smiled lightly. "I'm still trying to be at peace with that idea. I was brought to vessel twelve, along with countless others. I spent the first day just trying to figure out what was going on. There were fights breaking out everywhere, and I witnessed two murders in the first two days alone. I never even tried to stop the young man from killing the other guy. I don't think anyone was expecting it. He just clocked the older guy and went straight for his throat with his hands. The kid wasn't big, but he had a sinewy strength to him. Before we knew it, the older man was on the ground, unconscious. The kid took something from his pocket and ran out of the room. Pills.

"The room was full of people, and no one stopped him. We all just stood there with our jaws open, like we didn't understand what had happened. Finally, a burly man ran after him, but I guess the kid was long gone down the corridors. I decided, then and there, I wasn't going to be a passive prisoner.

"After exploring the vessel and talking to a lot of people, I knew our prison was huge. Gargantuan, with hundreds of thousands of people, maybe millions. We didn't know the scope, but we were trying to figure it out. So that meant the area they beamed us up from must have been a large one. That meant my wife might have been there with me." Skip stopped, and I almost said something comforting but decided to hold off. "My ex-wife, I meant. So that was my new goal. Find her among the throngs of matching rooms full of people. Some of the rooms seemed to have expelled a gas into the rooms, because people were down all over the place, seemingly at random."

We knew now that the Kraski were planning on moving their whole species away from their home, and they were going to put everyone in some sort of stasis using this gas. It basically slowed down the metabolic functions and allowed them to keep humans alive without food and water for prolonged periods of time. Quite a cool concept, if it didn't mean the death of so many people. It turned out a percentage of people were deathly allergic to the alien toxin, and about five percent of Earth was lost just from that alone, among the already sick who just couldn't survive, the vessels we'd lost to the sun, and the mass firings the hybrids had rained down on some vessels.

"Quite the needle in a haystack," I said, getting up to make myself a coffee. I asked if anyone else wanted anything, and after a pause, the dean asked for a splash of Scotch. I wasn't going to judge the guy for taking a pinch at eight thirty in the morning as he told us a story; I expected it wasn't going to end well for anyone involved.

He continued as the single-serve machine whirred and poured. I passed him the Scotch, and he swirled the brown liquid on the bottom of his tumbler and watched it as he spoke. "I tried to find the upper corner – the top floor and far left room. It took me hours to get there, and when I did, I searched that first room. People were milling about: some in the halls, some fearful of leaving the room for fear of retribution from an alien host we hadn't seen yet.

"Some people thought it was a crazy government experiment, and others thought they were just dreaming. I called for Marcie. When I entered a room of the unconscious people, I searched through the piles of them, hoping to see her lovely face. I never did find her. She didn't make it. They killed her." His eyes moved once again to Mae's face, hard lines etched on his forehead. "I found her name on my vessel list after it was over. If only I could have made it to her, I could have protected her."

"Or died yourself," Mary said softly – perhaps to make him feel better, but it didn't work.

"I would have rather died trying to save her than lived and not been there," he replied.

I wondered how this traumatized man had ended up running the camp there, but in the end, everyone was traumatized by the same event. Almost every single person in the world had been through similar situations and had lost someone close to them. My mother, cousins, old co-workers, friends, and countless others. We were all bonded in our loss.

"I'm really sorry, Skip," Mary said. "Losing a spouse is one of the hardest things anyone will ever endure. Dean and I have been through it too."

He frowned. "Weren't you guys married to some of

them?" He nodded his chin at Mae. "I'm not sure it counts."

"Now wait a damn minute," Mary started. I set my hand on her shoulder and could feel how tense she was.

"Skip, I think we can agree to disagree, but this isn't conducive to what we're doing here. Now can we see the video surveillance, and then talk to those two that seem to be causing all the stir from inside *your* gates?" I added emphasis to the word "your," so he knew I tossed a little blame at him. He might have been through a hard time, but he was still being a jerk, and had likely been one long before the Kraski had lowered to our world.

With a swift motion, he slid the Scotch down his throat, quietly setting the glass on a wooden coaster on the desk. "Of course. President Dalhousie says you're members of our new Earth Defense, and she evidently trusts you, so why don't you follow me?"

We left the office and were soon walking through a long hall with a freshly polished floor. I noticed someone who looked just like Vanessa sweeping the corners of a room as we passed. We continued on, and there were plenty more hybrids with familiar faces doing different tasks; some were unfamiliar outside of the news feeds. There were six different "models" of them. Janine had been one of them, Bob another. Then, of course, our friendly neighborhood saboteur, Vanessa. Ray's girlfriend Kate was the other model, and I had met her once at my wedding so many years ago. After that, we had an Asian man and an Indian woman, whom Magnus had described as matching the two he and Natalia had known overseas.

Mae smiled at some of them, and a few waved to her like they were old acquaintances. I was sure most wondered what one of their own was doing with the visiting strangers, but many recognized her as their savior. A lot of them knew it was with her help that they were alive. Others blamed her for their imprisonment and wished they had burned in the sun like planned. Those were the ones we were after.

"Mae," someone called as we passed a gymnasium. There was a group inside playing a strange-looking game, with four small nets and a silver disk. It looked fun, and maybe a little dangerous. The man was sweating profusely but had a wide smile across his face. "Hey, Mae. I'm not sure if you remember me, but my name's Richard. We met...well, right after we arrived. I was from vessel seven. Anyway, I just wanted to say thank you again. And to you guys too."

He extended his hand, and I shook it despite the sweat dripping from him.

"Of course I remember you, Richard. How are things going here?" Mae asked.

The game had paused, but when they saw Richard was tied up, someone sitting on the sidelines jumped in and the game started up again. I looked at Skip, and he clearly wasn't enjoying the delay. Mary, noticing this, smiled at me and took the dean aside, speaking softly to him and taking him away from us. Richard guided Mae and me into the gym, and we sat down on one of those wooden benches I hadn't sat on since my days of riding the pine on my varsity basketball team.

"This is a nice place to live. We work a bit each day, but I mean, it's no slave labor." He paused, looking embarrassed at his choice of words. "I just want you to know that most of us are so grateful for your part here. We were real slaves before this. Genetically created to invade a planet and act like humans. The Kraski never cared about us. There are a few who drank the Kool-Aid, if you will, but they're few and far between. They also seem to know to keep it to themselves, because I guarantee you, if I heard someone plotting against Earth, I'd string them up and call the dean over there to send his guards. This is our home now."

It was nice to hear this from one of them, but it didn't mean he was being one hundred percent honest with us. Even if he was, it didn't mean there weren't more of them against us than he knew about.

"Do you know Leslie and Terrance?" I asked him.

He shrugged. "Yeah. I mean, I know of them, but not close to them or anything. I think I saw Terrance walking around last night. He looks like me, but I'm sure it was him. We all have our own way of things, slight differences in hair, clothing, walk. Why, do you want to talk to them about something?"

Mae looked ready to say something, but I tapped her with my hand, without Richard being able to see. "Nothing important. We'll find them later. Thanks for stopping and chatting, Richard." I held out my hand to shake it again. The goodbye shake.

He smiled widely, and said he looked forward to talking again sometime. Mae gave him a quick hug. It held for just longer than seemed normal, and I turned away, trying not to watch. Mary was in the hall, still with the dean, who was waving his arms around and smiling.

"…and my tennis game sure has improved. There you guys are. Care to come and do what you're here for?" His good mood dissipated as Mae and I approached them. Mary gave me a cute look and crossed her eyes when Skip was turned around.

We followed him outside and into the fresh air once again. The sun was now over the buildings, casting its warm glow on our faces as we walked down the cobblestone pathway to a small brick building with a plaque saying *Alumni* on it. Two guards stood on either side of the door, beads of sweat dripping down their faces in the morning heat. I wouldn't have wanted the afternoon shift if it was that warm already. I gave them a quick nod as we passed by them and through the thick dark wooden doors. There was something I just loved about the turn-of-the-century architecture in this part of the country. It was also nice to be back in the state of New York, even though I'd just left upstate a couple of days ago. It felt like home.

"We have our guard station here, and our camera sur-veillance. The actual security office was across campus and consisted of a fourteen-inch television and a grilled cheese maker." Skip led the way through a foyer with a twenty-foot ceiling, and into a room on the left side. Another guard was stationed there.

"Where's Clendening?" Skip asked the woman.

She shrugged. "Didn't show up, so they called me in. Rayez thought he might have come down with some-thing. I guess he was talking about feeling a bug coming on at the end of his shift."

The room beyond was dimly lit and had about a doz-en flat screens mounted on the far wall. Inside were a few desks; computer fans whirred in the otherwise silent space. Three white-shirted people sat at desks, each with large headphones on. One of them turned to us, and he had a shocked look when his eyes stopped on Mae. It probably felt like he was showing the hybrids behind the Wizard of Oz's curtain.

The dean tossed him a thumbs-up, letting him know it was okay. I'd judged the man a little harshly, and maybe he wasn't quite as bad as he'd initially let on. He did have a big responsibility here.

"Good morning," he called to them, just loud enough

for the other two to hear him, and they also turned around. "Louise, can you bring up the Level Seven file for our guests, please?"

She gave him a look, as if to make sure he wasn't asking her to show the strangers in the room a classified piece of information. I noticed Skip nod lightly to her, and she brought it up, taking her headphones off. Three of the screens flashed to different scenes. The top left was playing, and we could hear some grainy sound. It was taken with night vision, and there were two people in the shot. One looked like Janine and Mae; the other looked like Richard, the Asian man we'd talked to in the gym. Leslie and Terrance, no doubt.

"Is it going to work?" a female voice asked.

"It has to. Everything is a go. We don't have much time. He's going to tell our contacts the details tomorrow." Terrance rested his hands on her shoulders in an intimate gesture.

"Did you…" She paused, looking down at the ground. "Get the outpost location?"

In the green light of the night vision, I could see his posture straighten, and I swore he was smiling. "No, but I know where to get it now. The plan stays the same, just a small detour. This is an all or nothing play."

"I'm for the cause the whole way," Leslie said with conviction. "The Bhlat…" The rest was indiscernible.

They spoke for a few more minutes in hushed tones so we couldn't make out what they said, and then quickly went their separate ways.

The video feed went dead.

"And you didn't think to instantly contain them?" Mae yelled at the dean, who shrank back at the sudden outburst.

"That's enough, hybrid! You don't think I'd thought

of that? We have more at stake here than the dreams of two aliens. They are stuck here! Do you understand that? They have no way to communicate with the outside world. We've been tracking them and keeping an eye on anyone they talk with." He was inches away from Mae's face, and I jumped between them, setting my hands on Skip's chest.

"You're done, Skip," I said, holding him back as he pushed at me. "Listen, where are they now? People are dying out there, and we have every reason to believe those two, maybe more, are behind it. There must be a reason for it. It's almost as if…" I stopped, my mind reeling for a second. "I think they're trying to distract us from something."

"Distract us from what? They're stuck here behind gates and guards," Skip said, stepping back away from me and Mae.

"Louise, can you show us where they are now?" Mary asked, in a calmer voice than the rest of us had been speaking in.

"Sure thing," she said, moving her mouse around and clicking some keys. The top left screen showed us a video of the two of them working in a garden. "See, they're right where they're supposed to be, on garden duty. Did you see the size of those tomatoes they have out there? Best I've ever tasted."

Skip rushed over and tapped the screen. "Garden duty doesn't start for another hour. Zoom out!"

She hit a bunch of keys, but nothing happened.

"Goddamn it." Skip ran his hands through his hair. "Switch to the next camera. We have one from the other end of the garden, don't we?"

She did so and turned the camera to the end where we'd just seen the two hybrids working. There was no one there.

"Switch back," he said.

The camera showed the two of them watering the plants.

"They've hacked in. We need to find them now." This from Mary.

The second screen had started playing that same video from before, with the night vision. I looked at it and saw something move I hadn't seen the first time. There was a third person there with them.

"Louise, can you zoom in on that second screen?" I asked.

Skip looked at me with annoyance. "Look here, Dean. We have more important things to do…"

"Just zoom in," I cut him off. "There's someone there with them."

The screen zoomed. The picture, while in high definition, was in night vision, and they were some distance away. By the time she zoomed in enough to see them up close, the image was slightly pixelated. The third person was in the dark between and beyond them, but just as they went their own ways, the body turned. "Pause it!" I called. There was writing on the jacket.

"Security," Skip muttered under his breath. "One of ours is in on it."

Louise went forward frame by frame and stopped on one where we could see him closer.

"Boss, I know who that is," she said. "It's Clendening."

That was the name of the guard the woman out front had said hadn't shown up this morning.

"That bastard. Any sign of either Leslie or Terrance yet? You two get on the cameras and find me Clendening too!" he called to the other surveillance officers.

"Nothing on any of them, sir. It's like they vanished," Louise said.

Skip grabbed a landline from Louise's desk. After a moment of rushed conversation, he had jotted down some notes on a pad of paper. "Send guards to Clendening's room in the barracks. If he's there, hold him until I get there."

"Can we get this show on the road?" Mary asked, obviously anxious to track down the hybrids we were there to get before they could do any more harm.

It appeared they were getting messages out by the guard we'd just spotted meeting with them in the middle of the night. A couple of them with a network out there and a guard on their side, and they could make things happen, even from behind a fence with no phones or web access.

"Are any of you armed?" Skip asked matter-of-factly.

I shook my head. "Nope, we haven't been given any firearms yet. I'm guessing the president thought you would be generous enough to set us up if we needed them, at least until we get to the base after this trip."

He waved us forward. Soon we were through the foyer and into an adjacent room, which Skip had to use two keys to open. It was lined with locked gun racks. In moments, all of us were armed, Mary and I with Glocks, and Mae with a Beretta.

"I'd been holding on the hope they were just all talk, and thought if they were trying something, we could maybe identify any other hybrids in on it. With Clendening in on it, we have no choice. We're going to take them down. If they had anything to do with those shootings out in the real world, they'll quickly learn to regret their decision to act as hostile terrorists on our world." The dean was working himself up, and I just hoped he would keep a level head once we found where they were hiding.

We left the building, and a group of four armed guards crossed the university grounds with us as we headed to the residence where the hybrids slept.

SEVEN

*D*ozens of the hybrids watched us as we made our way through the halls.

Skip told a couple of the guards to go to room thirty-seven and sent Mae alongside them to Leslie's listed residence. We continued to Terrance's room. When we arrived, a hybrid that looked just like Ray's girlfriend Kate walked up to us, arms held up, letting us know she came in peace.

"There's no one in there. He didn't come back last night." She kept her hands up as she spoke.

Skip turned the handle, finding it locked. He stepped back, and in a moment, he had kicked the area just under the handle, sending shards of wooden frame away as the latch broke and slid through the thin recessed hole. That suit had some fire in his veins.

A guard entered with her gun pointed forward, and we followed into the cramped space when she said it was clear. I'd somehow expected the random mess of a madman, but what we found was an extremely clean, organized space. Their rooms were small, much like the one Mary and I had slept in the night before, and inside the bed was made as if by a hotel chambermaid. Some papers were set in straight lines on the small desk to the left of the door. Inside the closet everything hung nicely, but I noticed half of the clothes hangers on the bar hung empty. The drawers had few items in them, telling me this guy had packed what few belongings he could possibly have, and was gone.

Skip's radio chimed, and we were told they'd found much the same at Leslie's room.

Grabbing the papers from the desk, Mary made a move for the door. "Let's go see what the guard's room looked like." She was off, Skip trailing her determined strides, even though he knew where the guard barracks were, not her. I could see her frustration. We were sent to do what initially seemed like a simple task but were being handed something much bigger. It was going to be a lot harder to track these two down out there than inside a fenced-off university campus.

The guard barracks were across the grounds, and we took four-seater golf-style carts to cross the area quickly. There were already guards stationed at Clendening's door, and when we approached it, the room was open. A large man stood in the opening, and when he turned to face us, he was white as a ghost.

"Sorry, boss. He's dead." The man stepped out of the way, and Skip rushed past him in the small dorm-style room. The man we'd seen in the surveillance video was slumped on the single bed, throat slit. Blood covered everything and had dripped down into a sticky puddle on the ground beside him. It was a callous, brutal murder, and I knew in my gut it was Leslie and Terrance who had done it. I pictured them smooth-talking the man, getting his help to spread their words across the fence; then, when they got his keys to leave, they'd killed him. In my head, I saw Terrance holding him down, a look of terror on the man's previously trusting face. Leslie showing a hint of remorse as she slid her knife across his throat, ending the one man who'd been willing to help their cause. It was sick, and I fought back the bile that was threatening to push out of my mouth.

I left the room and walked down the hall, my ears ringing. The hallway was spinning ever so slowly, and I pushed past the dozen or so guards and made my way to the doors that led outside. I thought I could hear Mary calling my name, but I kept going. The image of the guard was stuck in my mind, and the horrible way the hybrids used and discarded him made me despise their cause all the more. We had to stop them.

*I*t was a couple of hours later that we were in the surveillance room, combing through anything with Leslie, Terrance, or Clendening from the past week. The AC was cranked as the hot sun blasted the brick building, creating an oven simulation, and we sat in the cool room hoping to find a sign of where they might have gone. But nothing they'd done was out of place, other than that one thing we'd already seen. Clendening's room had brought up nothing of use, either.

Dalhousie had called Mary, and we filled her in. She asked them to have Skip and his team continue to look for leads while they left, and met up at the secret facility. I wasn't sure how they expected it to actually be secret with a massive transport vessel sitting in the desert, but it wasn't any of my business.

"Stop that one again, the screen second from the bottom," Mary said to Louise, who promptly zoomed in and paused the other screens.

"It's on a loop! Where is that?" Mary asked.

"That's the loading dock. Where we get food and

supplies delivered," she responded. "I think you're right about the loop. They did a good job, because the clock on the feed is still going, but there's a clock on the wall." She zoomed more, and we could see the second hand smoothly ticking by. After thirty seconds, it was back on the twelve and heading for the one.

"Get guards to the loading dock! We don't know what time they actually left. That loop could be from any feed they hacked into. Maybe they couldn't get out." Skip rushed out of the room, and we followed him. I was eager to find them and get back to Magnus and Nat, and I missed Carey at that moment.

Once again, we were heading across the grounds, and there were no hybrids in sight. Skip had ordered them all to their rooms for the time being. If Leslie and Terrance were still there, they could be pretending to be someone else, and it wouldn't be too hard, since they looked like a hundred other people.

The sun beat down on us from its high perch in the middle of the sky, and I could feel the sweat already soaking through the lower back of my shirt. The fact that I was nervous and excited that we might find the two outlaws didn't help the perspiration.

The warehouse on the edge of the grounds wasn't huge but was large enough to accept multiple pallets a day and store anything that came in for a while. I imagined trucks backing up before the semester started, unloading skids of textbooks newly revised for that year, and the smell of paper and forklift exhaust sailing through the air.

We entered the main doors, using keys from Skip's belt. The other guards were standing there waiting for his word. As soon as the doors pushed open, they quietly ran in along the large room's walls, guns raised, looking for the threats. Mary raised hers and started in, and I set my arm on hers, shaking my head. Instead, I waved her to follow me, and we hugged the wall of the building toward the fence. I wanted to see what was on the other side there.

The fence was chain-link there, about twelve feet tall, topped with that dangerous-looking wire you always see around prisons. No one was getting in or out with that stuff on the top of the fence. I looked to the left. There were multiple unlabeled white trucks, two backed up to loading docks, and one dock was open, with no truck in front of it.

We went back to the entrance. Skip was standing at the open loading dock, his hands sitting on top of his head in an exasperated gesture. "How the hell did we let this happen? Clendening didn't have the keys to get in here." He stared out the door, and we walked up to the tense man.

"I know you don't want to hear this, Skip, but I think someone else here must have been in on it. Unless your dead guard stole the keys, or Terrance and Leslie did," I said.

"Clendening never seemed smart enough to arrange something like this, but obviously I've been wrong before. Like when I thought no human would betray us all by catering to these damned hybrids." He walked to the office area, and we followed him, Mae staying back after his last comment was dipped in venom.

Gun raised, Mary stepped in front of us and tested the handle. It was unlocked. Wait, no, it was broken. She didn't even have to turn it. She pushed it instead, and it stopped short of opening. I saw her give it a heave; something pushed back, and the door closed again.

"What the hell is that? Get the lights," Skip said.

He reached his arm into the dark room and turned

them on. The door had a small glass window and he peered through it, turned to us, and vomited right at our feet, Mary and I both jumping back to avoid getting splashed. When he ducked, I could see what he'd seen: the bloated face of a hanged woman, swinging softly in the doorway.

The guards pushed past us, and soon she was cut down. It was evident she'd been hanged alive, as we saw the claw marks and boot scuffs on the inside of the door. The sadistic duo had really done a number here.

"Why put on all of this show for us? To make us mad? To throw us off?" Mary asked, her voice quiet.

Mae stepped toward us and said through pale lips, "To make you hate the hybrids. They hate us for giving in and not following through with killing everyone. They want to turn you against all of us and won't stop until whatever they want is done."

I hesitated, not sure I wanted to hear the answer to my question. "And what is it they want done?"

"What we were brainwashed to do: end humans," she said. For a moment, I forgot she was our friend, the words came out so coldly.

My phone rang, and it was General Heart. I filled him in on what had transpired, and he said a helicopter was coming to bring us to the secret base. Skip sent out an APB on the missing truck, and said they had a GPS unit in it, but it appeared the password for the tracking app had been changed. They were bringing in an IT guru, former CIA, who said it wouldn't be a problem to hack into.

The guards continued to search the whole campus for any signs of them, or more bodies, but came up empty. Leslie and Terrance were gone, and as the copter came down in the field, the sun was going down in the distance.

71

I couldn't help but feel we were leaving the camp in far worse shape than we had arrived in.

Skip approached us, bags heavy under his bloodshot eyes. "Catch those bastards. Catch them and make them pay," was all he said before turning and walking away.

I'd be telling Dalhousie she might want to replace Skip as the man in charge of the camp. I imagined life for the hybrids would get worse before it got better, especially with Skip in charge.

Mae followed us in. For the first time, I noticed she had an extra bag with her. I made a mental note to ask her about that later, when things were less tense.

We left at dusk, with more questions than we'd had when we arrived.

EIGHT

"*D*ean, wake up," Mary said through the headset, light-ly nudging me with her hand.

If I couldn't hear the whirring of the helicopter, I might have forgotten where I was. My head throbbed as I looked around the dim back seat; the soft lights of the pilot's dash were the only source of ambiance, and I wanted to close my eyes and go back to my dreamless slumber.

"Dean, we're landing for a refuel. Let's get something to eat. The pilot said he would be a while, and that the food was good at the station. If my memory serves me right, I've been to this army base before. It's in southwest Kentucky," Mary said. "It was top secret, but I'm guess-ing that doesn't matter anymore."

At the thought of food, my stomach growled and wouldn't stop.

It was close to one AM when we landed and were ushered to the base's kitchen. It was quiet there, few peo-ple were out, probably all sleeping for an early rise, but I was surprised to see the lights to the kitchen still on.

Mae hadn't spoken since we'd left Long Island, and I was worried about her for more than one reason. I knew it was hard on her to think about what she was, feeling out of place among the humans when the rest of her kind were caged up like animals, set to menial tasks to keep their bodies occupied. Then the fact that two of them had escaped now, setting up assassinations and terrorist threats out in the real world. It was enough to drive me mad, so it could only be eating her up.

"Mae," I said, holding back as Mary followed a private, sent to get us fed, through the kitchen doors. "I want you to know we're here for you, and together we'll find these two. Then we can rebuild the foundation of a long-term partnership between all of you and us." I meant it, but she almost rolled her eyes as I said the words.

"Dean, do you really think it's going to be that easy? Even if we do find them, which I doubt we will, the stigma was already against us. We were never going to be left to roam free amongst you. They only let me walk around because they can trust you two, and Dalhousie knows I'm important to you and Mary. Otherwise, I'd be in that fenced POW camp just like the rest of them. I'm here to keep you on their side, nothing more."

Her words stung, and hard. I stood there outside, with nothing but a small lantern fixture on the wall by the door giving Mae a stern, shadow-covered face. Moths flitted around the light, casting even stranger shapes over her.

"I hope you're wrong about that, but if you aren't, we're still here for you no matter what. You have my word." It was all I could say, and she walked past me, eyes downcast, and entered the building. She would get better; it was just too soon.

The smells of camp rushed back to me, and that was all I could equate it to, since I'd never been in the military. The mixed scents of many different foods floated along the air, throughout the mess hall, and from the cook's kitchen in the back. We walked down the center of the large room, tables and chairs lining the hall, all ready for the morning breakfasts.

The kitchen was immaculate, and Mary was chatting with the private. An alert cook smiled at us as we entered, whisking away in a stainless-steel bowl.

"Omelettes? I make them better than anyone here, and since I'm prepping for the morning, it's what's on the menu," he said with a slight southern drawl.

"Sounds perfect to me," I said, sitting down at the stools lined up before a metal table, which was covered in flour and bowls.

The smell of fresh brewing coffee wafted over and made me all the hungrier. I knew Mae had a newfound love of the roasted beans, so I got up and gathered a bunch of cups, asking the cook if I could help myself. He showed me where everything was, and soon we all sat with steaming cups of the good stuff in front of us.

Soon we were eating what might have been one of the best omelettes of my life. Mae was almost smiling at the private's stories about growing up as a military brat, and Mary was on her third cup of java. For a moment, it felt like life was real and normal, and then my phone rang.

A New York number came up, and I slid the bar, answering it.

"Dean, we have some news." Skip's voice called through the phone's speaker.

I muted it. "Guys, Skip's on the phone. I'm going to speaker him."

"The IT guy from the CIA has hacked in, and we now have a GPS reading on the hybrids. We have them halfway between Lexington and Nashville right now." His voice carried through the kitchen, and I turned the volume down, not wanting the whole base to hear.

"That's only an hour or so south of us. Maybe we can

catch up to them," Mary said, pushing herself off the stool. She looked so beautiful, hair tight in a ponytail, eyes alert. "Private Sama, can you point us to our transportation?"

★ ★

*T*he clock on the dash read four AM as we raced down the 9002 toward I-65 south, which would lead us directly to Music City USA. I drove as Mary kept track on her borrowed tablet of Leslie and Terrance in their stolen delivery truck. Skip told us their models had a built-in governor, which wouldn't allow the vehicles to go over sixty-five miles an hour. It was a safety feature they'd needed for insurance before the Event, apparently, and it was one we were thankful for. With those limitations, we could catch them shortly after they hit the city.

"Are you sure we shouldn't alert the local authorities?" I asked, not sure we were equipped to take these dangerous hybrids down even if we did catch up to them.

"Dalhousie wants this under the radar. We can't afford to have the link to the hybrids revealed, or else it will be pandemonium… and unfair to the rest of them." Mary looked back at Mae, who was sitting in the back seat, eyes closed.

"Just where do you think they're going? What's in Nashville?" I asked.

Mary shrugged. "Maybe nothing, maybe everything. Maybe it's just a city on their path to somewhere else."

I thought about this, and then wondered at the convenience of them being on the same path as we were flying in the helicopter. Did they know where we were going? Were they trying to be obvious? Maybe they weren't even in the truck but had swapped it out with a waiting vehicle.

"Where do you think that secret base is? It looked like desert, so if it's in the States, I have to guess New Mexico or Arizona, which would put us on a straight line from New York to here, then to one of those states," I said. "I wish they would just tell us, but I suppose that's a risk if someone captures us." I pictured the two dead bodies we'd just crossed paths with the day before and didn't want to be on the receiving end of the two we were chasing.

"That's the deal. Too many loose threads. I tried to text Nat but got nothing back. I'm guessing they have a block on the whole area, which I don't blame them for," Mae offered, finally talking. It was good to hear her voice without sadness laced through it. I smiled at her from the rear-view mirror, not sure if she could see it or not from where she was sitting.

"How much farther? I could use a coffee and a pit stop," I said.

"We're an hour out of Nashville but closing in on them. I'd say we catch them twenty miles before city limits, but we have time to stop really quickly, because I imagine we aren't going to ram them off the road if we do find them." Mary fidgeted with the tablet, zooming in on their location.

"They have to sleep just like us, so they might be taking turns, but if they're heading to a big city like Nashville, I'd say they're meeting someone," Mae said from the backseat.

The dash lights dimly glowed against my face, and I remembered driving a Jeep on our journey a year ago. It had been a lot different, but somehow the tension and the adrenaline were now familiar to me; my days of counting beans for people's small businesses in upstate New York felt like a lifetime ago.

We pulled over at a truck stop outside of a small town named Portland. It always struck me as amusing how we loved to recycle our town and city names, but then again, how many people in the world were named Dean? Or Mary? I shrugged it off and noticed the gas station lights weren't on. We had enough fuel to get us to Nashville, but since we'd stopped, I wanted to take advantage of the lost time.

"Dean, I think the pumps are still on," Mary called.

Turned out they hadn't been turned off, and we could use our credit cards to pay for the gas. It was more than I expected from an old truck stop, but we were close to Nashville, and I imagined a lot of trucks came that way, judging by the volume of them sitting in the lot across the street. Most of them probably had sleeping truck drivers in them at that moment, and my eyes felt weary as I thought about it.

The lights came on in the attached diner, and the ladies went inside to use the restrooms and beg for some coffee to go. At that moment, I could hardly think of anything other than coffee.

My cell phone vibrated in my left front pocket and I pulled it out, wondering if Magnus had broken free and found service. The number said UNKNOWN, but there was a text message. *Don't trust her,* was all it said. Don't trust who? And who the hell was sending me a text an hour before the sun came up?

Care to elaborate? I sent back. By the time the ladies came back with cups of coffee, there still hadn't been a reply. Mary was almost running to me, passing me a cup after nearly spilling it.

"I'll never understand why some places don't have

those little cardboard slips to put around their cups. Seems like almost everyone buying one of these would prefer to not be burned." She frowned at me, softening when she must have seen my off expression. "Everything okay?"

"Yeah," I lied and hated myself for it. I just needed to consider the obscure message before I said anything aloud about it. "Bathrooms out back?"

"Just inside to the left. The nice lady said we could use them even though they aren't open for another thirty minutes," Mary said, still giving me a sideways glace.

As I walked, the phone vibrated again, and I was anxious to see what the mysterious "helpful" stranger who was sending me cryptic five AM messages had to say. Once inside the doors, I reached for the phone, but stopped short as I saw the middle-aged woman waving at me. The restaurant had that classic Middle America feel to it, and I loved the way the booths lined the walls, and the four-seaters were huddled around the middle of it all. I longed to go sit at the barstools like my father and I used to do when we'd head into town to get something for the farm.

It started off as a benefit to helping my dad do errands and fix something, or do yard work after, but as I got older, we just started to make it our tradition. My mother would often be invited, but she would just shoo us away, knowing it was a special bond between father and son. That, to her, was priceless.

The smell of oil on the grill in the back, right then, reminded me of the last time I'd had breakfast with my old man. I'd headed back to the country the year after Janine and I were married. He was sick but wouldn't let it stop him from going out for a big breakfast at the diner, just like always. When I tried to tell him we could just stay in, have some oatmeal or something, my mother just shook her head at me, and I knew what it meant. He wasn't going to live for long. It was prostate cancer, and it hit fast; faster than we could have imagined. I knew he wasn't well, but my mother, most likely trying to protect me, had kept the severity of it from me for too long.

My little sister had called me, frantic, but she had always been an overreactor. Thinking of her then, I decided to text her as soon as I'd used the washroom. I had a longing for the one family member I had left, even though she resented me for not following her and Mom to California after my dad died. It'd been hard to explain to a heartbroken fifteen-year-old that I couldn't uproot my life.

When we stepped into their house, the sights and smells of being a happy kid filled all my senses, and then I saw my father. He was sitting in his plaid chair, looking like a skeleton with skin. His sunken eyes creased as he smiled at us, and it had taken all my strength to not fall to my knees in tears.

Janine had held my hand firmly, and I knew she was feeling a portion of what I was. It was so strange, because as soon as I saw him, I felt an overwhelming layer of sadness, mixed with a heavy sense of missing him, even though he was right in front of me. I really just missed the fact that things were never going to be the same, and I could see in his eyes he felt that way too.

"Can I help you with anything?" the lady asked, as I stood there staring at the empty room like a crazy man.

"Sorry, just tired is all. Thanks for the coffee. I needed it." I smiled and went to the bathrooms, checking the message once I was inside the small room. *Think about it and all will be clear.* Not wanting to get into a message war with someone I didn't know, I put the phone away. A minute later, I was heading out the front doors, and back to the Jeep.

The message could mean anyone: Dalhousie, Leslie, Mae... though I didn't want to go there, it could even mean Mary. There was no sense in speculating. We had to get back on the road.

"You good to keep driving, or do you want to switch off?" Mary asked as I was about to get into the driver's side door.

"I'm as good as I'll ever be," I said, giving her a smile. I popped the top of the coffee, took a sip, and off we went, heading for Nashville.

*T*he sun was rising as we approached the city limits, farmland and small town being replaced with suburbs and chain stores. I'd never been there before and was glad I had someone navigating my way.

"They came this way and seem to veer off toward this industrial area. Looks like nothing but warehouses for a few miles," Mary said, pointing to the exit east.

Morning light blasted me, and I flipped the visor as we made our way down the secondary freeway. We were catching up and still didn't know what we were going to do if we caught the killers.

"They're stopping!" she called with a little more excitement than I was used to from her normally calm voice.

I slowed and exited off the freeway, now driving the large Jeep wheels over potholed, worn asphalt. It was Sunday, so traffic was light so early in the morning, and there wasn't a car in sight in the many parking lots we were passing by. Soon we were nearing an old building, an auto repair shop by the look of it.

Mary gestured to our left, and my heart raced when we spotted the bare white truck: the missing one from the camp in Long Island. Pulling behind a large cube van, I kept my distance and turned the engine off. There was no one in the truck, but that didn't mean they didn't have eyes on the street. For all we knew, they saw us driving up.

The sun was still low on the horizon, and here it was blocked by large buildings between us and the rays. I hoped being in the shadows would help us.

"We don't know what we're up against here. They could just be hiding out, or they could be meeting more of their brainwashed humans. We have to be careful." Mary looked at me and held my gaze for a moment longer than she normally would, emphasizing the word *careful.*

"I'll go," Mae said. "Recon, right? And if I get caught, I'll claim I broke out too, and tracked them. I know for a fact that the one right across the hall looks just like us, and my hair is pretty much the same length." She pulled her hair into a ponytail, and she was taking off her shirt. I averted my eyes, noticing how much she looked like my wife. I'd spent so much time with Mae that I rarely thought of her and Janine on the same wavelength any longer, but seeing her pulling her shirt over her head reminded me so much of Janny. "I borrowed some items from Donna that Leslie would recognize. I also have some of Leslie's stuff. You know, just in case."

I almost laughed at the ingenious planning. *Don't trust her.* The words echoed in my mind and I shook them out, knowing it couldn't be either of these women. They were as trustworthy to me as Magnus and Nat.

"Great thinking, Mae," Mary said, smiling through an

otherwise worried face.

"Just be careful, okay? Take a quick look around and come back. Take the walkie and let us know if you need us. Just hit the talk button twice, and don't say anything if you aren't able to speak," I told her. Just like that, she was out the door, quietly stalking across the road, out of view of the warehouse's windows or the truck. She hugged the neighboring building's wall, and before we knew it, she was out of our sight.

"Mary, I got a text a couple hours ago. It just said to not trust her."

"Trust who?" she asked.

"I don't know. The number was blocked, and they weren't very open about it." I handed the cell over for her to look for herself.

"You don't think they mean…" She left Mae's name unsaid.

"I'm not sure. I imagine that's who *they* mean, whoever *they* are. I don't believe it for a second, though. It could just as easily mean Dalhousie." I held the radio in my hand, anxious to hear from Mae. I hoped she was just going to find them sleeping in the empty warehouse, and we could go in together silently, taking them quietly and safely.

The walkie-talkie alert sounded, then another one in quick succession. Mae needed help.

We were out the door, running with our guns in hand, and I was thankful for the daily runs Mary had forced me to do over the last year. It helped me breathe and focused my nervous energy out of my body.

We'd seen Mae go to the left side of the warehouse, and scanned for her, seeing nothing but some stacked pipes and an old forklift.

"Open window over there," Mary whispered.

Backs to the wall, we listened and could hear voices. They were getting closer, and I could make out the words after a few seconds.

"They followed you?" a woman's voice asked.

"Yeah, I think they were right behind. I don't know how they knew where I was going." It was Mae's voice, and I cringed that she had to attempt this ruse.

"And just how did you find us?" a male voice asked with an edge to it: Terrance.

"Like I said, I stole a truck right after you guys. I knew what you guys were up to, so I was watching you. I thought I could catch up, but the damned truck wouldn't go over sixty-five," Mae said as Donna.

"We had a guy kill the GPS," Leslie said.

"Must be a separate circuit within the trucks to each other. I wondered how they didn't find us. I kept looking over my shoulder, expecting sirens." Mae was pulling off the role well.

"I'm going to check this out. Where's the truck?" Terrance asked.

"Just out the main doors, across the street."

"Why didn't you just pull up beside us?" he asked.

"Because it's Sunday, and I didn't want to draw any attention to a closed warehouse," Mae said with ease. I was very impressed with her quick repartee, and her ability to slide into someone else's skin. Her cadence was even different.

"Fine. But if there's anything at all fishy about it, it's over," Terrance said, and we could hear his heavy boot steps crossing the hard concrete floor of the warehouse. He was heading for the door near us. Inside, Mae spoke to Leslie in hushed tones, and I could tell she was leading her further into the warehouse. I looked at Mary, and she nodded, holding her gun firmly against her chest, ready to piston her legs up at the sight of Terrance. I mimicked her, and when the door flung open, she went high and right, and I stayed low and left.

He didn't have time to draw his own gun, as Mary pointed hers at him and smiled. She motioned for him to set it on the ground and kick it over, which he did. His face didn't betray his emotions for a second, and I knew I didn't want to play poker against the guy.

In a matter of seconds, Mae was leading out a pissed-off version of herself.

"You have no idea what you're doing, Donna. You're really helping these humans, the same two that stopped us from doing what we were born to do? You're as bad as her." Leslie didn't have to say *Mae* for us to all know who she meant. The look on Mae's face must have given something away. "Wait a minute. You're not Donna, are you? You're that traitor!" Leslie lunged at Mae, almost connecting a shove, when Mary shot the ground behind Leslie's feet.

"Get back!" Mary yelled. "And never call her that again. You don't have any power anymore."

Leslie's resolve slipped and her shoulders slumped. Terrance's firmly gripped fists loosened, and I hoped we were done with any altercations. Grabbing the zip ties from Mary's pack, I went behind Terrance first and tied his hands behind his back, followed by Leslie's. Guns were aimed at them the whole time.

"Let's get them in the back of the truck and get on the road. We'll call in and let them know we've acquired the targets," Mae said without emotion. I figured she felt like a part of her was betraying her kind again, but I also knew she wholeheartedly disagreed with what they were doing.

"I'll take the Jeep, if you guys don't mind," Mae said

as we slid the back shut on the truck and padlocked it. There had been nothing back there, and we checked thoroughly for any hidden compartments where a weapon might have been stashed.

"Everything okay?" I asked her softly.

She just nodded glumly and touched my hand for a second, before heading across the street with the Jeep keys jingling along the way.

Soon we were heading back to the main highway, en route to New Mexico where, we'd been told, a location would be sent when we were within a hundred miles of the secret base. It was all a little too covert for me, but alien security was probably a good idea given the Event, and the stuff the hybrids just tried to pull off. We didn't really know exactly what it was they were going to pull off, but we had to hope it could be stopped if the wheels were already in motion. I was happy to bring them to Dalhousie and General Heart, and let them deal with that part. I just wanted some sleep.

"Dean, let me know if you need to rest for a bit. I don't mind driving," Mary said from the passenger seat. It was stuffy in there, and I rolled the window down, letting in the warm morning air.

"Sounds good. Maybe in an hour or so. I'm too wound up to rest anyway." It was the truth.

"I love you," she said as she closed her eyes and turned from me.

"I love you too," I replied. The words from the text message hung in the front of my mind.

NINE

*I*t was a long drive to the border of New Mexico, and we had to fill up a few times. The truck's mileage was terrible, and each time we stopped at a near-empty, out-of-the-way gas station in hopes that no one would hear the two prisoners in the back if they decided to shout or cause a scene. Lucky for us, they didn't make a peep, and when we opened the door on the side of the road halfway through our journey, they were both cross-legged, leaning against the far corners, staring at us. They seemed surprised that we would offer them water and a bathroom break, but they took both with caution. I figured maybe compassion would soften them up, even though I knew they didn't deserve anything but the worst treatment for what they'd done. My mother's words rang in my mind as I tipped the water bottle slowly: "You catch more flies with honey." I'd never understood that as a kid but did now.

Mae seemed more like her old self; the time alone must have helped. We passed the border into New Mexico well past sunset, and because of the stops and the governor on the truck, it was around eight at night when the text came in from General Heart's people. Mary had a location sent to her tablet, and before we knew it, we were heading off the main highway, and onto a back road in the rocky, hilly landscape.

The dusk sky turned to darkness, and with no lights on the roadsides, I struggled to make sure we stayed on the road.

"How far now?" I asked for the fifth time in the last half-hour.

"Looks like we should be up on it soon. I have no idea how they've kept a whole facility hidden out here. There aren't a lot of homes or anything, but those vessels aren't small. Testing the ships must get seen by the people in the area," Mary said.

"Yeah, we saw a town, what, ten miles back?" I asked, not expecting an answer.

The road we were on ended, with a large cement barricade preceded by some reflective construction signs saying "Road Ends."

"What do we do now?" Mary asked, zooming in on her tablet.

"Pass that over, please," I said, reaching for it. "Looks like there's a dirt track here, and if we follow that, we should be there in a couple of minutes. I know it's dark, but I don't see a damn thing out there." It was pitch black out here by then, but the sky was full of stars out in the middle of nowhere, and the moon hung low in the sky, half-moon but full of reflective light.

"Just be careful," Mary said, reaching for the radio. "Mae, we have to go left here onto the dirt road, and I use the term 'road' loosely. Do you mind going ahead of us in the Jeep so we don't go bouncing into a big rock and end up stranded with Bonnie and Clyde in the back?"

"You got it. Just let me sneak around you. Where do you think it is? Shouldn't we see it by now? Guards? Lights? A fence?" Mae asked over the walkie.

"That's what we thought, but the map says we're almost there. All I see are rocks, dirt, and stars." Mary set the walkie down, and Mae pulled ahead of us, driving slowly over the bumpy terrain.

We bounced along behind her, the truck's old suspension not made for this kind of travel. Five minutes of that, and we were coming to another barricade. Mae slowed before us. It was the strangest thing. Our lights blasted the back of Mae's Jeep, and I turned them down. For a moment, I thought Mae had turned her lights off, but then saw they hit the construction signs but didn't travel beyond them, like some sick science experiment my brain couldn't comprehend.

"What is this?" I asked, getting out of the truck, almost stumbling as I looked forward. Mary was right behind me, and we walked over to Mae, who was also looking ahead, jaw dropped down in wonder.

Twenty feet in front of us, the air shimmered, and the light from the Jeep dissipated into nothing, like it was sucked into a black hole. I could see rocks and dirt beyond it, but it didn't look right, like we were being tricked with an optical illusion. Looking up, we could see the stars in the distance.

"Look," Mary said, pointing upward. I didn't know what she meant, but then I saw it. A blurry line straight across the sky, like something bent at that point.

Before we could try to figure out what it was we were seeing, a noise like a garage door squeaking open hit us, and forty yards to the right, a door *was* opening; a door out of thin air. Three people came out of the doorway, which was large enough for vehicles to pass through. I saw Mae bring her hand to her gun, which was tucked into the back of her pants. I wondered if I should do the same but recognized the man at the forefront of the three. The other two were holding assault rifles, and stood half a foot taller than Trent Breton, one of the engineers from our meeting with the president in Washington.

"Glad you could make it," Trent said, smiling wide. "Do you have the package?"

Mary nodded and pointed to the truck.

"Slate, do you mind pulling the truck to the compound? Henrik, take the Jeep, please." Trent was still smiling as he motioned for us to follow him. "Don't worry, your belongings will be brought to your rooms in a few minutes. Patrice asked me to meet you out here and show you the wall." He led us to the slightly shimmering façade and ran his hand along it, where I noticed a small, almost indiscernible ripple, like a crease in a bedsheet. "Pretty cool, wouldn't you say? We found some truly remarkable technology lodged in the ships' computers. Things we could never have imagined working so easily. Being an engineer, I always dreamed of inventing or working on something like this, a cloaking device of sorts."

I was finally picking up what he was saying. "Are you telling us there's a whole facility hidden behind this wall that looks just like the distant desert?"

"That's exactly what I'm telling you. I won't bore you with all the details, but it involves refraction, thousands of reflective cameras imaging other points, and a net of sorts. We actually have a solid wall with the device draped over it."

Mary lifted an eyebrow. "How do you keep people from seeing inside from above? Planes? Drones?"

"It covers the base in a dome. Think of a football stadium with a retractable ceiling," Trent said, seemingly very pleased with himself. I didn't blame him, because I was thoroughly impressed with it.

"And just how big is this dome of yours?" Mary

asked.

He paused, as if thinking, and continued walking until they neared the open bay door. The truck passed through, and we waited to the side as the Jeep followed it. Once they had safely passed us, he stepped forward and smiled widely once again. We followed, and I was amazed at what I saw.

From the outside, we just saw a representation of the night, complete with hills, rocks, landscape, and stars; but when we looked inside, there was a huge structure, lights high in the roof, which had to be three hundred feet in the air. It went on for as far as I could see in all directions, and off what must have been a few miles was one of the transport vessels. Though I'd seen them countless times over the past year, my pulse still quickened at the sight of the gargantuan ship.

"It's about twenty square miles. We had to make it big enough to house the vessel for testing, and everything else we're doing here, including weapons testing. We couldn't have anyone seeing what we're doing. And for all we know, we're always being watched, maybe from space right now. Even by the Bhlat. We don't know enough, so we erred on the side of caution," Trent said. He wasn't kidding.

"How was it possible to cover that much space with this net?" I asked.

"Once we had it figured out, it came down to 3D printers… a lot of them. It's amazing what you can accomplish with some of the world's foremost engineers and a lot of resources. We had printers sent from all around the globe, and it only took two months to make it. After multiple glitches and setbacks, we were up and running six months ago," he said, walking into the base. We followed behind. The doors slid shut as we cleared the opening, clinking shut with finality, and we were closed in.

"What about people in the area? How could you keep this secret?" Mae asked. We were all full of questions.

"We picked an isolated spot, but one that was quickly accessible from most of the United States. It had a low ratio of people per square mile because of the hard ground and lack of farmable land, so Dalhousie took a tenth of the state and relocated everyone within a hundred-mile radius, or wherever they wanted to go. With half the houses vacant in the States, it wasn't that hard. Now, if you'll come with me, I'll show you to your rooms to freshen up. I heard you had a long day." Trent didn't pry any further on our adventures, and I was thankful for it as we made our way through the rocky terrain, on foot at first, until one of the carts we'd seen on the video in Washington swung by and picked us up. It sat the four of us with no problem, and we were whisked away to a group of shipping containers a mile or so away.

We'd headed in the direction of the vessel, and now I could see the large building beside it: the warehouse we'd seen the ships in on the video. I got a tingle thinking of those gray ships, red lasers blasting out of them, cutting the ground in front of us on our way south to get to Florida.

There weren't many people lingering around, and those that I saw were uniformed like the guards had been. Not quite military, and not quite police, but something in the middle. The accountant in me wanted to see the books for this place, if they even bothered keeping track of it anymore.

The shipping containers were stacked on top of each other, so they were around ten high, and twenty left to right. There was an intricate step and balcony system, making them all accessible from the ground, and each had its own door. I remembered seeing an article on the web a couple years before about people using containers like this for homes, and I could now see they'd done the same thing. If I wasn't in a dome hiding alien spaceships, I would have been more impressed.

"This is an interesting setup. Who stays here?" Mary asked Trent from the backseat.

The cart stopped, letting us out. I said thank you to the driver before he took off, leaving us standing at the base of the Lego-like structure.

"We have a more permanent structure for the staff, guards, engineers, and physicists. Dalhousie and the General have another complex where they stay if they're around these parts for a visit. You guys are the first to stay here, with the exception of your friends." As if on cue, a dog barked, and in the artificial daylight, I saw Carey bounding toward me, tongue flopping out the side of his mouth, his ears flapping up and down with each hop.

"Carey!" I called to him and lowered to my knees, enveloping him in a hug as he jumped on me, getting a wet face for my efforts. "Who's a good boy? I missed you, bud." He seemed to like that as he wiggled around me, rolling on the ground before saying hi to Mary, with a hesitant greeting for Mae.

Magnus and Natalia walked toward us, coming from behind the container complex, holding cups of coffee. Magnus had a tennis ball in his hand, and I assumed he'd been playing fetch with Carey in the grassed area behind the buildings.

I had a vision of a bad sitcom taking place here, about the crazy characters living in a complex of shipping containers in an alien ship research facility. I'd call it the *Earth Defense Farce*.

Nat picked up her pace when she got closer, and Magnus raised an eyebrow at seeing her obvious concern. Her having friends had thrown him for a bit of a loop, seeing a new woman blossom in her. She gave us each big hugs, and Magnus came in and did the same.

"You guys do know we only parted ways two days ago, right?" Mary asked, and it surprised me it had only been that long. It felt like at least a week.

"But you got to do all the exciting stuff, while we were cramped up in…" Magnus waved his arm in the air. "Whatever this is. Everything go okay?"

Trent stepped forward, and it seemed like we'd forgotten the engineer was present. "I'm going to bed now, but I'm sure I'll see you in the morning. Choose whatever rooms you like. They're unlocked, and the keys are inside the desk drawers."

We said goodnight, and before we knew it, the gang was back together.

"Welcome to the Earth Defense Unit," Trent said before walking away.

The words were meant to be friendly, but they carried a weight with them: a sense of finality.

"Well?" Magnus prompted.

"Yes. It went well. Almost too well," Mae said. "Do you think we could freshen up and get something to eat? Maybe we can tell you our tale with Dalhousie there to save the redundancy."

Magnus looked a little taken aback, but he let it slide. "Sure thing. You guys have had a stressful couple of days. Take a unit. Nat has eleven, and I took twelve." He smiled at me. "What? We like to be close. It's safer that way."

Mae was already walking to the complex, and soon she was inside the bottom left unit, Number One.

"Is she okay?" Nat asked Mary in hushed tones.

"I think so. The hybrids are in a tough spot, and those two crazy bastards aren't helping things. I'm just glad we caught them before they could do any more damage." Mary walked on, taking Unit Five. "Dean, you coming?" she asked, and for some reason, I wasn't sure if she was going to take her own room or not. I guess that answered that.

"We'll just be a few minutes. Then you guys can call us a cab, and we'll go for dinner and drinks, maybe some dancing," I joked, and Magnus guffawed for my benefit.

"Sounds like a plan, I'll bring the Hummer around," Magnus said, and Nat gave us a small wave. Carey looked confused for a second, but soon he plopped along, following us inside the room. I shrugged at Magnus and shut the door.

The room was bigger inside than I would have guessed. To the right was a living room, with a door at the end of it, leading to a bedroom. The kitchen was on the left, and a bathroom straight ahead. Overall, I was thoroughly impressed with the effective setup.

We found food on the kitchen shelves, mostly stuff with long shelf life, and the bathroom was stocked with toiletries. It was like our own little hotel in a dome in the desert.

Ten minutes and a hot shower later, I was snacking on some crackers, while Mary was drying her hair. A knock clanged on the door, and Carey ran to it, giving it a bark for good order. Mae was there, in a uniform like the ones the guards were wearing.

"Did they not bring your luggage to your room?" I asked, since ours had made it there five minutes ago.

"They did. I just wanted to be in the part. If I'm Earth Defense, then I'm Earth Defense." Her back straightened as she said it, and I thought there was a sense of pride emanating from her.

"It looks damn nice on you," Mary said as she stepped into the room. "Mae, are you okay?"

Mae stepped in, grabbing a couple of crackers and leaning down to pass one to the begging cocker spaniel. He graciously accepted. "I will be. I feel responsible for what Leslie and Terrance have done, killing those people, working with humans to attack. We have to find out how deep the web goes."

"Maybe it was just the one in Washington. It seemed like they just wanted to distract the country with some random shooting. Or give people the impression they had more power than they actually do," Mary said.

"I hope you're right. Either way, I do feel better now that we're here, and they're locked up." She smiled and set her hand on my arm. "And thanks for saying it looks good on me." She spun around, and we laughed.

A horn honked once, and I looked at my watch, worried it was a little late to be honking a horn.

"Don't worry, Dean. There's no one sleeping nearby right now. It's only ten thirty. Let's get some food and see what Dalhousie has for us," Mary said, and with that, we left our newly-discovered temporary home.

TEN

*T*he lights were dim in the sterile room, and crumbs were all that was left of my late-night sandwich. I sipped the bottom part of my coffee as Dalhousie and General Heart listened to us tell our tale from the start of the mission to getting to their base. She wrote some notes as we spoke, and I could see her write with fervor as we told her about the erratic behavior Skip had displayed.

"Good thing you had that CIA IT guy," Mary said. "We would have been searching for a needle in a haystack otherwise."

The president nodded slowly, a frown crossing her forehead. "It was just too easy. Don't you think murderers would have gone with a fight? Especially since it was you three who went to get them."

"Did you want them to fight? Dispose of us?" Mae asked, taking the comments a different way than I had.

Dalhousie shook her head. "Mae! I'm just saying it seemed a little too simple. Did they say anything at all about other contacts outside? Any big threats they're planning to set off with some human help?"

"We didn't really have time for a big conversation out there. We just wanted to get them into custody and brought to you. Where are they now?" I asked.

Tapping her finger on the desk, the president looked deep in thought, as if calculating something important.

"Sorry? Oh, they're in some makeshift brig. We've added some to the ships and vessels. If we ever make contact out there, we want to be able to lock an enemy up if needed. On the ships, we've made prison sections. For the same reason, or for our own people if needed."

This reminded me of all the atrocities humans had done against themselves while in space the first time.

"Why would we need the vessel ships any longer?" Magnus asked quietly.

"Because if the Bhlat do find us, we don't have enough protection. We're sending a colony ship out to Proxima b," Dalhousie said with finality.

All my life, I'd thought about exploring the stars, since I was a kid wishing I was on the bridge of the *Enterprise*, and we were going to do it. My eyes shifted to Mary, and she was looking back at me, as if we had some unspoken agreement.

"Who's going on this trip?" Mary asked for us.

Dalhousie paused, looking over at General Heart. With a gesture meaning *go ahead*, Heart took over. "Proxima Centauri b is liveable."

"How do we know that?" Magnus asked gruffly.

"Because I've been there." Heart sat up straight, looking us in the eyes one by one, as if to gauge a reaction. "I went with Slate and Jeff Dinkle, along with Allana and Clare." He referred to the burly guard we'd met on our approach, and the TV host obsessed with aliens. The other two had been at our meeting in Washington: physics and engineering.

We all sat on the edge of our seats, blown away that there was a whole planet that we could access at our fingertips.

"Well?" Mary blurted, and cut the tension in the room.

"It was everything we hoped for. Lush green land, water, and breathable air." Heart, normally a stoic man, smiled widely.

"Were there… other life-forms there?" I asked, curiosity burning my veins.

"Yes. No intelligent life, and by that, I mean we saw no signs of humanoid or bipedal life. They do have a wide assortment of insects and wildlife, like any planet with a healthy ecosystem would," Heart explained. It was a lot to take in.

"I'm not sure why everyone is so surprised. We were invaded, had half our world killed by an alien race who in turn had hybrid human-aliens, and they were being chased out by an even bigger, badder race. God knows how many worlds are out there, but one thing we do know is we have faster than light travel now, and this opens the universe to us. To all its wonders and dangers." Dalhousie looked like she was going to start standing in her speech but stayed sitting at the last line.

"So those ships had FTL?" Mary asked. I knew what FTL stood for from the mass of science fiction I'd devoured as a young single man. Accountants have all read the classics, no matter what they tell you.

"Yes, it turns out the input Teelon supplied you and Natalia didn't explain everything about the ships. Whether this was a glitch, an issue of compatibility with the human brain, or a conscious decision by the creature hellbent on killing two races, remains to be seen. But we know we can travel around four light years in a month of our time." The president looked for a reaction, and she got it. We couldn't hold back our surprise.

"You're telling me we can get to this planet and back in just over two months?" Magnus asked.

"Not in the vessel ships. Their tech is a little more

dated, but they can do it in twice that. I don't understand it all, but the team tells me it harnesses singularity: the power of a black hole. If they had this technology, and were afraid of someone, we should be afraid too. I take that back… we have to be cautious," Dalhousie said.

"Damn right we have to be afraid. Let's not beat around the bush here, Madame President, some bad mamas are out there, and they want to kill us and take our world. Probably for resources, or maybe they want us as slaves, like the Kraski did for the Deltras. Either way, we're hooped unless we figure it out before they end up on our doorstep." Magnus reached for his cup, finding it empty.

"You didn't answer my question. Who's going to Proxima?" Mary asked for the second time.

Heart looked at the president and pulled at his collar in a nervous gesture. "Magnus and Natalia will be going with Dinkle," he said, and I leaned forward as he continued, "as well as other key parties who will specialize in setting up Earth's first-ever colony. Mae will also be going with them." He said the last part as if it was of second importance. I thought he was trying to just slip it in there at the end.

"What about us?" I finally found my voice.

"We need you and Mary here. You're the face of the resistance against anything alien to our people. We're putting you two in charge of the Earth Defense Unit, and you'll work side by side with General Heart here. What you don't know about training pilots and intelligence officers, he and his team will help you with." Dalhousie took all the wind out of my sails as she spoke. I'd been relegated to becoming a pencil pusher even after saving the world. That was a full three-sixty.

Carey was at my feet, and his chin moved and set

down on my shoe. I'd missed him too. Finding a small piece of leftovers on the table, I brought it to him, and he happily took it without complaint. At least I could stay with him through this training.

"We're also working on expanding the fleet. So far, we've been able to duplicate the ships with success and are designing them with humans in mind. I think you'll enjoy the tour in the morning." Dalhousie was ending the meeting with her comments, and though I wanted nothing more than to see what was inside that massive warehouse, I also wanted to close my eyes and sleep like a baby for twelve hours.

We headed back to the sleeping complex in carts and were quiet the whole time. There was a lot to take in, and the idea of staying behind while our friends left for a new world was something that would take getting used to.

After saying good night, and a quick pre-sleep routine, Mary and I were in bed, two single beds pushed together with a queen-sized sheet overtop. Her hand rested on my face, and we looked at each other as Carey snored at our feet. "If I have to train an Earth Defense unit with anyone, I'm glad it's you," she said.

I didn't reply, just kissed her softly and closed my eyes. I saw ships in the skies, strange planets, and the burning sun as I dozed off to slumber.

*T*he morning air was dense and warm, instantly making my new uniform cling to my skin as we made our way toward the ship hangar. Beside it sat the transport vessel, just like the one I'd floated in space to affix the tether to, saving a large chunk of lives. It seemed such an insanely immense task now, but then it had just been the end goal of a long journey. The outside of the vessel was the same matte black I remembered, and I was curious to see the adjustments they'd made to the interior. They had been functional before, but they would need better plumbing and other systems to make them work for a large group going for an extended trip. We learned that the Kraski had been planning on moving their whole population in them, but where I thought of interstellar travel using cryogenics to put the travelers out, they were going to just gas their people with a drug that would keep them in a sort of stasis that wouldn't need food or water for extended periods of time. They'd tried to use them on the humans so they wouldn't know what hit them as they ran into the sun, but almost all of them had failed.

I supposed the Kraski would have been upset if they got their people on board, only to find out many would die before arriving because of a lack of supplies. Turned out they didn't need them, because the mystery race called the Bhlat ended the need when they invaded and killed the whole planet's worth of Kraski. They'd already left in anticipation, since the vessels were being stored deep in their system.

Could I blame them for being an ornery bunch, wanting a new world? No. But I also wouldn't let myself feel bad for killing the ones that had come to Earth. Karma and all that. I just hoped it didn't come back to bite me, but if it did, that was the universe.

"I can't believe you guys are going to another planet," I said to Magnus and Natalia as we approached General Heart and Clare, the other main engineer alongside Trent. She smiled widely at us, and it was nice to have a friendly face around. Heart seemed to have a perpetual scowl that wouldn't lift.

"Yes, my friend. I wish you three were coming with us. Maybe we can talk them into it. Won't be the same without you all there." Magnus smiled as he spoke.

Heart looked extra perturbed and he motioned me aside.

"Why don't you all go ahead? I just have to speak with Mr. Parker for a moment," Heart said, taking my arm in a light grip and walking me twenty feet past the door. When he spoke again, it was in hushed tones. "Dean, something is off about our guests you brought in. They claim they did have a part in the shooting, but it was intentionally not deadly. They wanted to escape and create chaos among us while doing so, but they also said they really just want to get their people, the hybrids, off-planet. There's somewhere else they know out there that will take them in, and they don't want to be a burden to us any longer. They feel like sitting in a prisoner of war camp, though we aren't calling it that, but let's call a spade a spade here, is a horrible fate. They understand now that they were brainwashed their whole lives, and they're acting remorseful."

I held up my hand. "Wait now. General, if you saw the bloody corpses they left in their wake back in Long Island, you wouldn't believe a damned word those psychos said."

"That's the other thing. They say they had nothing to do with those deaths. When we brought them up, they genuinely looked shocked and upset at Clendening being dead. Leslie cried, saying they'd been lovers. I don't trust them, but something doesn't add up here." Heart wiped his forehead with a handkerchief.

The images of the dead guard on his bed and the other hanging in the loading dock office hit me, and I felt sick to my stomach. If they hadn't done it, then who had?

Could Skip have been off his rocker enough to do it, so he could blame the hybrids he hated so much?

"We'll keep it up, but I wanted to let you know. They asked me to tell you specifically that they're innocent and just want to leave Earth. According to them, most of the hybrids from Long Island would leave willingly. They also don't trust Mae."

I thought about this and didn't blame them. She was the first one to help us, and without her, they would have succeeded in killing off the human race.

"They just see her as one of us now," I said, and Heart and I made our way to the hangar doors.

"Maybe you can talk to them later? They asked for you," he said, looking desperate for answers. I got the feeling that Heart was happy to have someone else there to divert the hybrid or alien business to. While I was sure he made a hell of a general pre-invasion, he looked older now than even the few days earlier when I'd met him, and much older than the interviews I'd seen with him on television months after we were returned.

"I'm not sure what I can do, but I'm here to help," was all I could think of to say.

He looked relieved and together we walked into the building. Its ceilings must have been one hundred and fifty feet high, and inside were half a dozen of the Kraski ships. There was a charge of energy inside the room, causing the hairs on my arms to lift a little bit.

Heart passed me a green pin, and I placed it on my uniform lapel. I was looking forward to someone explaining the technology behind these devices that allowed us to pass through a solid wall.

The ship closest to us was black, not the silver-gray of the other Kraski ships.

"What's this?" Mary asked, running her hand over the

smooth surface of the ship. Where the original Kraski ships were about eighty yards long, this one was almost twice that.

Heart smiled wide but waved his hand over to Clare to take over the answering period. "This is our newest design. We took everything you know and love about the original Kraski ships, and we've integrated some great features for humans: toilets, Bluetooth speakers for music, and just the right amount of mix in the air."

"Why does the outside look different?" I asked, seeing not only a color difference, but a texture variance.

"You know the technology we use to stay hidden out here in the dome? This ship has the same thing. It isn't as effective in a closed building, but out in the sky or space, you have to literally run into the thing to know it's there. We also found a way to block it from the Kraski and Deltra radars, and we're hoping that means it will stay hidden from other potential threats out there." Heart didn't have to say that he meant the Bhlat, because it was obvious.

Carey pulled against his leash and barked at a Kraski ship near us. It looked a lot less ominous on the concrete floor of a hangar than searching for us on our journey, ready to blast us into oblivion... if that had even been their plan. In the end, they were only trying to herd us to Machu Picchu to turn off the Shield. I wondered where the Shield was, guessing it was probably safely tucked away somewhere nearby.

Magnus and Natalia stood to the side, and she slipped her arm around the large man's waist and pulled him close. He leaned down to kiss the top of her head, and I couldn't help but feel happy for the two of them. They would be among the first people to go to a new world, and I couldn't think of anyone I'd rather have relish an experience like that than them. The fact that I'd miss

Nathan Hystad

them went without saying. The urge to call my old best friend James overtook me, and I shoved it down, deciding I'd ask for a way to reach outside the dome later. While I was at it, I'd call my sister, whom I also needed to talk to all of a sudden.

"We won't need the pins for this, but they might come in handy, like in your adventures." Heart clicked a button on a keychain, and the ship raised up off the ground quietly, followed by a ramp dropping to the ground under the new ship. This way, you could bring goods on and off the ship with a dolly, and not need to float through like an alien wizard. The technology the Kraski had was cool, but not always practical.

Carey hesitated on the grated ramp, but when he found his feet wouldn't fall through, he ran up in excitement. Though Magnus and Nat were leaving us behind, I was grateful that Carey could stay with us, and we could stay an odd little family. Mary was ahead of me, her uniform hugging her curves, making the whole picture look far more flattering than my uniform on me. She'd told me it was hot, and passed me her aviators back at the room, slapping me in the butt and calling me Maverick. We'd laughed, and I couldn't help but think of how lucky I was.

I was the last up the ramp to the ship, and as I'd expected, we were in a small bay used for storage and supplies. The lighting was soft and less sterile than the Kraski ship had been. Essentially, we were in the middle of the ship; behind us were the crew quarters, which consisted of four rooms with bunks. Two rooms had four beds, and the other two had two each, making room for twelve to sleep at the same time, but with most crews, I imagined there would be shifts. The space was twice the size of the other ships, but the idea of sharing the space with twenty people over an extended period of time was enough to make me feel claustrophobic.

Mary held up, and after a nod from Heart, she let Carey off his leash to explore. He barked in excitement and took off. "Quite the different experience, huh? I honestly hardly remember what the Kraski ship we flew in looked like, I was so invested in flying it and trying to stop what was happening. Basically a trip fueled by adrenaline, stress, and fear. I remember lying in those beds and talking to you. I think I started to fall for you that moment." She said this, and I remembered it all vividly. The ship, the sterile smell, sharing that moment with Mary was when I'd really started falling for her too. I also remembered tethering myself up along with Magnus to find a vessel half-filled with dead people.

"I fell for you too," was all I could bring myself to say.

Before we got back to the loading area, Heart showed us the small room that housed a dozen or so suits, designed specifically to fit human males and females, with built-in body fluid recyclers and radiation protection like the Kraski suits. They also had the thrusters attached to the hand controls, which would come in handy if you were floating uselessly in space. I hoped to never be in that position again.

"These kick ass!" Magnus said, sifting through them, probably seeing if they had one large enough to fit his big frame.

I noticed a cabinet, but when I tried to open it, I couldn't pull it open.

Heart put his thumb to it. It beeped, then unlatched. "We'll get you guys set up on the system when we're done here. You'll have full access." I caught an underlying sense of unease in the general at giving a civilian access to all of this, but Dalhousie had him sold on us working on the Earth Defense Unit. In time, I was sure he would grow to trust, and hopefully even like us.

Inside what looked like a large custom wardrobe from a high-end house sat a line of weapons, each larger than its predecessor. Magnus nudged me and whistled as he saw the arsenal.

"Not planning on meeting any friendlies out there, are we?" he asked as a joke, but it sat at the pit of my stomach. He was right.

We continued the tour, crossing up to the front half of the ship, where we passed by an engineering room. Clare glowed as she explained the propulsion system. It was all over my head, but Mary looked enthralled; I'd ask her to spell it out in layman's terms later. What I did understand was that each of the ships had FTL capability. When activated, the propulsion boosters opened from behind the ship, and it took hours to charge the drives, depending on how long your trip was. Otherwise, they could travel any direction with all the mini-thrusters we'd been using, and they were quite fast, from my experience.

The bridge came next, and it was gorgeous. Instead of the small space we'd been in, with two seats and a computer screen, it was like something out of all the science fiction movies I'd seen. Large viewport front and center, with five seats, each with their own workstation. Fashion added to function, since it was the first model Earth had built themselves. Brown leather trimmed the swiveling chairs, reminding me a bit of my office chair at my old company.

Heart and Clare showed us around, and I was only half-listening as they clicked controls and showed viewscreen options. I didn't expect to be flying one of these ships myself, so I'd leave it to the professionals. As it went on, the walls felt like they were closing in on me, and before they were done, I slipped out, with the excuse I was going to find Carey. As I neared the ramp out, Carey found me, nuzzling into my leg. Together we walked down and outside – if I could call it outside, since there was a ceiling over our heads high above. They'd done a great job of having soft light, imitating the sun, and then I realized it was sunlight we were seeing. The canopy reflected and emulated the other side of the net they'd installed. I could even make out clouds. It was amazing.

"Dean, they want to show us the newly renovated colony ship." It was Mae. She'd approached so quietly while I was looking to the *sky*. When I turned to her, I could have sworn I was looking at Janine, but I pushed the memories away.

"Sounds good." It came out choked.

She rubbed Carey's head, which caused him to follow after her as we made our way to the modified transport vessel.

I'd originally underestimated the size of the things when they'd first lowered to Earth, and though the news had given a solid estimate, they could realistically hold about a million people in comfort. The sheer volume cramped on them a year ago had been deadly in many ways.

"How many people are you bringing on this first venture to Proxima?" I asked Clare, who in return beamed at me, running her fingers through her short bob-cut brown hair.

"The plan called for around one hundred, but as we got deeper into it, with maintenance, construction, botanists, air and water purification, and all the other boxes, we needed about one thousand to check them all off. I wish you were coming with us. I mean, the hero of mankind and all. Would be nice to have you alongside us as we find a new home." Clare turned a bit red, and I wasn't sure if it was from her gushing to me, or because she might have let some secret information slip.

Mary was behind me, rolling her eyes as soon as I looked back. She didn't seem the jealous type, and why should she be? She was a strong, beautiful woman, whom I didn't even deserve.

"Wow, one thousand? Do all the people who are going know it yet?" I wondered how they would all take the news.

"Most of them. Some of the roles, we asked for volunteers. Doctors, veterinarians, teachers…" She looked me in the eyes. "We need certain people to come, and most wouldn't come unless their families were able to join. We want this to be a wonderful experience for everyone, and the future is there, so having families and schools will give us a foundation to build our new home on." I could hear Dalhousie's passion through this young woman.

"It all sounds great. I can't wait to visit," I said. I had an idea. "My sister, Isabelle Parker, is a veterinarian in California. I think this is the type of thing she'd love to do. Can we pose it to her?" The last time we'd talked, she seemed so down, and she had always been more of a space nut than me.

"Of course." Clare beamed at me. "Anything for your family, Dean. Send me her number and we can contact her. Unless you want to make the invite?"

"Sure, how about I call her and ask? I've been meaning to talk to her."

Clare smiled and walked ahead, talking to Natalia now, and I slowed, letting Mary catch up. "Oh, Dean, I wish you were coming with us," Mary said in a light pouty voice, pushing her chest against my arms and giggling.

"That's enough. I'm sure it has less to do with her wanting to sleep with me, than it does that I'm some sort of idol. God knows I deserve their attention less than any of you guys do, but if all the women in the world now want a piece of me, then I suppose I'll just have to make myself be permanently unavailable." I blurted the words without thinking what they meant, and when it clicked, I surprised myself by not regretting what I said. After Janine had passed three or so years ago, if you'd have asked me, I would never even have looked at another woman. Mary had changed all of that in the most unbelievable of scenarios.

"Are you saying what I think you're saying?" Her joking tone was gone. "Or should I say, are you asking what I think you're asking?"

We were twenty feet back from the rest of the group by then, and I stopped her, holding her hands in mine.

"Mary Lafontaine, would you do me the honor of being my wife?" I whispered beside her ear, my lips lightly touching it.

She nuzzled in, and now her lips were on my ear. "Yes. Yes, I will do you the honor," she whispered back before biting my lobe.

"General Heart, you guys go ahead. We'll be right there. We just... forgot something back at the room," I called before we turned back, almost running to the hangar where a cart was waiting for us to borrow.

As the rest of the group went for a tour of the colony ship, all I could think about was how much I wanted to see my new fiancée's pants on the floor of our little room.

ELEVEN

The next few days were spent with me going over training plans, Mary getting lessons on the new ships as well as the old, and Magnus and Natalia helping organize the colony supplies' loading. It was a busy time for all of us.

It wasn't until day five there that Heart came knocking on my door early in the morning. Mary was already out, and Carey sat at my feet as I ate a light breakfast, hoping I would give in and share with him.

Heart looked tired as I opened the door, seeing him outside his uniform. He shrugged when he saw me appraising him. "I'm supposed to be leaving today to see my family for the weekend. Before I go, I wanted to ask if you would visit the prisoners. They've asked after you, and frankly, we're of two minds on them. If they *are* telling the truth, we'll be doing something horrible. We don't have a judiciary system set up for something like this. If they did kill those people, then we have to decide what to do." He said the last sentence gravely.

Against my wishes, I said, "Sure. I'll stop by this morning."

Just like that, I found myself standing in the prisoner area an hour later, waiting to be let through a secured door. It was more than secure, it was like Fort Knox; steel doors two feet thick were the only way in, with thumb and retinal scans, as well as a passcode. They weren't messing around. We had been given clearance for most things around the base, but not for this area.

As I waited, I pondered my engagement to Mary, knowing it was what my once-broken heart wanted, but wondering if that was the most opportune time for such an announcement. We'd decided to keep it secret for the time being, and it wasn't easy since we were surrounded by our closest friends.

The door buzzed, and the guard on duty led me through. I saw myself on screens along the wall, being filmed as I walked.

"You guys take this seriously," I said to the guard, who just grunted his assent. In a moment, we were at the end of the hall, past six or so empty cells.

"He's all yours. Just holler if you need anything." With that the guard was gone, back down the hall. Terrance and I were a few feet apart, separated by nothing but what appeared to be a thin wall of plastic. I knew better than that.

A folding chair was propped against the wall, on which I flipped down and set before the cell.

"Where is she?" Terrance asked. He looked sickly: pale and slick with a light sheen of sweat.

"Who?" I asked, before noticing Leslie wasn't in any cell down the hall. "Leslie?"

He nodded. Sitting on the edge of his small cot in the tiny room, he looked half the size he had when we found them in Nashville.

They hadn't filled me in on any of this. I imagined the two prisoners would have been kept apart so they could interrogate each alone.

"She's fine." I didn't like making it up, but these people killed in cold blood, and I didn't think a white lie was tipping the karmic scale in their case.

Nathan Hystad

His head hung down below his shoulders. "Dean, we just want to leave Earth."

"And where do you want to go?" I asked.

"There's a place. Just get them to let us go, and there will be no further trouble." It sounded like a veiled threat.

"What makes you think they'll listen to me? I'm just an accountant."

He made a noise like a snicker. "If you ask, they'll consider it."

These guys really gave me more pull than I had. I felt like an outsider at the base, but also knew that might change the longer I was there. Not that that was comforting.

"Why should I? We talked to Clayton in D.C. and he blamed you guys," I said, voice rising slightly.

He looked up from his stoop, making eye contact with me. "The shooting in D.C. was our doing. We knew it would get your attention. There was no other way we could get you in front of us to talk."

There had been a couple other shootings around the country in the past week, and Heart thought they might be connected to them. "Do you have anything to do with the other recent shootings?"

He shook his head. "No, we don't. You know how people are. Once a rumor starts, it spreads like wildfire. You don't think there are hundreds of people in the US that wouldn't conspire to frame the hybrids for something like this? They hate us. They blame us for all their loved ones being dead, for them being ripped from their homes into the sky, and the torture they endured as they starved in space. Can you imagine their hatred? It's venomous, and we just want to leave."

He made a good point, but something was missing. "If you wanted to get our attention, why did you run

114

when we showed up? Kind of defeats the purpose, doesn't it?"

He shrank back. "We had our reasons, and they'll be clear to you soon."

I hated all the vague talk, and told him so, to which he just shrugged.

"If you want me to believe you, you better damned well give me something more than your word and a shrug," I barked, standing up quickly. The chair flew back, clanging against the metal floor.

Terrance stood too, face right against the plastic wall between us. "Dean, they're probably coming, and I don't want to be here when they get here. Is that what you want to hear?" He was yelling, spittle hitting the barrier.

My pulse raced at his words. He was right. I could almost feel it in my hybrid blood. With each heartbeat, the Bhlat were closer to Earth, or closer to finding our location.

"They told me you claim you didn't kill those guards in Long Island. Tell me." Our faces were inches apart.

"We would never have hurt them. They were our friends. Where all the rest of them looked at us with contempt, they were always nice to us. They understood our plight more than anyone. Someone set us up, and I bet it was that piece of crap, Skip." His anger faded, and he was moving back to the cot's edge. If I was ever going to read someone's truth, at that moment, I would have said he wasn't lying. But how did the guards end up dead just as the two of them were leaving? Skip was an odd man, but was he capable of a setup like that… and murder?

"Tell me everything you know about the Bhlat," I said, grabbing a notepad from my back pocket.

Dust flew in the air behind our truck tires as Magnus drove down the side road away from the base. In the daylight, the dome just looked like more rocky terrain, and I was once again amazed at the technology.

"We're leaving in a couple days, Dean." Magnus tried to sip from his coffee travel mug, and almost splashed on himself as we hit a bump.

"How much more do you need?" I asked. They'd had an endless train of materials coming to the base over the last month. All of the product was being sent to a warehouse in Santa Fe. From there, Heart's crew picked it up.

"There were a few items they couldn't procure, or wouldn't, so here we are," he said, grinning widely.

I knew this to mean cigars, Scotch, and a less than palatable Scandinavian beer.

"I wish you were coming with us, bud," Magnus said. "I can't believe they're breaking up the Beatles. You know, we thought about turning them down." This was the first time he'd told me that.

"It's a once in a lifetime opportunity, and they need you two out there. If anyone can kick some ass if needed, it's you two."

"Well, I hope there are no asses there that need kicking. I kind of just want to play colonist farmer. Build a cottage on the beach. Maybe start a family." He looked at me in his periphery.

A family. I knew they were a couple, but the idea of Magnus and Nat sitting on their porch drinking sweet tea while the kids ran around the yard was a strange image, though also one I truly wished for them.

"You'll be a great dad. That much I know," was all I could say.

"How about you two lovebirds?" He was fishing for information, and I wondered if it was coming from his own curiosity, or if Nat had given him a mission. They had their suspicions about our new engagement but had been nice enough to only ask indirectly. I wished he would just ask the question straight out.

"Magnus, you're my best friend, so I'm going to cut to the chase. I asked her to marry me…" I was cut off by him almost driving into the ditch. He'd been staring at me, not the road.

"Really? Who did you ask?" he asked sarcastically. As we swung back to the packed-down dirt road, he looked at me apologetically, but his grin was as wide as I'd ever seen it. "I knew it! Nat owes me ten bucks!"

We laughed and chatted about the future over the next hour on the way to Santa Fe. It was so nice to put all the other stuff aside, and just be friends on a road trip.

We entered the city, and Magnus had me check the nav system for something I hadn't even thought about, mainly because Mary said it wasn't necessary: a jewelry store.

We passed by a school just on the border of the city, probably catering to all the deep-dwelling super-suburban families, as well as the rural ones. Some children romped in the playground, but the few that were there seemed subdued, swinging in silence. Teachers had always been an important commodity, but now their task of helping educate these traumatized youths was a huge task. Magnus had brought up children, and I wasn't sure I could ever go down that alley. With Janine unable to have kids, I'd thought that ship had sailed. Of course, now I knew why. Because she wasn't human. I thought the world's birth rate would either take a drastic nose dive over the next year, or people would be happy to be alive, and take pleasure in the fact.

Magnus must have looked at a map before we left, because he seemed to know exactly where he was going without checking the GPS. Soon we arrived at a strip mall on the outskirts of Santa Fe, lined with generic franchises, some of which weren't open, the windows boarded up.

Other stores were doing business as usual. After the Event, so many business owners were no longer with us that their companies were sometimes handed to family members, who often didn't want the burden of running a post-Event-world store, which I didn't blame them for. I could hardly go back to bean-counting after everything we'd been through, so I understood completely. But life did need to go on, normalcy and routine were necessary to rebuild our world, and many businesses did end up running after it was all said and done.

The first stop was a liquor store. The building looked new, but it'd seen better days, like the whole area. A couple down-on-their-luck guys hung out on the sidewalk in front of it. With all the housing and new jobs becoming available, it made me sad to still see what looked like poverty, though I could probably attribute it more to addiction.

"Good thing they gave me a company card. This could get ugly." Magnus smiled widely as he flung the door open. "Come on," he called as he walked past the two sitting men.

The liquor store was half empty, but considering logistics were just starting to get back in order, that wasn't a surprise. A lot of these places were looted in the weeks people arrived back on Earth. Newfound life, and all some of the population could do was steal from each other. I thought about the colony ship leaving and felt a stab of guilt as I wished I could leave Earth behind and just start fresh somewhere else.

"Hello, good sir." Magnus walked up to the cashier, who looked almost as large as his new customer.

The man grunted. "What can I do for you fine gentlemen?" he asked, eyeballing us suspiciously. I was grateful we'd decided on not wearing our uniforms. Something told me we might be dealing with some more hostility if we had.

"Scotch. I want it all." Magnus raised his eyebrows as he spoke.

"Sure thing. We got some good stuff left over here." The man started to walk to the next aisle.

"No. I don't think you understand what I'm saying. I want it all. The stuff out back." I had no idea what the hell Magnus was talking about, but he seemed to.

"Who are you?" the burly proprietor asked.

"Let's just say, the president would be very thankful if you could supply me with what I need," Magnus said, and the man took a step back.

"Look, I ain't doing nothing the other stores ain't," he said, hands raised in the air as if to feign no responsibility for something.

"Relax. I just heard through the grapevine you had the best selection of 20-year-old Scotch in the area, and a lot of it, I might add. I'm paying, and I don't even need a great deal on it," Magnus said, and the man's tense posture did relax.

"Why didn't you say so? Drive around back. I'll get you set up." The man was now smiling like he'd won the lottery. "Name's Gus."

I followed Gus, our new friend, through the staff-only doors, and into the small warehouse space. He slid open a door, revealing a semi-truck trailer full of liquor. Magnus popped through the steel door beside it and whistled when he saw the stacks of hazel liquid he was after.

Twenty minutes later, we were leaving, our truck canopy three-quarters full of various booze bottles. I'd even grabbed a few bottles of some nice Bordeaux for Mary and myself. A few was actually a case. We had no idea how long we would be cooped up in that dome, so I couldn't be too careful.

"Next stop coming up," my big friend said, once again grinning like a school kid who'd just pulled a prank.

We drove through what was once an affluent neighborhood, only half the yards were untrimmed, and nature was on the warpath after being left for a year. The houses were large, with great yards and long driveways. After a few lefts and rights, Magnus pulled over as we approached a dark Spanish-style house.

"We're here," he exclaimed, as if I'd know where *here* was.

He took a case of Scotch out of the truck and nodded me to follow him up the driveway. A dog barked from inside the house, and it warmed my heart a bit. So many animals hadn't made it after being without food or water for so long.

Magnus trudged up the steps, setting the case of Scotch down, and knocked on the wooden door. Moments later, it opened, and a German Shepherd growled cautiously from behind a screen door. I eyed him warily.

"How can I help you?" an old man asked, and I noticed him for the first time. Through the screen, he wasn't much more than a dark top and a wisp of white hair.

"I'm Magnus. My friend Slate told me you could be of service." He lightly kicked the box of liquor at his feet.

The man's face came closer and he unlocked the door, pushing it open slowly. We ceased to exist as he licked his lips and looked down at the step.

"Yes, yes, come on in. Jasper, be good to these fine folks." With that, we entered the old man's large home. It was tidy, but I got the sense it hadn't been cleaned in a while. An odor wafted to me, reminding me of my history professor at university: seeds and shuffleboard dust.

"Don't mind the mess, I don't get much company any longer," he said, and led us past the large two-story foyer and into an office on the right. It was full of built-in cherry red bookcases and a large desk. The kind that didn't hold a computer, just papers and a phone.

He gestured to us to sit in the matching leather chairs on the opposite side of the desk, and we obliged him, Magnus leaving the Scotch on the floor near the door.

"What's this all about?" I asked Magnus, who still had that big goofy grin covering the lower half of his face.

"You'll see," he replied.

"I'm assuming you heard of me through some reliable source or another, which hopefully means you're trustworthy. My name's Herman, and that furry fiend is Jasper," the older man said. I scanned the walls and saw pictures of what I could only assume was family. The big house seemed empty now except for Herman and his dog.

He seemed to notice me looking and cleared his throat. "My daughter is still with us. Moved to Africa to help with those remaining there. Water wells are their priority, but most of the population has now moved to plumbed-in areas. She says that in a few years, they should be able to cut back deaths related to bacteria in water by ninety percent over there." He paused, and his eyes were misty with emotion. "My wife passed before everything... five years ago. Anyway, down to business. You need a couple of rings?"

Rings? What did he mean?

"Yep. Two of your finest engagement rings. Then some matching bands. For me and my partner in crime over here." Magnus winked at me.

The man leaned back in his chair. "Oh. I see. Well, congrats on finding each other in this tumultuous time."

Finding each other? "I think you may have the wrong idea. I'm recently engaged, so I get that, but Magnus…" I stopped and his smile grew even larger.

"Going to ask the question right before we go. Figured we could have a big party," he said.

"I'll be damned. Nat's going to make an honest man out of you after all!" I was on my feet and so was my big friend. We were hugging, and I saw Herman looking at us like he knew a secret we didn't. That look was enough to get me to stop our man hug.

Herman used a key, turning it to reveal a sliding drawer. From it, he pulled a briefcase, which was also locked with one of those old spinning combination locks. He spun the individual rows until he had the right passcode and clicked the case open with his back to us.

"Here we go," he said, spinning around and setting the display case down on the desk. My breath caught as I saw a wide assortment of ridiculously large stones in various cuts, in numerous settings. But those weren't what I saw first. A ring with a large green stone sat among the plethora of pink and white diamonds.

"Where did you get that?" I asked, heart stuck in my throat.

He looked at me for a moment and didn't say anything. I could feel the pendant against my chest and had forgotten I'd even been wearing it. It was as if it knew another like it was around, causing it to make tiny vibrations. Probably just my imagination.

"I've procured some interesting items over the last year. You see, I was a jewelry and stone trader before." He didn't have to say before *what*. "I heard about these magnificent stones and had to have one for my collection. I haven't shown another soul, until I saw the Hero of Earth show up at my door. Thought you might appreciate it, Dean." His voice was calm, a contradiction to what I was feeling.

"Wait, I thought the government got all the stones back. Unless someone chosen didn't tell them about it, and kept it," I said, seeing the picture of his grown daughter on the wall. She looked athletic, strong, and just the type of person the Kraski would have selected for the mission. And she was now conveniently in Africa, away from prying ears and eyes. "Are you willing to part with it?"

His eyes misted over lightly, just for a moment. "That depends on the bargain."

I hardly heard them negotiating, but in a few minutes, Magnus had the green-stoned ring in a bag, and we were looking at the other rings. Mary had told me she'd never cared about huge diamond rings. It was something she'd told Bob, but he hadn't listened, and she'd spent the next few years walking around with a carat and a half on her hand. When I picked out a small pink diamond set on a thin band, they gave me inquisitive looks.

"Oh, very elegant," Herman said.

Magnus had a huge princess cut for Natalia, and when we had matching wedding bands to go with the engagement rings, we were back at the door, the Scotch still in Herman's office. Jasper got a last scratch behind the ear, and we were off.

"What else did you give him in exchange?" I asked as the door shut on us.

"I told him the Earth Defense wouldn't come turn his house upside down looking for more alien jewelry. He was all smiles after that," Magnus said, hefting the bag of rings in his left hand.

"You knew the whole time?"

"They were talking about a ring seller under suspicion of having one. Not sure how they knew. Maybe they found a way to track it, or they heard rumors of his daughter being one of those left behind. Either way, we have it, and I figured while we were at it, we can get our beautiful ladies some bling." The word sounded quite funny coming from my large friend. I couldn't fault his motivation.

Herman's daughter had been left behind like us. I wondered about her story and wished I could talk to her. Working on wells in Africa was something worthy of the title Hero of Earth, and I hoped she found what she was looking for. Most nights as I went to sleep, I dwelled on what it would have been like if someone else had gone to space and I'd been left back on Earth.

We made a couple more stops, nothing too important, and in an hour, we were heading back to the base for the second-to-last night before the colony ship left for Proxima b.

TWELVE

"*I* can't believe I let you talk me into this," Mary said between big fake smiles.

"Don't blame me. Blame Magnus. It's their last night, and he wanted a send-off. Our engagement was the perfect ruse for it," I said, instantly regretting that phrase.

Instead, she just visibly calmed and slid her hand into mine. That meant all was right in the world. We walked into the hangar, where a couple of the ships had been moved out. It was lightly decorated, and half a dozen folding tables had been placed inside, covered by some obviously borrowed tablecloths from what looked like an Italian restaurant from the seventies. LED lanterns were draped across the room, giving it a cozy backyard patio feel. It was perfect.

Mary was wearing her ring, and the other Earth Defense members flocked around her, asking for a look, and I realized something like this was a great distraction for the whole base. It was an event that could make them forget for a night that Earth had been invaded, and that we were now fighting for our lives.

Even President Patrice Dalhousie was there, with General Heart at her side. Slate, the oversized ED sergeant, loomed beside them. They waved at us, Heart sipping what looked like a Scotch while he stared at us over the edge of the glass.

Natalia walked in wearing a sleek black dress, the skirt slit to the thigh. I let out a low whistle, getting an elbow for my efforts. Nat was smiling widely at the beautiful setting, pointing at the lights and decorations. Magnus stood tall and wide beside her, filling out what could only be a custom tuxedo. I laughed, knowing how much the man hated confining clothing on his large frame.

"Congrats, you two lovebirds," he said giving us a wink. "Dean, let's go get a drink."

"Nat, you look beautiful," I said, before being pulled away by Magnus. Mary and Nat were hugging and chatting. I hadn't told Mary about the surprise engagement.

"Change in plans, buddy." Magnus shifted side to side, either nervous or excited about the proposal.

I didn't like the sound of that. "What do you mean? Don't tell me you're not going through with it. She loves you. You guys are perfect for each other." I looked back, getting a wave from Mary, who was beaming at all the attention.

"I really hate to do this at your engagement party, but just remember it was all my idea," he said.

The bartender walked up to us, and I ordered a beer, getting Magnus a double Scotch, and wine for the ladies.

"Spit it out," I said, tired of the drama.

"I'm not just asking her to marry me." He paused, a big grin cast over his face. It was infectious, and I was smiling now too. "I'm asking her to marry me *tonight*."

"Yeah, that was the plan."

"No. I'm asking her to marry me, then getting married tonight." He was almost jumping up and down in joy, and I put my hand on his shoulder, trying to calm him down. Only then I noticed the white-collared young man leaning against the far wall, chatting with Clare.

"Congrats to you, then. Don't mind us. We're the last

people worried about wanting to be in the limelight. Take the spotlight. Take all of it!" I yelled the last bit, the room looking my way like I was crazy.

Lowering my voice, I told him he had my blessing. This got him laughing, and we hugged, quickly brushing it off as the room's many eyes once again looked to us.

"You will be my best man, right?" he asked with a raised eyebrow, as if he had to ask.

"Only if she says yes," I replied, and got a light shot in the arm.

Mary and Nat crossed the room to join us, and I passed them each their wine glasses. I raised my beer glass, the other three following suit. "To us. May we find new happiness in our new worlds." We all clinked glasses and took a drink.

"Where's Mae?" Magnus asked, and I felt a fool for not having noticed she wasn't there.

"I haven't seen her. I think she's getting her stuff together for the trip. I have seen her canoodling with a guard, so maybe she's having her own little love connection," Mary said, trying to divert how upset she really was by Mae not being there.

The night was getting on, Dalhousie gave us a nice speech about love and hope, and we drank to it, me starting to get a little lightheaded with all the liquor and ambiance.

Music played through some speakers, the hangar becoming a dance hall, and couples and friends alike paired up, slow-dancing to some nice music. This was when Magnus did his business.

In the middle of a song, everyone walked away, circling the couple. Nat didn't seem to notice, her eyes closed, her head nestled on his big chest.

He stopped moving, got to his knee and held her

hand.

A tear slipped down her cheek, and the room was silent for a moment.

"Nat, baby. I've loved you for years. The second I saw you…" He stopped, probably not wanting to ruin it by reminding her of her capture at the hands of Russian mobsters all those years ago. "My heart loved you even then. A scared young woman, who took that negative part of her life and turned it from a scar to a badge. You are the single strongest person I've ever known, and the most beautiful soul I can imagine. I know I'm just a big oaf who sometimes speaks before thinking, and shoots before negotiating, but I'll be there by your side for the rest of your life. You may think that I rescued you all those years ago, but the truth is, you rescued me. I'm forever in your debt. Will you make me the happiest man on Earth, New Earth, and Proxima b, and marry me?"

Natalia was openly crying by then, but so was the whole room. I unashamedly wiped a few tears from my face alongside everyone else, knowing how much the two of them had been through. Mary squeezed my hand tight.

"Of course I will," Nat said, letting him slip the ring on her hand. He got to his feet, picked her up, and spun her around in a hug.

"One more thing, baby," he said. "How about tonight?"

Music started up again, and the partygoers rushed to line up their chairs on the empty dance floor. The priest stood at the front of the rows, smiling widely.

Natalia blushed but shrugged. "Let's do it!"

Soon Magnus and I were at the front of the group, Mary opposite us as the maid of honor, and when the here-comes-the-bride music kicked on, Natalia was there looking resplendent on the arm of General Heart, who was walking her down the aisle.

The setting was beautiful, and I took it all in, knowing everything was about to change with them leaving us here and going on a crazy adventure to another world. It didn't seem real.

They went through the process, quick but classic nuptials. Mary was dabbing her eyes as they kissed, and the whole room stood up and cheered them on.

It was official. Natalia and Magnus were married.

Before the noise died down, Mae came into the room, bleeding from the face and limping. Her clothing was torn, and when she was close enough, I saw her eye was swollen.

I ran to her, the crowd spreading apart. "What happened?"

Mae pointed toward the sky. "They got away. Terrance and Leslie escaped."

We sat in Dalhousie's office, discussing what to do. Leslie and Terrance had somehow gotten free from their cells, stolen a ship we'd moved from the hangar, and gotten out the ceiling.

"How did this happen?" The president sat with her hands on her face. I'd never seen her so flustered. "They just happened to get out when we had the ships outside, and conveniently escaped as the hatch up top was opened for a nighttime test flight."

Heart assured her the pilot was one of his best and wasn't involved. They must have had secret information, and someone on the inside. That didn't bode well for the base's security.

"We need to go after them," Mae said, repeating the same thing for the tenth time. No one seemed to be listening. She was right.

"If they left, as you say, and aren't hanging out at Earth, hell-bent on blowing shit up, then we need to go after them before they get word to the Bhlat, or anyone else for that matter." I would be the voice of reason and back Mae up on this. She looked at me, her eye covered with ice, and her smile quickly turned to a grimace as the pain of moving her mouth registered.

"You're right." Dalhousie looked over to me and Mary, and I got that almost-regular sinking feeling in my gut. "The colony ship must go now as planned. It's even more imperative. As for the hybrids, we need to tail them, stop them at any cost. They're in the original, unaltered model of ship. Ours will be able to track it anywhere, and they won't even know you're coming."

"Wait. *You're* coming? Who do you mean when you say 'you're'?" Mary asked.

"I need the best on this. We can't take any chances. Mary, you've flown the ships before, and have experience in fighting on Earth in jets and out there in space. Plus, you've been practicing these last few weeks. You know that ship. And Dean has the kind of mind that will keep you guys on top of them, one step ahead." Dalhousie sounded much more confident about our chances than I did.

"Don't you guys have people for this kind of thing?" This from Magnus, who didn't look very happy to have his wedding night interrupted.

Heart spoke up finally. "We do. That's why Slate's going with you, and Clare. Slate is as big as an ox and will be your feet on the street, should it come to that. Clare will be your engineer wizard, able to fix things, and adapt the ship's needs to yours. The longer we talk about this, the farther they get from Earth. You're Earth Defense now, so do your job. Defend Earth!" He was red-faced by the end of it, and so was Magnus. He looked like he wanted to punch the older man. Hell, so did I.

"Look, no one is questioning your integrity. We need you guys again. Earth needs you." Patrice Dalhousie stood up now, looking Mary right in the eyes, then me.

"We better get going, then. Dean, you can stay back if you like," Mary said, breaking my heart a bit.

"You don't want me to go with you?" I asked.

"Of course I do! I just don't want anything to happen to you," she said, grabbing my hand.

"Nothing's going to happen to either of us. We can go stop them and be back sooner than you thought possible." I said the words but didn't believe them even as they left my mouth.

"Then it's settled. You guys leave now," Dalhousie said, a tired look in her eyes.

It was midnight by the time we packed up our few belongings, and the crews at the base loaded the ship with enough supplies to last a long time. Heart never did tell us how much food they loaded on, but the storage area had a lot of crates in it. He told us Slate knew what it all was, and since we didn't have time to go over the itinerary, we trusted they were prepared for this.

"I can't believe you guys are leaving. And before us!" Magnus said, walking with us to the ship. He was still in his tuxedo, the tie conspicuously missing.

Carey followed alongside us, wagging his tail. I couldn't believe that after all we'd been through, I had to leave him. I couldn't bring him on the ship with us. It was a dangerous trip, not one for my new best friend to tag along on.

I had an idea. "Magnus, would you take Carey with you?" I hated to ask, but I had to.

He looked at me, his features softening. "Dean, are you sure? He could stay here. I'm sure you'll be back in no time."

"But what if we're not? What if something happens to us out there?"

"It won't. I know you guys."

"But what if? We could be following them a long way. To God knows where. Just take him, please." My heart was freezing up at having to pawn off the little guy. He meant so much to me.

"Of course I will, buddy. We love the little rascal too. When it's all over, come to Proxima, and he's all yours again." Magnus clapped me on the shoulder. His words rang a finality over my mind, and I worried I'd never see Carey again. That I'd never see any of them again.

I took a knee and Carey rubbed his face into my stomach. He loved it when I got down to his level. He licked my face, and I laughed, giving him one last big hug before I left. At that moment, I told myself I would get back, stop the Bhlat threat, and make it to Proxima to see my friends again and get Carey.

Mary walked up, pack slung over her shoulder. She seemed to get the sense of what transpired, and she gave Carey a big hug, letting his sloppy tongue give her a lick before leaving.

"Nat, I also need you to watch over my sister. She was supposed to get here today for the party, but they were delayed. I still can't believe my little sister is going with you guys. Take care of her. Please," I said, wishing I could see her just one last time before leaving.

"Of course. If she's anything like you, we'll have a lot to pick on her about." This from Magnus. "Dean, take these." He passed me a small cloth bag covertly. I snuck a peek and saw some of the green gem jewelry used to counter the Kraski beams. "You never know when you're going to need them." I spotted my pendant in there and wondered how he'd managed to pilfer them.

"Goodbye, guys," Mary said, and everyone got in for a last hug.

Mae approached, and I went in to give her a hug.

"What are you doing?" she asked. I shrugged, taken aback. "I'm going with you."

"Did Dalhousie approve this?" Mary asked.

"I don't give a damn. I'm coming with you. They're hybrids, and that makes them my responsibility. I know them, can understand their motives. So I'm going."

It made sense, and to be honest, I was happy to have her along. Mae had proven herself invaluable many times over.

Clare was on board and called to us from the top of the ramp. It was time to go.

Dalhousie was nowhere in sight, and when I spotted Heart arriving on his cart, I pushed Mae forward onto the angled ramp. "Get on the ship," I said through clenched teeth.

She didn't argue or say anything, just ran up the length into the ship, limping on her left leg ever so slightly. I guessed it hurt more than she was letting on.

Magnus stood at the base of the ship, arms crossed, looking like a guard.

Heart's cart stopped, the soldier staying in the driver's seat.

"You have a monumental task ahead of you. Take heed in knowing we'll do what we can to protect Earth, should anything go wrong on your mission. The colony vessel will be leaving tomorrow, and that brings new hope into our situation. Sorry for the speech." He rubbed his temple with his hand. "This is all just so important. I couldn't ask for better people to call on. And I mean that."

His words touched me, but at the same time, I wished he were speaking to someone else.

"We'll do what needs to be done, General," Mary said.

"Joshua. Call me Josh," he said before turning around and heading back to the cart. "Slate, take care of them for me. For all of us." The big man emerged from the ship a few steps and saluted his general before heading back inside.

Dust was kicked up and the general was off, leaving a few people milling about, loading the last of the supplies.

"I guess this is goodbye. See you on the other side." I scratched Carey behind the ear one last time, and when he started to follow me up the ramp, Natalia grabbed his collar, pulling him back and crouching down with him. His head turned sideways, wondering what was going on.

Mary was in front of me, and she patted me on the arm. We turned around, waving at our friends while the ramp lifted. Before it shut completely, I heard one last bark from Carey, and I wanted nothing more than to get back out and tell them to hunt the hybrids down themselves.

"We'll be back soon," Mary said, the ever-caring fiancée. If she was okay with it all, what use was there in me moping about?

"You're right." And just like that, we were loaded and in one of the new ships, heading back out to space on another impossible quest.

THIRTEEN

*W*e were gathered on the bridge for pre-flight: Mary, me, Mae, Clare, and Slate, as well as Doctor Nick Ellis, whom none of us had met before, though I had seen him around the facility over the past month. We were sure to have enough space on board, especially since the ship slept a dozen.

Slate stood tall, intimidating as he silently seemed to assess each of us, his military-trained mind looking for value or weakness. He wore a black vest, holding what I could only assume were multiple dangerous and deadly devices on it, overtop of his Earth Defense uniform. We were all wearing the body suits, and it actually felt like we were a trained team about to head into space rather than a rag-tag group of survivors who'd just met, looking to stop escaped hybrids from camp.

I wondered who was in charge of the mission. After a few moments of dead air, all eyes ended up on me. They were looking to me to lead the charge? How was that even possible?

I cleared my throat, hoping someone else would speak, but when no one did, I began. "I don't have any idea how I ended up here, on the bridge of a human altered Kraski ship, about to go back to space, the one place I truly have no desire to ever see again. But here we all are. Leslie and Terrance have left us no choice but to stop them. We can't have the Bhlat know where we are. This is imperative at all costs." I stopped, coming to accept the facts I was saying. "We'll sacrifice ourselves, if necessary."

The doctor fidgeted with his sleeve and kept his eyes to the floor as I spoke.

"Everyone good with that?" I asked.

One by one, everyone agreed. The last was Nick, who finally met my eyes, and I was happy to see resolve in them. He nodded once, firmly.

"Good. Mary, let them know we're ready to go. Mae, on screen, please," I said, sitting down in a chair. Not the one in the center, which I could only assume, from years of *Star Trek* watching, was meant to be the captain's chair. I hadn't earned that spot yet.

The curved viewscreen showed us the inside of the hangar.

"All clear. You're ready for takeoff," came through the speakers on Mary's console, and she tapped the green glowing console tablet. The ship came to life, lights firing up around the bridge, giving us a green and blue glowing aura. It was spectacular.

Everything hummed lightly as we began to move, and moments later, we were in the field, directly under the open base ceiling. The viewscreen showed a line of base workers, all watching us depart. I picked Nat and Magnus out of the crowd, Carey at their feet. *Godspeed, my friends.*

Our black ship hovered and raised upward to the opening.

"Return to us, Heroes of Earth," Dalhousie's voice cut through the speaker.

"We will, ma'am," Mary returned, and lifted us out of the secret base and into the night sky above New Mexico.

The stars were white and bright against the deep black

backdrop. Here we went again. I remembered back to a year ago, when Mary had flown the smaller ship from Machu Picchu with Magnus and the Shield, a crazy elaborate and desperate plan to save the world. It had half-worked too. Better than the alternative.

A blip flashed on the 3D map on the bottom right side of the viewscreen: the same map that showed on my chair's sidearm console tablet.

"That's them. Setting course for intercept. They haven't hit the high-velocity drive yet," Mary said. They were more than a few thousand kilometers away, with a two-hour head start on their side.

"I've started to charge the drive. Should be operational for in-system FTL in two hours." Clare stood at a console to the port side of the bridge, stood straight-backed, wearing her uniform with pride. She knew that ship inside and out, and I was sure she was going to be a great asset to the team. Not only that, but she was always a positive presence in the room, no matter where she was. It was hard to be in a bad mood with her energy lifting up the people around her.

We lifted through the atmosphere and shot into the massive expanse of space. I stood, seeing the moon ahead. It was such a different experience this time. This time, we knew what we had to do. Mary shifted the trajectory, pointing us away from the sun. The map showed the current position of the solar system's planets, each on their own pattern of rotations around the system's star, our sun. The blip of our target Kraski ship was on a line toward Mars.

"Slate, can you give me a tour of the supply room?" I asked the beast of a man. He'd just been standing, there watching space through still eyes.

"Sure thing, boss," he said, and I thought it might be

the first time I'd heard the guy speak. His voice was higher-pitched than I'd expected.

"I'll be in the storeroom," I said to Mary, who just nodded, focusing on her task at hand.

Slate led the way out of the bridge, down the hall, past the engineering room, and into the center of the ship. Crates were strapped to the walls. Upon closer inspection, I saw they were labeled. Food products on the left, from floor to ceiling.

"Boss, here are the clothing crates. We have medical supplies here," he waved to the stack of crates on the right side of the room. "Toiletries here. And you saw the food supplies."

"How about those?" I asked, nodding toward some large steel boxes in the middle of the floor.

He shook his head. "You don't want to get into those yet. Armaments. Lots of them. Grenades, more pulse rifles than the few of us could ever use. Always better to be overprepared than underprepared. A few secrets, I'll show you later." Slate had a twinkle in his eyes, and I saw what turned this man's crank.

Nick Ellis, the doctor, sauntered in, whistling when he saw the crates piled up.

"How about we get some of this sorted and organized?" I asked them. "There's a small medic room near engineering. How about you start there, Doc? Slate, let's get this kitchen set up, and the beds while we're at it."

Nothing was ready in the ship. The president hadn't expected a long-range venture with a crew, so nothing was set up for us. I didn't mind, because it allowed us to bond by setting it up. Some sweat equity at the start of the journey.

"Sounds like a plan," Nick said, grabbing a crate down with Slate's help.

Soon we were organizing what we needed, Nick setting up the medical station, then adding linens and pillows to the bunks. Slate and I filled the shelves of the kitchen and I found a coffee maker, brewing some fresh-ground beans to keep everyone going. All in all, it took us just over two hours, and I brought coffee up to the bridge for the ladies on duty.

"Dean, I've been thinking," Mary said, smiling at me as she took the coffee cup. "If we can't catch them here, maybe we should follow them secretly. We might want to see where they go. It could teach us a lot. Maybe we can find where the Bhlat are and take the offense to them."

I hated the idea but didn't want to dismiss her right off the bat. Maybe she was right.

"Let's see how this goes. Maybe we catch up today and stop them, even if it means I'll never get to eat the dehydrated food I just lined the shelves with. Patrice and Heart wanted us to stop them right away. I'm not sure I'm up for breaking those orders. Especially with the huge guy in the store-room on their side," I said.

"Just think about it," Mary said quietly.

"Clare, how are we doing on the FTL drive?" I asked.

She smiled. "Under an hour left before we can fire it up. What's the plan?"

"Mary, what do you say when it's ready, we jump closer to them? I have to think they know how to use their drive too. Maybe they just haven't yet because they don't know we're coming after them. Appear right up their ass and blow them away." I knew it wasn't going to be as easy as capturing them. I wasn't going to even try to kid myself.

"That's exactly what we should do. I just assume they'll …" The blip on the screen flashed. "Shit. They activated it."

The blip was accelerating faster. We traversed through space toward their trajectory, and all we could do was watch as their ship kept getting farther and farther away.

"That's what we have tracking for," Clare said as we watched the blip get smaller as the map expanded. My gut was telling me we were in for quite the chase.

"We wait until the drive's charged, then follow them just like the plan accounted for. Is there something to eat in the kitchen?" Mary asked, stomach growling at the mention of food. As if on cue, mine followed suit.

"I'll go whip up some omelettes. Nothing like pre-beaten eggs from a cardboard container. Everyone good with that?" I asked.

Clare said she was, and I walked over to Mae, who was still nursing a swollen eye. "Mae, why don't you let the doctor assess you finally? Maybe take something and rest for a bit."

She looked at me, her one open eye intense. "I just want to catch them, Dean. I want to go home. I... I let them get away."

We hadn't heard the whole story from her yet. She got up and followed me into the kitchen, where coffee still sat in the maker. I offered her another cup and she nodded to me. I wanted to give her a big hug and tell her everything would be okay, but I could tell it would only upset her more.

"What happened?" I asked, grabbing a frying pan.

"I know you had your big event, but I felt like it might be just the time someone would make a move. With the whole base distracted, it only made sense." Mae sipped her coffee.

"If you thought that, why didn't you tell anyone? It does make sense, but sometimes the most obvious things are the ones we miss first."

"Everyone was just happy, and I didn't think there was a way they could escape, so I hung out by the prison, just laying low. At the ten PM guard switch, it went south. I snuck in behind him and saw him let Terrance out first. I tried to intervene but got a beating for my troubles. Soon Leslie was there, kicking me too. That's who we're dealing with here. They'll do anything for their cause."

I cringed, thinking of my friend getting pummelled by two people. No wonder she had become so closed off-lately. She'd been through so much.

I walked over to her where she sat and pulled her toward me, being careful her bruised face didn't get hurt. I held her head to my stomach and leaned down, kissing the top of her head.

"I'm sorry, Mae. I'm sorry we weren't there for you. Never again," I said, and she cried into my shirt.

Doctor Nick started into the room, saw our intimate moment, and slowly backed away. I hoped he saw it for what it was, not something else. That was all we needed with a crew of six people.

"I love you, Dean," she said, her hand holding mine. I knew what she meant. We weren't in love, but she was like a sister to me, and I a brother to her. It was a bond we would never shake.

"I love you too," I said.

Mae got up, and we made breakfast for the crew in silence, working in the small space like we'd been doing it our whole lives. By the time we brought the food to the bridge, Clare had a look of pure joy on her face. It was a little unsettling, considering the circumstances.

"It's ready. Let's blast across this galaxy," Clare said.

Mary shrugged her shoulders and pressed the glowing green tablet button. Stars stretched out around us on the viewscreen.

"Anyone for eggs while we make history?" I asked.

FOURTEEN

"Don't look so worried. Mae has it under control," I said. We were lying on the bed in our own bunk room, face to face, heads on pillows. We had been soaring through space for hours now, not catching up to our target but keeping on their tail as best we could.

"I know. It just seems like so much. I still can't believe we're here, racing past Mars, only half a day after we watched our friends getting married. Do you wish we had gotten married?" Mary asked.

I hadn't given that a lot of thought. "I'm happy just being with you. A label at this time is really just that, a label. It doesn't change anything."

She closed her eyes. "You're right, honey. I'm going to sleep for a while, okay? Try to get some sleep yourself."

I closed my eyes too, noticing the missing dog at our feet. Even through all the unknowns, the body knows when it needs to recharge, and in moments, my mind stopped racing, drifting off into a well-needed slumber.

A few hours later, I was awoken to the sound of Mae's voice over the comm-system. "All crew to the bridge."

Mary was already up, putting her jumpsuit back on, and I fell right in behind her. I felt rested, but wished I had time to brush my teeth or freshen up. I made a quick pit stop in the washroom and did just that after relieving myself. I wasn't going to be of any use wetting myself on the bridge.

When I crossed to the bridge, Nick was behind me, and he called up. "Any idea what's going on?"

I looked back. He was in a bathrobe, toothbrush sticking out of his mouth. His eyes were sporting some serious red veins, and I expected his first attempt at sleep on a spaceship was a failure.

Slate was standing tall behind Mae's console, with Mary and Clare flanking her. They were all looking at the viewscreen.

"The icon blinked out here," she said, highlighting the spot on the map, "but the tracking still seems to be working, unless there's a major glitch in it." She looked over her shoulder to Clare.

Clare stood there, perplexed look across her face. After a moment, a light bulb went off, and I could see recognition wash over her. "Holy shit. The reason the map went all funky and tiny like that is because it was zooming out. Somehow they travelled from here" – she pointed to a spot on the tablet screen – "to here." Another spot way to the right.

"Just how did they do that? We're operating the same drive as them," Mary said.

"I have no idea. To travel that far would take something entirely different. Something we don't have. Maybe…" She stopped, tapping her finger on the back of Mae's chair.

"What is it? What could do that?" I asked, losing my patience. If we lost them now, on day one, we were hooped.

"The only thing I can think of is a wormhole of some sort. We didn't find the technology on their ships, though," Clare said. "That's the only reasonable explanation I have."

A wormhole. This just kept getting more convoluted.

"So what do we do? Wait until we catch up to the spot they disappeared at and see if we can duplicate it?" Mary asked.

"What's our ETA to that spot?" I asked, a nervous energy coursing through my veins.

"Just under two hours," Mae confirmed after tapping a few glowing buttons.

Two hours to travel FTL toward a spot where our target ship blipped out and moved thousands of light years away. If we didn't get the same hop, we would never be able to catch them. The whole escape would be successful, and we would be heading back to Earth with our tail between our legs, preparing for an all-out war.

"Then that's what we do. Pray for the same wormhole to be there," I said, and we all kept staring at the map, a light blip across the stretched-out expanse, glowing, letting us know our target was still out there.

"*I* hate waiting around," Mary said as we sat in the eat-in kitchen.

The table was bolted to the ground and would sit all of us if we crammed in there. We sipped tepid coffee and batted ideas back and forth. Really it was all speculation, because we couldn't know what we were going to arrive to.

"What are the options if the wormhole, or whatever the hell it is, isn't there any longer?" I asked, sure I could guess what they were. I just wanted Mary to reconfirm to me what I already knew.

"I'd say the first option at that point is to turn around, hightail it back to Earth, tell the powers that be what we found out, and hunker down, preparing for a war that may or may not ever come to us. I hate the idea of living in constant fear of invasion. The world can't deal with that after all we've been through." She took a drink from the cup and set it down, wrapping her slender fingers around it.

"Option two?" I asked.

"Option two: we keep going, take months to get where they are, thousands of light years away, and hope this ship is really built for it. We may be too late then, but at least we'll know one way or the other."

"Option three?"

"We say screw it, head to Proxima b, where we meet up with our friends in a few months, and start over on a new world." She smiled at this one, and I knew that option probably suited her as much as it did me, but we couldn't do that. We had too many people back home relying on us.

"So now what? We play the wait and see game?" I knew it was only a matter of minutes before Mae called us to the bridge and we saw firsthand what was left of the "leap" spot, as we started calling it.

Slate came in the room, and I noticed he had to turn sideways to get through the doorway. His short blond hair was a little messy. Probably coming from a quick power nap. I used to tease Magnus about being too big, but this guy was next level.

"Slate, what's your story? And where'd you get that name?" I asked, truly intrigued by the man.

He shrugged, grabbing a cup of coffee, and sat down at the end of the table so we could both turn and face him.

"Name's really Zeke Campbell," he said nonchalantly.

"You don't look like a Zeke," I said, trying to hold back a laugh.

"No kidding. My old sarge started calling me that when I was just a private. He found out I painted, and said I was like a rock but had many layers. Ergo, I was Slate from then on."

I did laugh then, and soon Mary was laughing beside me, and even the ever-serious Slate was grinning.

"Where are you from?" Mary asked. He was Army and she was Air Force, so they had more camaraderie between them than with an accountant from upstate New York.

"Grew up in L.A. near the water. Loved to surf," he said, staring into his cup. "My older brother shipped off to the Gulf War when I was just a kid and died two months later. It broke my mom. Anyway, at that moment, I started to plan my revenge. I was just eight years old, but in my heart, I told myself I was going to find who killed him and make them pay. I wasn't sure what that meant, but it was too much for a little kid. I started to work out as soon as my mom would let me, and against every wish of hers, I joined the Army when I was eighteen. I saw a lot of tours in the Middle East, and killed a lot of men, but none of it ever brought me the redemption I dreamt of as that little boy. It just… I'm sorry. I don't talk about it much, so when I get started on it, I guess I can't stop."

I thought about running through the massive Kraski vessel with the Shield, killing what was left of an entire race. "We do what we have to do, Slate, and we have to live with it after. I'm glad we have you along. I look forward to getting to know you better," I said, and meant it.

"Same here." He smiled again.

"We're about to shut the drive down," Clare said through the computer's wall speaker.

"I guess we find out what's next now. No more speculating." Mary stood, and we followed her out to the bridge, where Clare sat to the left, Mae still in the pilot's seat.

Mae got up, relinquishing the seat to Mary. Her face was impassive, impossible to read. She looked worried, and we all were at that moment, hoping there would be a swirling wormhole or something to carry us across the universe.

"Drive down, normal engines on," Clare said, and the viewscreen showed distant stars slowing from lines to points in space once again.

"Where is it?" I asked, looking around for a sign of the anomaly. I walked over to Clare, who was quickly typing in something on her console's tablet.

"I'm not picking anything up. Shit. It's gone."

We stood there, frustration enveloping us. The mission had failed.

FIFTEEN

"Where's the exact point they took off from?" I asked, curious more than anything. Before we started to debate the options Mary had suggested in the kitchen, I had to see it. I had to be sure.

Clare hit some keys, and a distant point on the viewscreen lit up. Mary maneuvered over to it, slowing the ship's speed as they approached.

"Try one of the probes, maybe?" Slate said.

"What probes?" Mary asked.

"They didn't practice with them, but we created some probes that are essentially nanotech. They're tiny probes we eject, and they act as sensors for surrounding areas. We don't have scanning technology like in the movies unless we're right up on something, but the probes can be sent into atmospheres and will send back weather, gas levels, that kind of stuff," Clare said.

"Clare, did you invent these?" I asked, and she blushed, answering my question immediately. "Good call, Slate. Send them off."

We watched the monitor as blue lights indicated where the probes were. Three went flying toward the mark, and readings were being sent back to our ship.

"Wait. There *is* something there," Clare said. "The radiation level changes."

I saw the middle probe disappear from the monitor.

"It's gone!".

"So it is. The readings from it are gone too. The others are still sending data back," Clare said, perplexed.

"Mary, can you take us in? As close as you can get to where the probe disappeared." I had a feeling we were right on it.

As we approached, the light changed, and a fold opened before us, just enough for us to see different stars beyond it. In my head, a wormhole was a dramatic swirling maw of light and energy, but what we saw before us was nothing but an illusion of space, a fold in the universe. It was amazing.

"I'll be damned," Mary said, and Clare literally walked toward the viewscreen, tears rolling down her face.

"It's beautiful," she said over and over.

"We have to make a choice. Do we go for it?" Mary asked.

"We know the other ship made it through, so by that, can we assume we will as well?" Mae asked.

"This is what we came for, and we have to stop them, so my vote is on entering the unknown," I said.

"You're in charge," Mary said, and it struck a chord. Did anyone really think I was calling the shots? "Don't panic, honey. I'm just kidding. Don't worry, I won't blame you if we disintegrate into a million pieces. Just give me a kiss before we do it."

"I don't remember Kirk ever kissing Sulu when they were going into a dangerous situation," Slate said as I bent over, kissing my fiancée.

We would have all laughed if our lives weren't at stake. Mary eased the ship forward, and we entered the almost invisible wormhole. I expected us to just appear on the other side, so when we started shaking, lightning flashing all around the viewscreen, it didn't quite register.

One minute I was standing watching the screen, the next it went blank and my head hit the ceiling.

★ ★

My eyes opened slowly, the soft alarm klaxons ringing in my head. I looked around and saw everyone strewn about. The viewscreen was blank. Getting to my feet proved to be difficult, so I stayed down, half-dragging myself to Mary, who was just starting to come to as well.

"You okay?" I asked. She just nodded, a distant look in her eyes.

I checked on everyone, and when I got to Mae, I knew it wasn't good news. She was already so banged up from the other day, and now her head was bleeding from a scalp wound on top of it. We'd been tossed about like rag dolls.

"I think we made it through," Mary said. "But the link to the viewscreen is broken."

"Mae," I whispered. Her chest rose and fell lightly. She was alive. "Where the hell is the Doc?" I asked, re-membering he wasn't on the bridge at the time. He must have been in the bunks.

Footsteps clanged from the hall, and he emerged, holding his arm up in a makeshift sling.

"Everyone okay?" he asked. "Thanks for warning me we were about to be tossed around like a sack of potatoes at the harvest festival."

"We didn't know it would do that. How could we?" Clare asked. "Help Dean get Mae to the medical lab, and I'll work on the inertial dampener. I'm hoping the con-nections just loosened and it didn't fry."

That explained the flying around the ship. I made sure

Mary was really okay, and headed with Mae down the hall, propping her up between Nick and me.

"I take it we found the wormhole," he said, voice thick with sarcasm.

"I'm sorry we didn't wake you. It just happened so fast. One minute we didn't think it was there, the next we found it." I felt foolish even saying it like that. He was right. We should have woken him.

We laid Mae down on the bed, and Nick went about looking over her. When he lifted her eyelids and shone a light in them, they darted around, and her leg kicked out at him.

"Mae! You're fine! It's just Doctor Nick," I called in an effort to calm her. She stopped flailing, and I stood by her head, holding her hand.

"All the blood is from this small scalp wound. Their bark is far worse than their bite. I'll have to stitch it up. You'll be good as new, but with your other injuries, we'll have to keep an eye on you for a concussion," Doctor Nick said. I appreciated his bedside manner, especially after nearly being kicked by his patient.

"I'll be at the bridge. Mae, let him do his job. We need you healthy," I said. She nodded softly and squeezed my hand before letting it go.

I closed my eyes in the hall, trying to determine my own injuries. I could feel some pain in my knee, but I hoped it was just a bruise from landing on it. My left shoulder was a little tight, but again, that could be from falling on it. Nothing seemed too serious or broken.

A quick stop in the kitchen, and I was heading to the bridge with an armful of water bottles for everyone.

Slate stood, looking no worse for the wear, and Clare was absent, talking to Mary through her console speaker. "How about now?" her voice asked, and the viewscreen flickered, cut out, then stayed on, showing up the view before our ship.

Black sky, stars in the distance. Yep, pretty much what we had been looking at before, only I knew it was far different. No one from Earth had ever been this far out, and when we brought the map up, it zoomed in from tiny specks to large blinking icons. We were right on their tail.

The icon had moved trajectory since we'd last seen it, and to my non-spatial, linear mind, they were heading deep south in the 3D map. At their speed, it was evident the FTL drive was back up and running. As if she read my mind, Mary said, "Our drive will be good to go in twenty minutes. We were still holding a charge."

I slumped down onto the console chair to the left of Mary, staring into the blank space outside, the blip of our target getting ever so farther away with each beat of my heart.

I wondered how long this journey was going to take.

*T*wo weeks later, we were settling into a routine. I'd become more of a scheduler than anything, shifts on manning the bridge swapping between all six of us. We took turns making meals and sleeping.

Slate had a great idea for training sessions, which not only allowed us to get in shape, but let us learn the ins and outs of every weapon on board.

I headed into the storage area, which had become a makeshift gym, mats layering the floor in a square. Mary and Clare were inside, doing push-ups with Slate counting them off.

"Time for hand to hand," he said, grinning at me. If there was one thing Slate loved, it was hand to hand combat. He lit up every time, and I was sure he wished there was some competition aboard for a man his size. There wasn't anyone close. I'd been at the bruising end of his moves a few times, but he had taught me a lot, and for that I was thankful. Now the smaller Clare was up, getting ready for some basic combat techniques against the better-trained Mary.

Watching Mary sweating like that, getting ready to kick someone's ass, was a turn-on. I wondered where that primal emotion came from.

Clare was thin, and her glasses were off to the side of the room. As an engineer, she said she hadn't spent much time worrying about athletics, but Slate said she was a natural. Mary wasn't the biggest fan of the upbeat nerd, as she called her, but was willing to admit she was a useful addition to the crew, especially since she'd helped convert some of the alien technology on board to better suit our human needs.

The two women strapped on gloves, and Slate made sure their headgear was on firmly. Mary tugged her ponytail and planted her feet. Clare moved hesitantly, a feint, before attacking from the left. Her kick hit Mary in the side, who grunted and jabbed with her right, catching Clare in the head.

The smaller woman went down, and Mary was on her, two quick shots, before Slate stepped in and pulled her off.

"She's down," he said angrily. Clare was down on the ground, turtling her head, and Mary moved back, hands in the air.

"I'm sorry, got a little too into it." She reached her hand out, and a heavily-breathing Clare grabbed it, letting

Mary help her to her feet.

"No sweat. I'll get you next time," Clare said before guzzling some water.

Slate looked at me and raised an eyebrow, as if to say he was impressed with their cordial behavior. Frankly, I was too.

Mary grabbed a towel and started for the washroom, where I knew she'd take a quick shower. I still couldn't believe we had a Kraski ship with a human shower and toilet on it.

"Everything okay?" I asked, when we were out of ear-shot of the others.

"What do you mean?" she asked.

"You just about took our engineer's head off back there."

"I just got a little too into it. And honestly, since you're asking, I'm getting a little frustrated. I'm a pilot, but I usually get to leave my jet, not follow a bogey across an unknown universe. To top it off, I'm tired of Clare giggling at every little joke you say and batting her eye-lashes under those Buddy Holly glasses she wears."

The truth came out. "I get it about the ship. We're all getting restless."

She sighed, closing the door behind us, and started to take her workout clothes off. I didn't want to be pre-sumptuous, so I hung back, thinking I might be reading the room wrong.

She stepped into the now-steaming shower and stuck her arm out, wiggling her finger for me to join her.

"You don't have to ask me twice," I said, shucking my uniform in record time.

There were still some things we could do to ease the tension, and it wasn't easy on a small ship with very little privacy. We chose our times carefully. This time, she just didn't seem to care. She was taking what was hers.

Fifteen minutes later, we heard the speakers throughout the ship. It was Mae. "They're out of the FTL drive. You guys are going to want to see this."

SIXTEEN

Mary's hair was dripping into a puddle on the bridge deck, and she was wearing a bathrobe, while I'd rushed and slipped my uniform back on. Doctor Nick winked at me as he entered the room, but I didn't care about any of that. We were about to find out where Leslie and Terrance were headed. Were there Bhlat down there? Was this one of their conquered worlds?

"Our cloaking tech is working, right?" I asked, wishing I'd asked when we came out of the wormhole.

Clare was on her tablet but nodded. "One hundred percent active. They can't pick up our signal, or see us, unless they fly into the side of the ship."

We had slowed to our normal drive, getting closer to the world below. The hybrids ahead of us were nearing orbit, and they hung there for a time, allowing us to get caught up.

The planet looked amazing. It had been one thing to see your own planet from outer space, seeing familiar clumps of land look so alien from that height. Seeing this new planet was life-changing. My whole perspective on life somehow jarred at the sight. There were other planets out there with life. Scientists and theologians had debated the point for centuries, and we were seeing one firsthand.

I looked over, and everyone's faces mirrored what mine must have looked like. Excitement for finding the hybrids but mixed with curiosity.

"Enough drooling, everyone," Mae said. "This could be a Bhlat world. We have to be cautious."

She was right. We waited, Mary having time to get dressed before taking over the helm from Mae.

"Can we send the probes down yet?" I asked.

Clare shook her head. "Great idea, but their signals aren't hidden. They only make a small signal, but we should still wait."

We didn't say what we were waiting for, but I kept assuming they were going to lower planet-side. As if they read my mind, the ship started moving, descending through the planet's atmosphere.

There were clouds on the large planet. It was hard to tell from our vantage point, but Clare said the world was a third larger than Earth. The system's star was slightly closer, percentage-wise, to the world, which would make it warmer than we were used to.

We kept tracking the target ship as it crossed across the planet, and once they were far enough away, we flew in closer.

"Launching probe now," Clare said. I stood beside her, watching the readout numbers scan across her screen. It only took a few minutes before we had the answers we needed. "Surface air temperature appears to be around 35 Celsius, and the air is within ninety-five percent of Earth's, surprisingly. No toxins read that can be harmful, but we'll get a better read when we land."

"We're going down there?" Nick asked, looking doubtful of the move.

"What choice do we have? Wait until they leave and blast them?" Slate asked, then answered his own question. "Actually, that's not a bad idea."

Mae shook her head. "We need to see what brought

them here. If there's a base, or a danger to Earth, it's up to us to bring the fight to them," she said, standing straight in her Earth Defense uniform.

"How about life-forms?" I asked.

"We aren't there yet. We don't have those kind of readings, but we're picking up some images." Clare pushed the pictures from her tablet to the main views-creen with the press of a button.

The shots weren't high-definition from this distance, but we could make out some buildings, and what looked like crops near a river. The green lush landscape overtook almost everything, and I was reminded of the thick deadly landscape in South America.

Clare switched to the map, and we saw the hybrid ship's icon land near the marker she'd placed on those structures.

"Bingo," I said. "What are we waiting for? Let's go in."

Clare looked ready to say something, but Mary cut in first. "Let's wait a few hours, until the sun is set on that part of the continent. The cloaking works much better in darkness, under the cover of the night sky. They'll never see us coming."

We spent the next couple hours planning our move, and when it was all settled, we lowered toward the planet, nervous energy palpable on the bridge of the ship. We couldn't make out a lot in the night sky, but the world was beautiful, unspoiled by pollution, and most importantly, humans. It made we wonder for a moment what would happen to Earth if the people were all gone from it. Would it reclaim the cities like in those post-apocalyptic movies? Would New York be covered in trees, and would deer walk down Fifth Avenue, making a home in Central Park?

We decided to scout a spot close enough to get to the village by foot, but far enough not to be spotted. The landing area was an empty copse of trees, which each stood over a hundred feet tall, surrounding the location. The ground was soft, and Mary decided to hover there rather than keep the weight on the grass. It was similar to a rainforest, and the chances of sinking into the bog-like terrain were high.

"Clare, you're sure you know how to fly this thing, right?" Mary asked for the fifth time.

"Yes. I did help create it, after all," Clare answered, impatience thick in her voice.

Nick stayed back, looking relieved that we didn't ask him on the away mission.

"We'll keep in radio contact. Any sign they're leaving in the Kraski ship, you tell us and come pick us up," I said, slinging a pulse rifle over my shoulder. I was thankful for the time Slate had spent with me, familiarizing me and the others with the vast array of weapons we had. My confidence holding the gun was much higher than it had been a year ago, when it was new and alien to me.

Mae had her EVA suit on, the door closing between her and us as the ramp lowered. A hand-held tablet in her hand, she walked down the ramp.

"Readings shows the air is breathable," Mae said, and I felt my shoulders loosen. Skulking around without the suit on was going to be much easier.

The door opened, and I felt warm air rushing up the ramp and into my face. A strange smell emanated from outside, a mixture of barn and swamp.

Stepping on the ground, I felt it give ever so slightly. The grass was more like moss, the water table evidently very high. The high humidity was almost a shock after spending a couple of weeks on a closed-system ship, where climate was controlled to a tenth of a degree. My uniform started to stick to my sweating body nearly instantly, and I looked at the others, seeing much of the same. Slate was the only one who kept stone-faced. He was a soldier on a mission, and his mind was extremely focused on the task at hand. Being on a strange planet with terrorist aliens on it, I was more than happy to have the gigantic soldier alongside us.

"Clare, come in," I said, testing the comm-system.

"Go ahead," the reply came.

"We'll keep our trackers on. Just don't leave us hanging if things get hairy," I said.

Slate took the lead with ease, and we followed him. I finally got a look around, which was hard in the dark. We were hesitant to use flashlights in case we were spotted, but Slate had night-vision goggles on. I felt mine strapped to my thigh and considered wearing them. Instead I followed the others, trying to not be distracted by the brand-new surroundings.

We were on another world, walking on the mossy ground. It was an amazing feeling to see the strange massive trees looming around us, a moist musky smell lingering in the air. The river was close, but I suspected smaller ponds or swamps nearby, judging by the dampness.

As we got near the tree line, I stopped to touch one. The bark was smooth, slightly sticky. The branches were thin near the lower end of it, with slim leaves unlike any I'd ever seen.

"Dean, let's go. We can look at the flora once we nab Terrance and Leslie," Mae said.

I just shrugged and kept moving. The village was a couple of miles away; we'd expected to take fifteen minutes to get there at a good pace. Reality was different.

Three minutes in, the ground was too soft to walk on.

Slate's substantial bulk sank in as he stepped down, and we had to help him pull his right leg out of the mossy hole. A smelly mud stuck to his boot when he pulled free, and Mary wrinkled her nose at the stench.

"That's not something you want to walk in. Let's see if there's a way across this way." She pointed north, and we found much the same issue. Doubling back took valuable time, but the ground was eventually firmer, and soon we were making our way to the village in the right direction.

In a few minutes, we could see lights from the town: a soft glow in the darkness of an ominous world. It called to me like a beacon, and suddenly I remembered the time my car broke down on the highway in the winter when I was first off at college, right before the days when cell phones were in everyone's hand constantly. It was the middle of a snowstorm, and after seeing no one else was crazy enough to be on the main roads, I spent an hour walking down a gravel road seeking a house. Just when I thought my toes were going to fall off, I saw a light in the distance. I ran, more stumbled, toward it, and the family let me call a tow truck and stay there until the driver picked me up.

When I saw the village light, the same feeling hit me, and I ran ahead. A few steps into my sprint, I felt the ground make way for water and I fell forward, going under.

It happened so fast, my brain couldn't comprehend it. One second I was moving in the warm air, the next my head was under water, a thick sludgy liquid. I flailed my hands, trying to find something to push against, but they just sank into the muck on the bottom of the ground.

I finally swiveled my legs out under me and pushed up, my head breaching the muck.

Laughter shot at me from behind, and I turned to see Mary's outline snickering at my epic fail.

"Laugh it up, chuckles," I said, angry I was so stupid to get into this situation. That anger was heavily mixed with embarrassment. "Can you guys just help me out?"

It looked like I was in a small pond, only thirty feet across. All we would have had to do was walk a few steps to the left and avoid it. If I hadn't rushed forward, I would be up there with the rest of them, dry and clean.

Slate stepped forward and reached a hand out, when something brushed against my leg.

SEVENTEEN

"*W*hat the hell was that?" I asked, shaking my leg.

As I stretched my hand out to grab his, I felt it again, this time harder.

"Guys, something's in here with me." Panic was creeping into my voice, the embarrassment all but forgotten. Slate grasped my wrist and that was when the creature underwater made its move. It wrapped around my ankle, pulling at me. I still couldn't see it, but it was constricting tighter by the second. Another tentacle twisted around my waist and before I knew it, I was gasping in murky water, flailing for air.

I hadn't even noticed, but Slate was still holding my arm, tugging at me, a tug-of-war where I was the rope. I could hear shouting as my head ducked in and out of the water, me just trying to get air when I was able to. There were multiple tentacles now, and I had no idea if it was one multi-limbed attacker or a group of snake-like animals.

This was it. I was going to die my first hour on a new world. Water gushed into my nose, and I tasted the stale muddy water as I was tugged under it once again. The strong hard grip of Slate's hand was gone suddenly, and I was pulled down and away from my friends. Clenching my eyes shut, I tried to stave off the panic, and fought to pull one tentacle from its crushing force on my abdomen.

Nothing worked.

The water muffled sound, and I thought I could make out Mary's voice from the ground a distance away. The swamp area was far larger than I'd initially thought, and I kept being pulled farther in. My lungs burned for air, and I knew it wasn't going to be long. Light flashed in my closed eyes, and my body went from tense and flailing to calm and serene. The light was there for me.

Something splashed nearby, and I felt a surge of hope. The pressure on my waist ceased, and before I knew it, I wasn't being pulled any longer. Next the grip on my ankle was gone, and an arm was under my chest, lifting me to the surface. My feet found muddy purchase on the swamp floor, and my weak knees helped keep me in an upright position. It was dark, and I retched out water, bile mixing with the thick stinky liquid.

"Are you okay, Dean?" Mae's voice asked in my ear. She was panting, and my eyes made out her form beside me in the dimly-lit night sky.

"Mae," was all I could muster through my clenched teeth.

"Oh, thank God," she said quietly.

She was holding a knife in her hand, and that's when I saw the floating tentacles to the right of us. She'd dived in and killed the thing with a blade. The others were calling to us from forty yards away. Mae helped me to them, dragging the creature behind us like a prize kill.

Slate reached down, picking up a limb and pulling the thing onto the ground.

"Dean!" Mary called, her voice strained and tearful. "Are you okay?"

I was out of the water, pushing my body further away from the swamp just in case another of those monsters decided to swing an arm up and grab me.

"I think so," I said, lying on my back. For a moment, I just stayed still, staring at the strange star clusters overhead. I let my body tell me what, if anything, was wrong with it, and other than a tender abdomen and a pulsing ankle, everything felt normal.

"Mae, that was amazing," Mary said. "She didn't wait a second. As soon as Slate lost grip, she dove in, knife in her hand. I've never seen anything like it."

I turned my head and saw Mae's outline watching the water, still holding the knife. She was soaked like me, her hair hanging long and dripping with mud.

"Looks almost familiar, doesn't it?" Slate said, poking the dead creature with his heavy boot. It resembled a large octopus, but with six thick tentacles, each at least the length of a human. Beady black orbs sat on either side of its head, and even though the thing almost killed me a minute ago, I felt bad for it lying there dead. It was just doing what nature taught it to do, and we were the invaders.

"Amazing," Mary said, looking at it now too.

I finally got up, testing my ankle and feeling it take the brunt of my weight. I lumbered over to Mae and put my arm around her waist. "Thank you, Mae," I said. She was still looking over the swamp, and she leaned her head down against my shoulder. We stood like that side-by-side for a minute before Slate cleared his throat.

"We should keep moving. We're almost there." He took the lead, and I stayed back waiting for Mary.

"Dean, I'm so glad you're all right." Her fingers slipped between mine, and I squeezed her hand back.

"So am I. Mary, if anything ever does happen to me, just keep going on. We need to finish the mission." I felt foolish for saying it, but a near-death experience was sure to bring up a couple of unwanted conversations.

She shook her head. "I don't want to think about that. You're fine now. A little wet and dirty, and to be honest, stinky... but fine."

I sniffed, and the putrid swamp water that covered me did make me smell something terrible. A shower was probably out of the question. I laughed and pulled her close. "Now you can smell bad too." She fought me off, and we were so distracted with each other, we nearly walked into the barn-sized man, Slate. He turned and shushed us like an annoyed parent. His finger went to his lips and he held his hand up, telling us to stay still.

The village was a few hundred yards away, and we were coming up to the first building in the area. A few dim lights were on, a soft yellow glow making me wonder just how different the inhabitants were from humans. It looked like a scene from a hundred years ago. I took comfort in the similarities, but knew it was only right to be cautious at the same time.

Slate motioned for us to crouch down, and he took a pair of binoculars out. He found something. He passed them to me, pointing in the distance. I scanned the area his finger extended toward and saw it too. Terrance and Leslie's ship was there. They walked through the field toward a large dwelling built of logs, and smoke poured from a rock chimney in the roof. It looked like quite the quaint scene until I spotted the aliens beside them. One was insectoid in nature, legs bending opposite of ours like a chicken, large black eyes on an oval-shaped head, antennae poking up a foot into the night sky. There was another with it, and I recognized the race instantly. Delta.

Relief that there were still Delta out there washed over me, but dread quickly replaced it. The last time I'd seen a Delta, they were trying to kill us, after convincing us to murder the entire race of the Kraski. It hadn't ended well for them, and there wasn't a night I didn't close my eyes and see the explosion that had snuffed out their lives at our hands.

Mae nudged me, and I handed the binoculars over to her. So the hybrids had stolen a ship, traversed a wormhole, and traveled to a backwater planet. To what end? What did they want there?

"Just what are those bastards doing?" Slate asked, mirroring my thoughts.

"Let's get in closer," Mae said.

A voice spoke behind us in an unfamiliar language. My translator shot the words into my ear. "You're going to be much closer." We spun around to see two large Deltra holding pulse rifles toward us.

My eyes roamed to Mae's hand, which looked to be twitching near her holstered gun. She looked toward me and I shook my head, hoping she wouldn't get us all killed. She grimaced and raised her hands in the air along with the rest of us.

"Come with us," the translator said.

They marched us straight to the building the hybrids had gone to, and more insectoid aliens and Deltra sentries came out of the surrounding woods. They'd either been waiting for us or were a very cautious colony.

The building was large and looked more like a big house as we neared it.

"Weapons on the ground." The bigger of the two bald Deltra pointed from us to the ground with his gun. We obliged, even if I saw a second of hesitation from Slate. Every inch of him looked ready to pounce.

The front doors on the side building were large, on rails like a sliding barn door. Inside the garage-like hangar, we saw a ship unlike any we'd seen yet. It was about a quarter the size of our ship and had an insectoid frame, almost like a hornet. I suspected I knew which aliens it belonged to. A Deltra was inside talking with Leslie and Terrance. They stopped and looked toward us, surprise etched on both the hybrids' faces.

"Terrance, you left your wallet on Earth. I thought you might need it," I said, hoping a joke would break the tension. It didn't.

"What do we have here?" the Deltra said in perfect English. The guards walked us further into the room until we were only a few feet from the three inside. The Deltra was tall, very thin, and had markings tattooed on his neck and hands. He stood straight, confident. The energy this guy was pushing out was amazing, and I knew he must be a leader among the Deltra, or at least of the colony there.

"How the hell did you find us?" Terrance asked, shaking his head. He scanned the four of us, eyes stopping on Mae for a moment longer than the rest of us. He wouldn't have known about the new ships or technology adaptations.

I figured telling them wouldn't do any harm. "The smart people back home found a way to add a tracking system to our ships."

Leslie nodded. "I told you they might be able to find us. We were too careless."

"And you brought them here," the Deltra said. "What are we going to do with you?" he asked, walking over to Slate. He was as tall as our huge soldier, but about a third as wide, even with the billowing cloak he had on. The contrast was almost comical.

"Why can't you just let us be?" Leslie asked. "We just remembered hearing rumors of this place and wanted to ask Kareem if we could bring the hybrids who want to leave Earth here to start fresh. Somewhere we can be ourselves and forget about the Kraski and the human blood coursing through us. Live out our days as a free people."

"And to do this you would kill? You would slice a friend's throat, and hang another after gutting them? Then attack one of your own, leaving her pummeled on the ground as you stole a ship and killed more guards?" Mary was standing up straight, her voice loud and strained as she attacked them.

"We killed no one!" Terrance yelled. "And we didn't attack anyone. What do you mean?"

"Mae. You attacked Mae on your way out!" Mary yelled back. The guards got between Terrance and Mary, separating them.

"We didn't even see Mae. The guard listened to us, and he let us go. We left unseen, and quietly," Leslie said calmly.

My hands started to shake hearing this. If they didn't kill those guards on Long Island or fight Mae, then who had killed them? And who had attacked Mae? I turned slowly, looking for Mae so she could fill us in. We needed to hear her side of the story, to bring the truth out, and show these hybrids for the liars they were. But Mae wasn't there.

"Where's Mae?" I asked quietly. No one seemed to hear me. "Where is Mae?" I asked louder, and the others stopped talking. We looked around the dim hangar, and she was nowhere to be seen.

"Mae!" Mary called. Silence.

"Go find the missing woman," Kareem said, his cloak flapping as he pointed to the entrance in haste. The guards raised their guns and started for the doorway.

"It was her the whole time. She must have killed those guards after we slipped out of the University. She killed the guard at the base after we left, beating herself to make it look like there was a fight," Terrance said, and it all made sense. I couldn't believe it. I wouldn't. But the facts lined up. *Don't trust her.* The text I'd gotten from that unknown source at the gas station last month flashed through my mind.

We ran to the doors as we heard pulse rifles go off in the distance. Red beams shot toward the forest and moments later, a green light emanated from the area before a ship lifted from the clearing where we'd seen the hybrids' ship as we'd scoped out the village.

"She's getting away. And in our ship!" Terrance cried.

What just happened was taking a long time to process. One minute we were all there, and Mae used the moment the guards separated Mary and Terrance to sneak away. She got onto the hybrid ship and stole it.

"I can't believe it," Mary whispered. "All this time. All of this time. She gave you blood, Dean. She saved us after the Event. She stayed in our *house*." Mary ran her hands through her hair, tears falling down her face. I wiped the tears away with my thumbs and brought her in for a hug. "She was... our friend."

"What the hell is going on there?" Clare's voice came through our earpieces. "Are you all okay? Do you need a pickup?" The questions came in frantic succession.

"It was Mae. She ran off, taking their ship," I said in reply. The words didn't even make sense to me as they left my mouth.

"Mae. I knew those damned hybrids were going to be the death of us," Clare said, making my blood boil. Maybe she was right. Janine, Vanessa, Mae... they'd all used us.

"Why are you really here?" I grabbed Terrance by the collar, getting close enough to his face to touch noses. Anger flushed through my body so intensely I thought I might punch someone. As I stood there, waiting for an answer, I wished I was back home. Before any of this. Before the Event, and before Janine. I wanted to just go back in time.

"I told you! We just want to leave Earth. We need somewhere to go. Somewhere off the grid. This is it, a safe haven," he said, spittle hitting my face.

Maybe they were telling the truth. Probably not, since history had told me all hybrids were full of shit.

"Leave him," Kareem said calmly, and I looked back to see the two guards holding guns pointed at me. I wasn't going to give them the honor. I let Terrance go, and he straightened his shirt. The anger was still there, but muted. I shoved it down, along with all the fear and suspicion. Bottle it up. That's what a man was supposed to do, yet I felt worse for it, like I needed that anger to keep going.

"Come. We have much to discuss," Kareem said, motioning for the guards to lower their weapons. They did so, and I felt slightly better off.

"We don't have time for chit-chat. We need to go after her," Mary said.

"It won't take long, and I think you're going to want to hear what I have to say." Kareem turned and walked toward the home's front doors. We had no choice but to follow along, and soon were inside the large open foyer. He took his shoes off, implying that we do the same. Embarrassed, I remembered I was covered in mud and stank something fierce. Kareem didn't seem to even notice as he called to someone to bring *langols*, which my translator said was some sort of beverage.

Beside what looked to be a kitchen of sorts was a large wooden table. Some things crossed species well. There were a dozen chairs around it, and we sat, the three of us on one side, Kareem and the two hybrids on the other.

"First things first, tell me what brings you here." His voice was calm, soothing, and I found myself comfortable around him.

Terrance told him the story of the Kraski, and Kareem twinged at the name but pulled it together quickly. This guy had a hell of a poker face. Terrance told him of the plan to remove all humans from the world, sacrificing their own hybrids in the process. Terrance was passionate as he talked about being created for nothing but sacrifice and death, and how he wanted to lead the remaining survivors away to be safe and live their lives out in peace.

Kareem sat stone-faced as Mary and I told him of our journey, and the backstabbing of the Deltra. I didn't speak of them all dying, but he seemed to get the gist of it. He leaned forward as we told him about the final rescue, and how some hybrids came too, helping us stop the ships from exploding into the sun.

Leslie spoke of the year since, the internment camp they were at, and how for the most part humans had been nice to them. Kareem's face softened at this, and we drank our *langols*, which was much like a hot flowery tea.

"We really just wanted to stop these two, whom we thought were murderers and terrorists, from getting to the Bhlat and…" I was cut off by Kareem instantly after saying their name.

"The Bhlat! Don't speak that name here!" he yelled, getting to his feet. "If you thought the Kraski were bad news, you haven't seen anything." Just like that, the energy seemed to drain from him, and he sat back down, slumping forward. "I'm here because of them. My grandfather created the 'Shield,' as you called it."

"That means you would have to be…" Mary started.

"I'm over two hundred by your calendar years. Yes, my grandfather was the one to create the device that would save our race from the Kraski. Only hundreds of years under their oppression seem to have turned my people from a loving, nurturing race, to a blood-lusting race, just as bad as their tormentors." Kareem stopped, silence filling the room. The night's adventures and the retelling of our harrowing story had sucked the life out of me. I looked him in the eyes, and he stared right back as if seeking something deep within me. "Dean, can I trust you three?"

The question hung in the air a moment. "You can," I answered, wondering if I could trust him in return.

"Can I trust the rest of humanity?" he then asked.

That was a much more difficult question to answer. Humans had been through a lot, and most of my life I wasn't sure I fit in. I hated our internal strife, our abuse of each other, warring for things like salt or oil or just plain power. But my views had changed after hearing the stories of the vessel ships. We had so many heroes, ones that deserved the title more than I did, and for the first time in my life, I did think that as a species we could be trusted. Past Dean would have struggled to get the answer out, but I felt confident and powerful in my reply. "You can. I trust them. You can trust them too."

He looked me in the eyes, his pale thin lips pursing as he did so. His black eyes buried deep into mine, and eventually he sat back, grabbing his cup. "I believe you. I have a way for you to stop the Bhlat."

Just like that, I found myself wishing I was back home in another time.

EIGHTEEN

Our ship lowered in the spot where the silver ship had been sitting over an hour ago. The ramp dropped to the ground, Nick and Clare walking down to greet us. Nick's eyes went wide as he saw the alien beings around. The insectoids and the Deltra were quite the sight for someone who'd never seen them in person. Hell, I was still trying hard to not stare at them.

"I'm so glad you guys are okay," Clare said, looking toward the two hybrids we'd followed there.

"We have a lot to tell you about, but for now, let's get out of here," I said. Slate held his gun tightly in his large hands, and I knew he was still feeling like we could be attacked. The man hadn't relaxed since we'd landed on the planet. I didn't blame him.

"Come on, Slate," Mary said, and the big man walked aboard the ship.

"Kareem, we appreciate your help and advice. We'll do our best to keep your location secret," I said, and the tall Deltran man nodded to me in thanks. "Leslie and Terrance, I'll talk to Dalhousie and make her see the value in letting you all leave Earth. I promise this." I only hoped I'd be alive to keep the promise.

"I can see why people follow you, Dean. I'm glad we were able to find out we were on the same side of the fence," Terrance said, extending his hand. I shook it, but the nagging thought that I couldn't trust a hybrid took over my mind. It wouldn't matter, though. They could leave Earth, and that was enough for me. Everyone deserved a chance to be happy and free.

"Remember what I said, Mr. Parker. And never turn your back on a Bhlat. They won't lie to get on your side. They'll just shoot you from behind." Kareem turned, his cloak flowing behind him.

We walked up the ramp, the ominous words of the Deltra leader sinking in. The system's star was rising over the horizon as we rose up, shining into our viewscreen on the bridge.

With our small crew, Mae's absence was obvious; her betrayal still coursed through her blood inside me. Her ship's blinking icon flashed on the map, and as Clare keyed in the coordinates Kareem had given me, we saw her trajectory matched ours.

"Is it a coincidence she's heading the same direction as we are?" Nick asked.

"She knows," Slate said, his face a square block of intensity. "She knows where we're going somehow."

"Shit!" I cursed. Of course. She'd heard the whole conversation. "Everyone, change your frequency." I keyed in a new one and showed the rest of them. "She heard us talking with Kareem. How could I be so stupid?"

"None of us thought of it. We didn't have our earpieces on the frequency with each other, just the ship. She was smart enough to know that," Mary said as we zoomed through the atmosphere and toward the intense star in-system. The viewscreen dimmed as it grew, ever so slightly each minute.

"She's got a head start on us. A couple of hours. Let's just hope we're not too late when we get there. She hasn't hit the FTL drive yet. Leslie said it wasn't charging when they landed, since they hadn't been planning on leaving quickly. That gives us the advantage. Maybe," I said.

Clare confirmed this. "We can hit the drive in a few minutes. It should be enough to get us there first."

I looked at the estimated time of arrival to our new destination, a derelict Deltra station from fifty Earth years ago, and it said one hundred and sixty hours. Almost a week of twiddling our thumbs. A week to stew in anger at the betrayal. I sat down in the captain's chair for the first time, hardly aware that I'd done so. I was exhausted, and my clothing stank.

If she was just going to leave us, why save me at all? She'd risked herself again for me in the swamp. Was it just for show? Did she think the others would turn back if I was killed?

Someone tapped me on the shoulder, and I looked up to see Slate there.

"Let's get something to eat," his mouth said, but his eyes said he wanted to talk to me about something. I obliged and followed him down the hall.

"Slate, start the coffee. I'll be there in two." I headed for my bunk and grabbed a fresh uniform before hopping into the shower for a quick rinse-off. I rushed, hardly letting myself dry before suiting up and getting back to the kitchen.

"You'd make a good military man. That was as fast as any I've seen." He laughed, and I found myself joining in with him. I found myself really liking the quiet man. I'd expected him to be a lot like Magnus, but instead of the boisterous confidence of my Scandinavian friend, Slate gave off an aura of quiet confidence.

"I brought sandwiches to the bridge. Want one?" he asked, and I picked up a PB and J from the small stack in the middle of the table.

My stomach growled just at the sight of the food, and I ate half quickly, no words needed.

"Dean, I have a feeling when we get there, we'll be fighting. I don't know if Mae will be able to contact reinforcements, and at this time, we don't even know whose side she's on."

Don't trust her.

"The Bhlat," I said, my gut spitting out the name. "It has to be. There's no one left. If she's not with the hybrids, and we ended the Kraski, that leaves the Bhlat. We always said if the Delta were able to infiltrate the hybrids' core, the Bhlat could have too." Kareem had told us more about the alien race, and I almost wished he hadn't. They moved from system to system, destroying lives, using slaves to mine each planet for minerals so they could expand their reign of terror. So far, they looked to be centuries from coming near Alpha Centauri or our solar system, if ever. Kareem stated that the chances of them even bothering were low, but a race of humans that managed to stave off the fleeing Kraski might entice them to visit.

"I agree. I just want to see where your head's at. Can you pull a trigger if you see Mae's face in the crosshairs?" He asked the question so softly I had to lean in to hear him.

Janine's face. Mae's face. Could I? I nodded, saying I could and would, but words were one thing. Action was another.

"Good. What do you say we continue our training after some sleep? I'm going to relieve Mary from the bridge, and you two can get some rest." He didn't even look tired, and there I was, ready to fall asleep at the table.

"Thanks, Slate." He left me sitting there alone until a couple minutes later, when an equally tired-looking Mary came to join me.

"Let's get some sleep, babe," she said, coming over to me. I pushed my face into her stomach, and she ran her hands through my still-wet hair.

"I love you," I said, my voice muffled by her uniform.

"I love you too. Just think of the stories we're going to be able to tell our children," she said.

It was the first time she'd mentioned kids, and until then, I hadn't even realized they were a possibility. Maybe there was room for another life on our new world.

Standing up, I kissed her. "Take some pictures. There's no way they'll believe half of it."

I hit the ground hard, having been at the receiving end of Slate's demonstration.

"Now you try," he said, motioning Nick forward. The wiry doctor came at me, feigning a low kick, and struck out with his fist. I spun, mostly avoiding the impact, and followed through, momentum doing most of the work as I flipped Nick onto his back and pushed my knee onto his chest.

"Very good!" Slate yelled, clapping his hands together.

"Yeah, very good," the doctor said, his words short and terse.

I got up and gave him my hand, which he hesitated to grab.

"Do I really need to learn this? I mean, I'm a healer, not a hunter." Nick rubbed his chest with his palm.

"We don't know what we're up against. Nick, you've never told us your story. Why are you here?" Slate asked, surprising the doctor.

"I told you why. They needed a volunteer and I stuck my hand up."

"We get that, but what drove you to stick your hand up?" I asked, genuinely curious.

We sat on the crates, drinking water, and Slate tossed us a couple of towels. I was covered in sweat and laid the towel over my head while he talked.

"I suppose a lot of my life decisions led me to that point. Where do you want me to start?" he asked.

"We have another four days before we get there. Go as far back as you want," Slate said, leaning against the wall. "Tell us about your life. You know... before."

It was hard for some people to go back to that life. To dwell on what was, because so much had changed with the Event. Nick's eyes had that look to them, and that was probably why he was so tight-lipped about himself.

"I always wanted to help people. Even as a little kid. Where others would shy away from blood, it fascinated me. It was inside us, and if enough leaked out, we died. A weird thing for an eight-year-old to think, and my questions sometimes had my parents worried. They were simple folks from the Midwest. She worked part-time at a bank, and my pa had a small construction company. I remember the day he asked me if I wanted to take over his business. I told him I couldn't because I was going to be a doctor. He looked crestfallen, but he never told me he was disappointed. They both supported me, and while I worked summers and part-time anything jobs while I went to school, they paid the lion's share of my tuition." His gaze had taken on a longing look to the far side of the room as he spoke, and I didn't have to ask if his parents had survived the Event. They hadn't.

"That's great. That isn't far off my own story," I said. "Where did you go to school?"

"Medical degree at Stanford. I moved to California after pre-med for a life-changing experience. It sure was. I loved the beaches and people, but eventually got homesick and went back to Indiana for my residency." He took a drink of water before continuing. "I ended up joining the military ten years ago."

"What made you do that?" Slate asked.

"A girl... rather, a woman, but aren't we all just boys and girls at the end of the day?" he asked, a grim smile on his face.

"I suppose we are. Especially when it comes to following the heart," I said.

"We went to Iraq. Different stations, and she was killed by a goddamn suicide bomber before I ever told her I loved her." He stared at the wall, as if looking either of us in the eyes would open the bottled-up floodgates that were inevitably there.

Slate came over and rested his hand on Nick's shoulder. He didn't say a word, just let it sit there a moment before heading back to the spot he'd been leaning on.

"Not that any of that matters anymore after we got taken. The world was always an upside-down place. Now we just have to turn around with it, so we can see straight."

The perspective on things was a good one. "When was that?" I asked.

"Two years before *they* came. I was a wreck. When I got back from the tour, I could hardly function. I started drinking too much and almost lost my job." He stopped, just staying quiet for a few moments. "Then they came and changed it all. I was up there with people dying around me, everyone fighting each other like wild animals trapped in a corner. I helped save a few lives up there, and I got it back. That urge to survive, and to help others survive. It was like I needed that shock to bring me back to being myself. Anyway, here we are. I guess someone heard about my efforts on vessel twenty-six, and I was recruited to the cause."

It was a great story, and I found myself liking the already affable man a lot more for hearing it.

"Want to get back to it?" he asked. "I'm ready to learn to fight. Thanks for making me talk it out."

We got up, me doing a little stretch on my tightening back, and we got back into position.

"Go!" Slate called.

"*E*veryone to the bridge." Slate's voice carried over the comm-system.

"Mary, time to get up," I said, pushing the blankets off my body. The floor was cool under my bare feet, and in moments, I had the uniform on, socks included.

"Just five more minutes, Mom," she said, her eyes still closed.

"I'll see you up there," I said, leaving her in bed but turning the lights on. Oldest trick in the book.

Nick came out of the kitchen, shrugging at me as we made our way down the corridor onto the bridge.

"What's up?" I asked. Clare was at the helm, with Slate on the console next to her. Their faces were grim.

"Asteroid field. That bitch led us into it," Clare said. Hearing someone call Mae something derogatory stung for a moment, until I remembered she'd betrayed us. I still clung to a glimmer of hope she hadn't, that she had a good reason for what she'd done. My gut told me otherwise.

We were out of the FTL, stars slowed on the viewscreen, and the computer zoomed to pick out a few large chunks of rock, highlighting them in blue on our screens.

"They look easy enough to avoid. Let's go around," I said, sitting down.

Clare took us around them, the computer calculating a trajectory for each of the asteroid chunks, a stream of blue lines covering our viewscreen.

"She's heading right for them," Slate said, standing as he watched. "She must have a death wish."

We were only a day away from the location of the space station Kareem had told us about. What games was Mae playing?

We kept going, Mae's icon blinking along a thousand kilometers behind us now. She was getting awfully close to one of the asteroids. We saw her darting in and out of clusters, before the ship went straight toward a large chunk a few hundred meters across. Her ship's icon blinked rapidly and disappeared from the screen.

"What the hell was that? Did she make impact?" I asked. I felt a hand on my shoulder and looked back to see Mary standing there, dressed, her hair in a tight ponytail. Concern etched across her face, and I knew she'd been clinging to the idea Mae might still be on our side too.

"Looks that way. The tracking is far more advanced on this vessel. You remember those ships. They have a proximity sensor more than exact calculations. She must not have seen it coming, or thought she could sneak by it," Clare said.

"Keep going," I said, my hand mopping my face. The urge to yell at someone surged through me, but there was nothing anyone did wrong. Mae had been the culprit, and now she was dead, and I'd never be able to ask her what her truth was. I knew we wanted to stop Mae from making contact, but I still thought I was going to be sick. My eyes shut, only to see the icon lights of her ship still blinking on the back of my eyelids. It all felt so anti-climactic. That was life sometimes.

"We're clear of the debris field. Activating the drive now," Clare said. Otherwise, the room was silent.

NINETEEN

"Let's bring it in slowly," I said, standing behind Mary's chair. Our cloaking shield was running, making us look like the stars around us from a distance. Up close we would appear like an anomaly, and anyone seeing us would most likely investigate the disturbance.

Kareem claimed he'd abandoned the station over fifty Earth years ago. The translation wasn't clear, but it made sense with how long he'd been on that planet. They'd been fleeing a Bhlat sentry ship, which apparently caught on that the Deltra were in possession of some new weapon. He didn't know if the station still existed, but they wouldn't have the code to start the engines.

He'd had every intention of getting back to it, but by the time he'd made planetside, he wanted to put it all behind him. To live a quiet life away from the war. His wife and child were with him, and that was enough for him to stay hidden.

"Is this worth it? I mean, now that Mae is gone, and the hybrids don't want to sell us out?" Nick asked us for the tenth time since yesterday.

"If this thing will do what Kareem says it does, then yeah. It could secure our safety from invasion," Mary said, creeping our ship toward the system. A ringed planet hung in the distance, a gorgeous juxtaposition to the ugliness I was feeling. A large moon was nearby, and just where we were told the station would be, it stayed, orbiting the planet beside the moon, its massive wheel-shaped rim spinning still.

"It might still have gravity," Clare said, staring at the viewscreen, taking in the amazing piece of technology.

It had to be a hundred times the size of our ship, with no lights of any sort on the outside of it. It looked like what it was: abandoned. I couldn't take my eyes off the circular space station, rotating so slowly, but that was probably because of the size of it. It was flat dark gray in color, patches of different material on the outside layers. It looked like there was an unfinished section in the center of it, a section probably closed off from the interior.

It gave off a coldness, looking at it. For some reason, the station made me think of visiting my father's grave after he'd passed away, and I didn't like the comparison in my mind. Nothing about it should have made me feel that way; nonetheless, it did.

"I have a bad feeling," Slate said, mirroring my thoughts.

"Me too," Mary whispered.

We slowed the ship, all silently watching the massive stationary vessel's turbine slowly rotate.

"No signs of anything nearby?" I asked, knowing there wasn't, because the map showed no vessels flying out there.

"Nothing within range," Clare said.

"Okay, let's do this. We stick to the plan. Clare, you stay here with Nick. Mary, Slate, let's suit up." I walked past them, to the hall.

"Dean," Nick said, "take care, and good luck out there."

I turned and forced a smile. "Thank you. Should be back in a jiffy. I wouldn't mind a beer after all of this is over. Can you put some on ice?" I joked.

"We mean it. Be careful," Clare said.

"We will. We have each other's back. Right, Slate?" Mary asked, nudging him with her elbow.

"Right," he said, his face set in grim determination.

With that, we exited the bridge in a line, and made our way past the storage area to the prep room, where our three suits hung on the wall, already prepared over the week. The lapels had the buttons attached to them. I hadn't green-beamed through any walls for a while, and frankly, I wasn't looking forward to it. The last time had been stressful enough. At least this time we were going into an empty ship, and the imminent death of millions of people wasn't looming over our heads.

Our suits were much like the ones we'd used from the Kraski ship last year, only there were five fingers for the hands, and they fit us since they were custom-built. The material was light and thin, though protective from radiation and, as we'd learned, almost melt-proof. As I slid into the suit, I thought back to when Mae and I had harnessed up and shot toward the vessel heading for the edge of the sun, clipping it and saving countless lives. Why had she done it?

"Ready?" Slate asked. His helmet was clipped in, and he checked ours, ensuring they were sealed properly.

"I think so," I said.

"You remember all the training we've gone over?" he asked us both.

Mary nodded, and he handed her the pulse rifle from the weapons cache. We were strapped with a handgun, and Slate had an arsenal of other weapons: concussion grenades, clubs, knives, and anything else he could carry on his person. He made for quite the imposing soldier.

"Overkill?" Mary asked him. "Expecting company?"

He answered with a toothy smile. "You can never be too prepared."

I keyed into the storage room computer tablet on the wall, and we watched the viewscreen feed as Clare approached the Deltra vessel. Kareem had told us where the best spot to enter would be, and Clare hovered our ship just above it.

"Love you, Mary," I said, grabbing her hand and squeezing it for a second.

"Love you too," she replied.

"What about me? Am I chopped liver?" Slate asked, laughing at his own joke. It was nice to see him cracking a funny one, and suddenly I didn't miss having Magnus beside me quite as much.

"We love you, Slate," we said in unison, getting a laugh and an eye roll for our trouble.

We strapped the lanyards to the harness clip on our suits' waists, safety cords should something go wrong between here and there. We had to travel through a few meters of space, and I didn't want the beam to drop me out there.

"Here goes nothing," he said, pushing the pinned button on his suit's collar. Green light enveloped him, and he pushed off the bar as we lowered from the ceiling. He passed through the floor with ease, and we followed.

Mary went next, glancing up at me just as she was leaving through the floor. I couldn't help but smile at her as I pressed my own pin, green light covering me. It was surreal to be doing this again. I pushed and had the odd sensation of crossing through something solid, as my particles bounced around super-fast.

I closed my eyes briefly to avoid seeing outside the ships. Infinite space and I were still on tumultuous terms after last year. Counting three seconds, I opened them, and pressed my pin again as my feet touched down on the metallic grated floor. I scanned the room, and my brain took a moment to catch up to what I was seeing.

"Mary," I called into my headset.

"I'm here," she replied, and I saw a movement to the side of the room.

"What happened?"

"Someone was here waiting. They fired into the room, and Slate went after them," she said as I approached her.

"You okay?" I asked, worry creeping into my voice.

"Yeah, let's go back up Slate."

She raised her pulse rifle, and I followed suit, walking sideways to the doorway. "Slate, come in," I said into my helmet speaker.

"There were five of them. I took two down so far. I'm coming back." Slate's voice was calm and quick in my ear.

We stood in the hall, guns raised in each direction.

The night vision on our display glowed green, showing us a basic hall of metal beams and grates. The place was built for function, not fashion. Something caught my eye to my right and I spun, seeing the bulk of Slate backing toward us.

"You know where you're going?" he asked.

I tried to get my bearings and nodded. "He said it should be in the anti-grav generator halls. Under the level-three air ducts." I wished it was closer to our entry point, but Kareem hadn't counted on us being attacked when we arrived.

"Lead the way. I've got your backs," he said.

We moved down the hall, sweat dripping down my arms as nervous energy raced through me. "What are they?" I asked.

"Big. Bigger than me. Heavy armor. Nothing we've seen before, but they may match the Bhlat description we've heard. It was hard to tell with them firing at me," Slate said.

Bhlat. The name sent shivers through my spine; my finger crept closer to the trigger on my weapon. Our footsteps clanged on the floor, echoing down the quiet halls. I kept thinking how they must be hearing it, they would be around the corner; but for that first section, it was all quiet.

The anti-grav wheel spoked out at four points, and the door to the third one was my target. We made it there in peace, and I tested the handle. The electric pocket door hissed open, causing me to jump and almost fire my gun. My nerves were getting the best of me. We'd only been walking on the ship for five minutes and it felt like an hour to me.

"Go get it, Dean. I'll watch the door." Slate slipped inside after us, and the door hissed shut. The room was confined, with a manual hatch leading down the massive wheel spoke, for lack of a better term.

"I wasn't planning on having the Bhlat here. Kareem said we need their DNA to activate it." The device was awful in a humanitarian kind of way. The Deltra had built the Shield as a way to keep Kraski away from it, and in a small area, the high-density few-kilometer radius killing them instantly, as I'd seen when we'd destroyed them in their own vessel last year. The image of them melting from their proximity to the Shield still haunted me, and there I was, hunting for another weapon of mass destruction with even more power.

"I'm coming with you, Dean. We can't get separated. We'll be stronger together," Mary said.

Part of me wished she would stay behind and be protected by Slate, and another part was happy to have her by my side. I tried to spin the hatch wheel, grunting at the stubborn thing. Mary joined in, and just when I was about to ask Slate for a hand, it started to move. We spun it open and saw a ladder heading upward.

"I'll take the lead," I said, climbing into the tube. It was a few feet wide, but not spacious by any stretch of the imagination. The rungs were metal, coated with small flakes that gave it grip. I raced up the first few; but looking up, I saw it went on for what appeared to be forever, so I slowed, pacing myself for the climb. We passed a small hatch that would exit to level one of the grav-system. Level three was our destination.

Pulse laser fire erupted from below us, and I had the urge to get Mary to pass me so I could get between her and any potential fire. But they could be above us too.

"Just keep moving. Slate's trained for this," she said, pushing my foot lightly. I listened without hesitation, adrenaline speeding me up as we made our way past the second hatch.

"Almost there," I said, straining to hear gunfire below. Nothing. "Slate, come in," I said. Nothing but static returned. "We've lost contact."

The third hatch was upon us, and my muscles burned as I climbed toward it. This one spun easier than the one below had, and I climbed through the four-foot diameter hole, sticking my hand out to help Mary into the room. It was pitch black, and finally, I could feel the wheel we were in spinning. Our feet were planted on the ground from the gravity it was creating, and while I didn't quite grasp the science very well, I was happy for it.

"Where is it?" Mary asked.

"He hid it. For good reason, apparently." The room was bathed in green from my helmet display, and I scanned for the crate Kareem had told me about. It was there, right where he'd said it would be! My heart raced as I ran to it. There was another door to the room, a normal humanoid-sized one, perfect to accommodate the tall, lanky Deltra. As I approached the crate, the door hissed open. Mary was a few feet away, the doorway separating us. We both had our backs pushed against the wall, and I held my breath. Something walked into the room slowly, feet clanking heavily on the metal floors. It was huge: seven or eight feet when it stood straight after bending for the too-small entrance.

Mary didn't hesitate. She stepped out in front of it and fired. It grunted and pushed back through the doorway, hitting its helmeted head on the way out. Red beams shot from my rifle as well, and it lay there twitching before Mary fired a kill shot at its head. The helmet burst open, exposing a thick-faced monster.

Shots fired in the distance, and Mary stood like a superhero. "Get the device. You have your DNA right here." She kicked the body and ran down the hall, firing like a commando.

"Don't leave. You don't know what's out there!" I yelled to her, but it was too late. She was long gone.

I stood there like a fool, holding the rifle and staring at the dead Bhlat for at least a minute. "Clare, they're here. Keep your eyes out for any incoming ships." I finally had the common sense to tell the ship what was going on.

"Slate told us. We've lost contact with him. Is he okay?" Clare's voice came through, asking a question I couldn't answer.

"I don't know. Over."

The crate was heavy, full of maintenance tools and spare parts for the anti-grav system. I had to empty it before it would even budge from the spot it'd been sitting in all those years. Soon a pile of junk was spread around the room, and the crate finally moved. The whole floor was sections of metal grates, each about three meters square, attached to grooves in T-bar style metal beams that made up the subfloor. I tugged on the corner square, and it lifted easier than expected. Leaning it against the wall, I looked for the device as Kareem had described it. Where the Shield had been large and heavy, this device was made with similar engineering in mind, but a couple hundred years later. It reminded me of cell phone technology in a twenty-year span, going from the clunky brick design to a computer in your pocket.

Empty. There was nothing down there. I ran my hands along the edges, and just as I was about to get up, I felt a slight protrusion. Excitement raced through me. I had to slide my torso into the opening, leaving my legs and back exposed, but I got the device in my grip, unclasping it from its secure hiding spot.

"I got it, Mary," I said.

"I killed another one. But…" Her voice trailed off, and I could hear blasts echo from my earpiece and inside the ship.

I needed to get this thing going and help them out there. It had a metal case, made of some lightweight but durable black alloy. It unlatched, revealing a circular device the diameter of a coffee cup base. It whirred to life as I touched it with my nano-fingered gloves. Soft yellow light glowed from the edges, and a white screen blinked on the interface of it. Deltra words scrolled across it, and my heads-up display was kind enough to translate them for me. I hadn't had a chance to test out this technology, so I was thankful for it.

I clicked the icon that translated to *Genetics*. The image of a double helix flashed onto the screen, rotating around. Words slid onto the screen, and my HUD translated them to: MISSING DATA.

What had Kareem said? I flipped it around and saw a small button, which I pushed. A small probe extended from it, and bingo, I had it. Now I just needed to get a sample from the huge corpse at my feet, which couldn't be difficult with all the blood and gore at my disposal. Suddenly, the body seemed repulsive to me, and the power of the device in my hand scared the hell out of every inch of me.

I closed my eyes, seeing the Kraski victims spewing out green bile before crashing to the ground in heaps. Thousands upon thousands of them littered that vessel last year. So much death at my hands. The fact that they were going to kill us didn't ease my conscience all the time. It was nature. Kill or be killed. Mary was out there somewhere, and she needed me to stop being a baby and get this done. I could think about the moral ramifications later.

The Bhlat's helmet was half blown off, so that's where I went, pulling the rest off the corpse's head. Blood oozed out, red like ours. Its face had a dark pigment; where our noses were, it had three holes on an otherwise flat face, lips thin around a wide mouth, teeth sharp and twice the length of mine. But it was the eyes that threw me off. Swirling green- and blue-speckled eyes stared back at me, and I lifted my rifle for a moment, they looked so full of life. But they weren't. It was dead.

Cringing, I stuck the probe from the back of the device into the Bhlat's neck, where a blaster had hit it. The yellow light turned to red and it beeped, transitioning back to yellow. The words GENETICS CONFIRMED appeared on the backlit white screen of the device.

It kicked back to the main menu. ACTIVATE now showed highlighted, and when I hit it, settings appeared. I could adjust the strength, the distance to cover with the pulse, and could rotate through the DNA samples. This scared the hell out of me. With this, I could add human DNA and wipe out our entire race. I almost dropped it right then, but the sounds of battle in the ship through my headset kept me focused.

"Dean, is it working? I'm cornered," Mary said through my earpiece. She sounded panicked.

Boots clanked in the hall, moving slowly, and it had to be a Bhlat trying to sneak up on me. How many of them were there? And why were they even here?

The steps got closer, and I stood in the adjacent corner to where the floor was lifted, aiming my pulse rifle forward toward the door. The steps stopped, and I could almost hear the Bhlat breathing from just outside the room. The device was in my palm. One click and I could test it. I just had to press CONFIRM on the activate option.

One more step and a boot poked through. My heart beat heavily against my chest, one finger on the trigger, the other hovered over the device icon. I didn't get to do either as the ship's lights came on in a steady hum. My night vision gave way to normal as the levels of light increased in the room.

The Bhlat said something in its language, and suddenly, the wheel we were in stopped spinning, the force throwing me across the room fast enough to see the Bhlat's eyes widen at the sight of me before it went flying down the hall. Gravity was gone.

TWENTY

I'd hit my head on the wall, and my body expected me to fall onto the pile of tools and parts scattered across the floor. Instead, they floated beside me in the room, with no gravity present to keep us grounded. Someone had powered the ship back up and stopped the spinning wheel we were in from moving, stopping the artificial grav unit from doing its job. Air hissed into the room, the life-support system back up and activated.

As I floated there, contemplating what was happening, I noticed my left hand was empty. I'd dropped the device. Grunting echoed from the hall, and I remembered I wasn't alone. Scanning the room, I saw the device floating there beside a large wrench and a soldering iron.

I pushed off the wall, arcing toward the device just as the massive Bhlat came flying into the room. Its gun flashed beams at me, narrowly missing and cutting holes into the wall behind me. I fired back but missed as well, hitting the roof instead of the large target. I collided with the far wall, with the Bhlat soldier piling into me with some serious velocity.

It felt like being pinned to the wall by a semi-truck. My chest ached, and I nearly let go of my blaster. The training from Slate took over, and I gripped a metal rail on the wall, kicking out with all my strength, sending the Bhlat back a couple feet. It left me just enough time to grab the device.

The Bhlat said something aloud, and my translator attempted a translation but failed. A strange noise emanated from the alien, and I guessed it was laughter. I must have looked like easy prey to such a large creature. His long blaster rose as he floated there, aiming right for my head. He said something else, and the translator annoyingly showed an error again.

The device was in my palm, still waiting for the CONFIRM command to be hit. This time, I did so with ease of conscience. It was kill or be killed, and I understood that now more than ever.

Time seemed to slow. His finger bent to pull the trigger just as I pressed the icon. It hummed quickly, vibrating ever so slightly. I almost didn't feel the blaster beam rip into my side as the Bhlat nearly exploded before me. In my new slow-motion world, I saw his same green-blue swirling eyes widen just before his face pushed out, blood covering the inside of his mask. The rest of him seemed to melt, and when time started again, he was just floating lifelessly, a massive space suit of blood and bones. I nearly vomited in my own suit, and alarms were going off inside my helmet. The suit had been breached.

That was when I felt the pain in my side. My suit was torn open, blood seeping out into the room and floating around in tiny drops, each visible as I hung there staring forward.

"Dean." I heard my name in my earpiece over the internal klaxons. It was Mary's voice.

"Mary, where are you?" I asked, reality snapping back to my muddled mind.

"Main ship, near our entry point. They're all dead. Are you okay?" she asked, her voice strained.

"I'm okay. Just a little shot. I'm coming down." I

grabbed the Bhlat's weapon, knowing we wouldn't have any more trouble from them on the vessel. Getting back down was easier with no gravity, and I was thankful, since my wound wouldn't stop screaming at me. As I entered the tunnel spoke of the gravity wheel, I used the ladder rungs to pull me down the chute. Much faster than I'd gotten up not ten minutes before, I was back on ground level, in the center of the vessel.

"Where are you?" I asked, feeling like I might pass out. She gave me directions, but I could tell she was hurt. I pushed against the walls; every movement sent shooting pain through my abdomen. Blood trailed behind me, and I was thankful the life-support had come on; otherwise, I'd already be a dead man.

I heard something clank around the hall corner, and I raised my pulse rifle. Just because the device killed the Bhlat on board didn't mean they couldn't have had other friends on the ship with them. I moved slowly, my vision fading slightly. I'd lost too much blood. I needed to get to Mary. I needed to see her one last time. Ready to fire at an enemy, I pushed out, floating into the next hall, and saw it was Slate just before pulling the trigger.

"Dean!" he called, and I heard him with my ears, not my earpiece. His suit was banged up badly, and his left arm was floating uselessly at his side.

"Slate! Thank God, Mary is over here," I said, feeling a renewed sense of energy.

We headed to the third room on the right, where she'd described her location to me, and there were four Bhlat in there with her. Four large floating corpses.

Mary was floating lifelessly as well.

Through the pain, I made my way to her.

"Clare, tell me you're ready. We'll be there in two," I managed to get out, seeking a confirmation they were ready for us.

Mary was still breathing. Her suit was blasted open in a few spots, but none near her chest or head. Normally, I would have freaked out at seeing my beautiful fiancée's injuries, but I could hardly make sense of anything I was seeing, my vision fading quickly.

Slate took charge, grabbing her, and moved faster than I'd seen him move before, leading me back to the room we'd started the mission in. Our ropes were still there, and we clipped them in.

Slate looked at me with a grim, exhausted expression. Yet he still smiled. "You did well," he said, just loud enough for me to hear before my world went black.

*W*hite light. That was what I saw first. For a brief moment, I thought that was it for me, that I'd passed to the other side, and a small part of me was ready for it.

"Dean, can you hear me?" a familiar voice asked. That wasn't unusual. Theologians had speculated for years that we might be ushered into heaven by an old friend or loved one. "Dean, you're back on our ship. Your wound was substantial, but I've managed to stop the bleeding and patch you up."

So much for heaven. I was still on a trip to hell on board a small spacecraft in the middle of some unknown galaxy.

My bleary eyes cleared and I could finally make out where I was. The bunks were stripped of any clutter, and a form lay on the one across the room from me.

"The medic bay wasn't big enough for both of you, and I assumed you would both prefer to be in the same room, so we made do with the spare bunk room. Hope you don't mind," Doctor Nick said.

The both of us? It all came flooding back. The device, the massive Bhlat soldiers. Mary's limp body floating there, blood hovering around her.

"Mary!" I tried to sit up, but the pain in my stomach stopped me from lifting more than a couple inches before falling down on my back.

"Dean, you have to calm down. You've been through a lot, but you're healing faster than anyone I've ever seen."

The hybrid blood in me helped with the healing process. Mae's blood.

"Is she going to be okay?" I asked, seeing her chest rise and fall slowly. That was a good sign.

Nick stood between us, looking every bit the part of the doctor for the first time since I'd met him. He was a natural.

"She's sustained a lot of wounds, but none in themselves are life-threatening. She was shot in the legs and the left shoulder. The suits are made to prevent the serious burning from the beams, but flesh and veins were still seriously damaged. She'll be fine, but I have her sedated for the time being, while the grafting heals."

"Are you telling me you have the ability to graft new skin on this ship?" I asked, dumbfounded.

He nodded, smiling widely. "We do. It's amazing what we learned from the Kraski databases. I don't think we've even begun to scratch the surface. Give us another ten years to analyze and decipher it all, and we could be living in a world with no illness, disease, or famine for that matter."

The idea was a lofty one, but admirable. Earth needed hope now more than ever.

"Where's Slate?" I asked, feeling foolish for not having asked after him yet.

"I'm right here, boss," the big man said, stepping in from the hallway. "I wanted to give you some privacy while you woke up." His arm was in a sling. He saw me looking at it. "It's just sprained. I'll be back to normal in no time."

"Slate's being humble. He dragged you two onto the ship and hasn't left your side since," Nick said. "I'm going to go grab some sleep, if you don't mind. Dean, I left some painkillers beside you. If it gets to be too much, take one and rest." With that, he left the room, leaving me alone with Slate and my unconscious fiancée.

"How are you feeling?" he asked, sliding a chair up beside my twin bed.

"Do you mind passing me another pillow?" I asked, and he even stuffed it under my head. I cringed at the movement in my gut, but propped up, I could speak to him properly, instead of staring at the ceiling.

"I'm not sure how I'm feeling. We got the device, met the Bhlat, and survived." I looked over to Mary, hoping to God she was going to be all right. She should have stayed with me. She was always trying to protect others first, and it nearly got her killed.

"That we did."

"How many did you take on out there?" I asked.

"Killed five of them. By all accounts, there were about twelve or so on board – that we saw. There could have been more hiding out."

"What were they doing there? If they knew there was a device with the capability to destroy them, why not destroy the station and leave it at that?" I asked, stumped.

He passed me a bottle of water from beside the bed, helping himself to one as well.

"I'm not sure. That's above my pay grade."

"Take a stab at it," I coaxed.

He stared at the wall for a minute. Slate was a trained soldier, but from my experience with him, he was a lot smarter than even he gave himself credit for.

"Kareem said they were chased away, forced to leave the device hidden because they didn't have their DNA yet. The Bhlat are a big force, we can assume, so maybe they left soldiers here in the off chance the Deltra came back. They pretended it was dead, in hopes of luring them back. Or they're no better than space pirates, trying to get someone to board, and then stealing their ships. Either way, I doubt they knew about the hidden killing machine Kareem left behind," Slate said, impressing me with his speculation.

"But fifty years? It doesn't add up. Unless Mae was able to communicate to them?"

"There was no ship there. They had to have been dropped off some time ago."

"What happened with the grav-system out there?" I looked to the ceiling, even though I had no idea what direction the Deltra ship stood.

He smiled at this. "We were losing, and I wanted something to turn the tides."

"Thank God you did, because I was about to get shot."

"And how did that work out for you?" He nodded at my stomach.

"I got shot," I said, laughing along with him. "Stop, it hurts." My hand settled on my wound, which was extremely tender to the touch.

"Sorry, boss. No more jokes."

"Are we still at the station?" I asked.

"We moved away a few thousand kilometers." He

crossed the room and picked up a tablet. "See?" He showed me the image from the viewscreen on the bridge. The ship lingered there, just in orbit of a gorgeous, lifeless world, particles, water, and ice creating a visually stunning ring around the planet.

"I can't believe something so beautiful can be so treacherous at the same time," I said, still staring at the planet on the tablet.

"I had a girlfriend like that in high school," Slate said, straight-faced at first. Soon we were laughing, and I was literally busting a gut. The pills beside my bed were starting to call for me.

"You guys are going to want to see this." Clare's voice came through the room's speakers. Slate's tablet switched to the map mode; Clare was pushing through. A small icon blinked once again on it. "Mae's ship is back and moving fast."

TWENTY-ONE

"Mae's ship?" I blurted, hardly able to believe what I was seeing. "How is that possible?".

"We don't know. She's heading out from the asteroid field we passed just now. Maybe she found a way to hide from our sensors inside it." Clare slapped her palm to her forehead. "We should have gone back and checked. Sit a ship on a large enough hunk of rock, with just the right amount of radioactive metals inside it, and it would probably jam our sensors."

I nearly smiled at Mae's move. She'd hidden from us on an asteroid and was now getting away.

"Follow her," I said.

Three heads turned to look at me, propped up in the captain's chair wearing a cheap med-suit, and solemnly nodded.

"What choice do we have? If we want to keep the Bhlat from knowing we were here, she's the last moving piece," Clare said.

"She has to be exterminated." Slate stood tall, staring forward toward the map on the viewscreen. His words bothered me, but I knew they shouldn't. He was right.

"How do we know where she's going?" Nick asked, still wearing his scrubs.

"We don't, but we can predict where her current trajectory will take her. We'll aim for that path, and maybe we can even cross paths. We have the advantage because we can see where she is, but she can't do the same with us." Clare was taking charge, and I obliged her. With Mary incapacitated, we needed someone who could fly the ship and think outside the box.

"What do you think she's doing?" Nick asked.

"She has to be going to the Bhlat. The Kraski are gone, for all we know... but maybe that was a lie from Mae. She had no affiliation with the Deltra, at least none that we knew of." I thought back to my memories of the Deltra visiting Janine and convincing her to work with them. They, of course, tricked her, just as they had tricked us last year. I looked down at the new Deltra tool I held in my hand and wondered how I had trusted Kareem so quickly. Suddenly, the killing device I was holding made me want to throw up. How had it even gotten into my hands? For all I knew, they were tracking us with it. The urge to release it out the airlock passed over me, but we might still need the damned thing. After that, I was sure I needed to dispose of it, once and for all.

"Make that happen, Clare. Slate, can you give me a hand back to the room? I think I need to rest." My body was in serious pain, and the events were leaving me light-headed.

"For sure, boss." He took most of my weight and soon I was back in the room, lying on the bed looking at the ceiling. I took another pill, and before I knew it, my vision was fading, my brain getting foggy.

"Dean, I'm just going to go for a run. I'll be back soon, and I'll make breakfast." Janine walked over to me at the kitchen island as

I was pecking away at my laptop. She leaned over, resting her chin on my shoulder. I turned my head and she kissed my cheek, leaving her freshly applied lip balm. She always wore vanilla. I loved the scent.

"Have a good run. Can we have bacon with breakfast?" I asked. She rolled her eyes.

"Dean, do I go for a run just to counter a couple slices of bacon? Maybe you should join me." She prodded me in the side with her finger.

"I promise I'll go next time. I have some work to get done for this afternoon." It was mostly the truth.

"Okay, babycakes. I'll be back." She hopped from one foot to the other, warming up her blood flow. Her hair was in a ponytail, and she didn't have any makeup on. She was the most beautiful woman I'd even seen.

The door closed, and I went back to working on the Peterson file.

I awoke from the strange dream wondering why I'd remembered that brief moment of my past. It was from eight years ago, probably not even a year after Janine and I had met. The pain pills left my mouth dry, another side effect of the medicine. Finding the bottle of open water on my table, I guzzled half the bottle before setting it down.

The dream had left me shaken, seeing Janine again. Mae looked just like her. I always felt like there was a difference I could notice between them, but since I hadn't ever seen them together, it was hard to tell. Either that, or my brain filled in the Janine role in my dream with Mae's face, her nuances.

"Dean," a coarse voice whispered from across the room.

"Mary!" I exclaimed, so happy she was awake. "I'm here."

Getting off my bed proved easier this time than the last, and I saw from the tablet on the wall that I'd been out for four hours. The pills really packed a punch.

I pulled the chair Slate had been sitting in and brought it to her bedside.

Mary's eyes were closed, but she opened them when I touched her hand. It was warm, but not hot to the touch, and I took that as a good sign.

"How are you feeling?" I asked her, squeezing her fingers ever-so-lightly.

She groaned but smiled at me through the pain. "I feel like I fell from a cliff and landed on the ground in a poof just like a cartoon coyote. What happened?"

"You don't remember? You talked to me, letting me know which room to find you in."

"No. The Bhlat cornered me, and I tried to shoot my way free, then... nothing."

"The device worked, and they turned to mush in their suits. It was terrible and lifesaving at the same time. We found you unconscious, and I was barely hanging on. Slate ended up hauling us the pair of us, passed out and bleeding," I said, getting a slight snicker from her.

"We make quite the team." She rubbed the back of my hand with her palm.

"We sure do." I kissed her forehead, getting a shot of pain from my stomach wound, though it felt way better than it had. The hybrid blood was helping me heal from it at a welcome expedited rate.

We talked, and I filled her in on Mae's ship reappearing. I hated to tell her, but she swore she wanted to know everything. With any luck, we would have time to heal a bit before we were back in battle mode.

"I wish Magnus and Nat were here," Mary said, mirroring my own thoughts.

"Me too. I still can't believe they're married."

"I wish we were," Mary said. "I was running around that damned place trying to distract the monster Bhlats and all I could think about was walking on a beach with you, a little boy holding our hands between us. We walked, swinging the boy, sand warm and messy under our bare feet. It was wonderful and scary at the same time. I thought that was it. Like I was having an afterlife vision of what wouldn't be, if that makes any sense."

"It makes a lot of sense. I love you, Mary. Let's go stop Mae from doing whatever it is she's up to, and go home," I said, wishing it were that easy.

"Deal. Now where can I find one of those crazy pills you were talking about?"

★ ★

"*H*as she changed course at all?" I asked. We were all on the bridge, six days after the adventure that had resulted in two of us being badly wounded. Slate still had a few bruises, mostly healed by that point.

"Nothing substantial. She only moves when there's something standing between her and her target. Wherever that is." Clare had gone from bubbly engineer to focused pilot. Mary took some light duties now, but she needed to walk around with crutches, which they surprisingly had stored on the ship.

I passed around the freshly heated freezer-pack dinners, though we really didn't know what time our internal clocks were working on since we all had such different schedules. With just the five of us, we had to split the small number of chores.

I bent down, passing Clare a dinner plate, and noticed my side didn't hurt at all any more from the movement. It was almost entirely healed. I only wished Mary had the same success. She was still in a lot of pain, popping more pills than she thought was healthy.

"Where the hell is she bringing us?" I asked for the hundredth time.

"I guess we won't know until we get there," Mary said between bites of her heated-up quinoa mixture.

The map on the side of the viewscreen flashed, expanding at Clare's direction. Mae's ship icon blinked and was gone, the map zooming out once again.

"Son of a bitch. Another wormhole?" Nick asked.

Setting my plate down, I almost looked for Carey, who would inevitably come sniffing around looking for a way to steal the chicken off my plate. But Carey was on another ship heading to a new world. As the map expanded, and I saw the universe enlarge around us, I suddenly wanted to be sitting back on Earth with Mary and Carey, in front of a fireplace at a resort in Vermont.

"That slows us down a bit, since we were aiming to cut her off on her trajectory. Looks like we can get to that spot in an hour."

"At least we have time to eat," Nick said, nearly getting a smile from Clare.

TWENTY-TWO

The wormhole was hard to spot again, but there it was, a window into another galaxy.

"Sending in probes," Clare said.

"I'm no scientist, but even a theoretical wormhole is near impossible to work, let alone stay open," I said, baffled by the phenomena.

Clare turned while the probes shot back data. "You're right. They need an outside force."

I pondered that before standing up fast, nearly knocking my empty plate over. "Outside force like technology?"

She nodded, pursing her lips slightly. "Sure. If there was a way for them to keep the gateway open, that might make sense. Bear in mind, I have no real understanding of this other than the Hawking books I read in college."

"Send more probes out. Look for any electrical or nuclear radiance that isn't coming from us."

We waited for the results to come back.

"Probe 9351 found something. Wait." Clare was almost giddy with excitement. "9714 found the same results."

"Take us to one, please," I said, standing behind the helm's console.

Slate zoomed on the coordinates, and we saw a hovering satellite. No doubt this was one of the things keeping the gateway open.

"Look, I find this fascinating too, but every second we stay here looking at this piece of alien metal, Mae is getting closer to her target," Slate said, clearly agitated.

"Just record their emittance frequency, and let's get out of here." I had a plan for when we passed back through the fold in space. If we came back.

Soon we were hovering in front of the wormhole. I was holding the device with Bhlat DNA affixed to its sensors. Just holding it was making me feel better about going into the mouth of the beast.

"Everyone strapped in this time?" Mary asked from her seat.

"Affirmative," Slate said after a quick scan of the bridge.

"Three... two... one." Clare eased the ship into the opening, and it felt like we entered the gates of hell. The ship lurched back and forth, like a boat in a tumultuous storm on the sea. The inertial dampeners, already patched up after our last venture, kicked in and out, and it felt like my head was going to rip clean off my shoulders. As badly as I felt, I worried for Mary as we tossed about, but just as quickly as it started, it ended as we exited the other end.

"Are you all okay?" I asked, getting out of my seat to cross over to Mary.

Her eyes were closed, and blood ran from her lips. My hand ran to her face, and her eyes darted open. "It's all right. It's just me," I said calmly.

Her fingers traced her mouth, coming away with her blood on the tips. "I'm fine. I bit my tongue."

"Well, that was better than the first time," Slate said, getting up too. The map had zoomed once again, and Clare left the bridge to check on the engineer room.

"She's not using her FTL yet. That could mean a couple of things. Either she's having trouble with her ship or the target's near."

Slate looked every bit as imposing as I'd seen him before. If I didn't know better, he was itching for a battle; a final showdown.

Clare's voice came through the console speakers. "Everything checks out here. We should be good to go."

Mary moved to the helm position, though I could see her wince in pain at doing so.

"She's slowing down," Mary said, pointing to the map. "We'll be at her location in thirty minutes."

"It'd be a lot faster if we just toss this baby into FTL for a minute," I suggested, getting a smile in return from Slate.

"I like the cut of your jib, boss. I'll suit up. Care to join me?" he asked, and I didn't answer because he wouldn't like to hear what I really thought. I just nodded sullenly, anxious for a resolution to this chase, but worried about what that outcome would look like.

I felt my pocket for the Deltra device and couldn't find it. Panic coursed through my body until I found it on the ground across the bridge. It must have gone flying when we were jostled around in the wormhole.

I pressed the touchscreen, and yellow light glowed in a ring around it. Everything looked fine.

"Be careful," Mary said.

I leaned over, giving her a deep kiss, long enough to make a sailor blush.

"I love you," I said, hoping it wasn't for the last time. She mouthed it back to me, a tear falling down her cheek.

Leaving that bridge was the most difficult thing I'd ever had to do, and considering what I'd been through, that meant a lot.

"Nick, what are you waiting for? Suit up," Slate said, causing the doctor's mouth to fall open.

"What? Me? Out there?" Nick stammered.

"Why do you think I've been training you? So you can go home and win the Hill Valley state karate competition?" Slate asked.

"Oh crap, you're serious," Nick said.

"It's time for the big leagues, my friend. Don't worry; we just need you for backup. We still don't know what we're getting into," Slate said, and I saw Nick's tense look loosen up a little.

The corridor to the weapons room felt longer this trip.

"What do you think we're going to find?" I asked Slate while Nick was busy getting his assigned suit on.

"She might be bringing us right into the hive of the enemy. Good thing you have that weapon," he said, nodding his chin to the device in my hand.

As much as I wanted to protect Earth, I wasn't sure genocide of a race was the answer this time.

"Of course, we'll still need to eliminate Mae when it's said and done," Slate whispered in my ear.

I solemnly nodded, still not believing we had to kill my close friend. I felt so used by her.

"Don't worry, boss. I'll make the shot if that helps."

It didn't. "I'll do what's necessary." The words came out, but I didn't recall saying them.

We got suited up, leaving our helmets off, and lined them beside our weapons in the storage room next to the ropes and tethers. I pushed the pin on Nick's collar just long enough to see him glow green as Slate held him.

"I'm not looking forward to this," he said.

"Just press this, push yourself through on this bar" – I lowered the bar from the center of the room – "and don't forget to strap in. You don't want to end up floating around in space. We haven't had a chance to train you on the suit's propulsion system yet."

This just made him pale more, if that was possible. A year ago, I would have looked just like him, but I'd been thrown into a desperate position with no other options.

"You guys have to see this." Clare said through the speakers.

We crossed the ship and entered the bridge, amazed at what we were seeing.

"Our cloaking tech is functional, right?" I asked.

"They can't see us," Clare said.

The viewscreen showed us a planet in the distance, and one of the two stars in the system, on opposite corners of the planets, which made for a complicated orbit pattern and had to be hell on days and nights. Maybe whatever life was on them had adapted to that, if there was any life.

Before us was a satellite, a small moon for the closest planet, which reminded me of a sand-colored Mars. The viewscreen zoomed, and there was Mae's ship, hovering near the moon.

"Look." Mary zoomed closer and we saw a structure on the surface. It stretched out in an intricate system of halls leading to an assortment of outbuildings. There was obviously no atmosphere, and probably very little gravity, so they had a sealed colony.

Beside the structure, three ships were settled on the rocky surface.

"This looks like an outpost. We must be closer to their home galaxy," Slate said, clenching his fists. "We can't let Mae get to them."

Mae's ship was just hovering there. She was either contemplating her next move, or she was waiting for clearance. Clare tried to scan all communication frequencies, but nothing came across.

The good news was, they still didn't know we were there.

"What do we do?" I asked, looking to Slate for guidance.

"We go down there, activate that death tool you have, and blow up Mae's ship." He said it so straight-faced, it startled me.

"What if there are more than Bhlat down there?" I asked, playing devil's advocate.

"That's why we have guns," he replied, a smile crossing his face. It was more than a little unsettling.

"Does it end here? We stop Mae, we stop the outpost from ever passing on the knowledge we were here, and we go home. Right?" I laid it out and everyone nodded.

The device was light in my pocket, but the weight of what it could do almost caused me to sit down. The good news was, I would just need to use it one last time. To kill the potential enemy before they knew what hit them, in order to keep humanity a secret longer.

"How close do you think we need to be to use it?" Mary asked, not having to say what "it" was.

I shook my head. "I don't know, but I doubt it will work instantly from a thousand kilometers. I'd say we fly over them and hope they can't see us, turn it on, get Mae, and go home." It sounded so easy. Part of me was excited that we might be on the way home in a very short amount of time; the other was tired of having to kill.

"Bringing us in," Mary said.

Mae was still in space, and we went the long way to avoid crossing her path. The moon was rocky, small hills and mountains jutting out from it. The station was on the flattest part of the moon, which was even smaller in diameter than I had originally thought.

I tried to gauge the size of the room and hall structure as we approached, and put it at about six city blocks long with about twenty separate buildings, each connected with dark corridors, no glass anywhere.

When we hovered above the center of the area, I stood, sliding the device from my breast pocket. Tapping it turned the yellow ring on, and I scrolled to the icons, even though my helmet wasn't on to translate the text. I remembered which to press.

"God forgive me," I whispered as I tapped the confirm icon.

"Is it done?" Clare asked.

Nothing on the base looked any different. Were they dead?

The device ring shone red and started to flash. Text appeared over the screen. "I can't read it, but I think something's wrong." Grabbing my helmet from beside my chair, I popped it on, locking it in, and let my HUD fire up. I scanned the device text again. *DNA sample insufficient.*

"Shit. The DNA sample has failed. Must have messed up when it flew onto the ground when we were tossed around in the wormhole," I said, my hands nearly trembling. I tapped it a few more times, trying to get it to work, and the same result occurred. I even popped the sample tray open on the back, careful not to add my own sample to it. This thing was dangerous.

"You know what this means?" Slate asked, before answering his own question. "This means we go down there, kill one of them, and get a fresh sample. Then we beam the hell out and destroy them."

It was as sound a plan as we had. "Couldn't we just blow them to hell?" This from Nick.

"As much as I agree with the good doctor here, I think we need to get the sample. What if they do find their way to Earth? Having protection against them would be the difference between survival and extinction," Mary said. I found it hard to argue with her logic.

"Then it's set. Let's go, Slate. We'll be back in a few minutes. Don't leave without us." I led the way off the bridge, catching a worried glance from Mary. I knew she wanted to be down there with me, but her injuries weren't healed enough, and it was a lot safer on the bridge than in the spider's web we were about to jump into.

Nick was there beside us, passing us our rifles. He slid his helmet on. "Call me and I'll be right there."

Slate clapped him on the arm. "Dean, you ready for this? We isolate a Bhlat, incapacitate him, take the sample, activate the thing, and walk out of here."

"Deal," I said, pressing my pin, green light covering me once again. Nervous sweat dripped down my back and sides as I pushed on the bar, passing through the floor of the ship and into the light atmosphere of the moon, before crossing through the two-meter-thick ceiling of the building we hovered above.

I emerged in a room, gun ready to fire at will, but it was nearly dark, soft lights coming from some wall computers. Slate was beside me; we unlatched our belts and made our way to the doorway.

"All we need is one." Slate took the lead. The door slid open at our foot pressure, making more noise than I wanted. So much for stealth.

The hall went both directions, lights glowing along the floor. It was quiet. Left or right. Right would lead us to a group of larger buildings we'd seen from above, so Slate led us left, probably assuming there would be fewer enemies that way.

We walked quietly, our rifles held up, ready for action.

"Guys, Mae's on the move. She's landing in their shipyard," Clare said in my earpiece.

"That doesn't change anything," I said, Slate nodding firmly. He motioned to keep moving, and we approached another door to the left. Slate stepped in front of it, gun ready to blast, and it opened. He rushed in, gun moving from side to side, but the room was empty. It looked like weapons storage, and Slate's eyes widened at the sight of huge alien guns lining the walls.

"Later," I assured him.

Alarms clanged through the halls, and I winced at the volume. They knew we were here.

TWENTY-THREE

"What do we do?" I asked.

"We keep moving," was the reply I got.

We checked each room. Some were empty; each served a different purpose. Whatever this place was, these guys were there for the long haul, or at least intended to be. Bunks lined the walls of a massive open space, enough room to sleep fifty of the large warrior race.

Where were they all? We passed the kitchen and mess hall, and I couldn't help but feel they weren't so different than we were. Maybe there was hope we could all get along. Seeing the look of grim determination on Slate's face, I doubted it. Hell, humans couldn't even get along with themselves.

Slate slid a finger in front of his mouth in a shushing motion and crept forward slowly. "There's a group of them ahead. This is one of this side's larger rooms. Maybe an auditorium."

The alarms still blazed, but not as loudly, and soon the sound went away, leaving just the flashing lights to annoy us. I snuck a peek but quickly turned around, feeling like one was about to sneak up on us at any moment. The coast was clear. These Bhlat weren't uniformed. Instead, they wore something akin to a jumpsuit. They weren't carrying weapons, either.

They kept moving in the same direction as us, and we

poked our heads into the next room. It looked like a large laboratory, with indecipherable mathematic formulas on digital screens. The structure to them looked quite different than anything I'd ever seen, yet eerily familiar at the same time. My HUD translator read what it could understand to me, and it still made no sense.

"Maybe it's a science station," I said.

"It doesn't make a difference." Slate was trained for a mission, and he wasn't going to sway from his objective. His linear warrior mind was focused on the task at hand, and my mind was moving a mile a minute which, after our faster than light travel, might not have been so fast.

Alien voices flowed down the halls toward us, a deep vibrating language different than our own. My translator spilled out what it could, constantly getting better as it learned more.

She comes alone. Talleidudne will be happy shiguedbggr is here. Time poloo answers.

They knew Mae was there.

We ducked into the science lab and waited as two hulking forms passed by, talking away, their voices muffled so my translator couldn't pick them up.

"Keep going," Slate said.

We approached the space where the group had emerged from a few minutes ago and entered an amazing room. Chairs lined the center of the space, and a glowing platform sat in the middle of the room. Either a stage or... a projector. My gut leapt as I realized this was a communication hall. They had probably been in there talking with a leader from a faraway planet, but they didn't know the humans were here. They did seem to know Mae was, though, and it was only so long before they spotted the abnormal cloaked ship hovering above them.

Slate was right, we needed to end this now. Something rustled near the back of the room, and Slate fired a quick shot, killing the computer tablet on the wall, shutting the lights down. The helmets' night vision sprang to life, and we covered the doorway so no one could get through. I stayed at the door while Slate headed toward the noise. I heard and saw three quick red pulse beams, and then silence.

"Slate?" I whispered into my mic.

"I got one, boss. Get the device and let's do this thing once and for all."

I moved to his location, seeing a Bhlat smaller than I expected. It was slender, and less ridged than the ones we'd encountered. I almost dropped the Deltra weapon when I realized what that meant. It was a female of their kind.

"Doesn't matter," Slate said, "just do it." He was proving to be quite the robot, but that might have been what I needed right then.

Sliding the DNA sample stick from the back, I found a wound from the rifle, took a deep breath to stifle the wrongness of what I was doing, and jabbed it in. The device whirred to life again, following the same pattern as it had before.

"Make it snappy," Slate called to me as we heard the door slide open.

What is idpewa here? a Bhlat asked into the darkness.

Slate fired a few rounds, and I heard two forms slump to the ground before the alarms raised again.

"What's happening down there, Dean?" Mary's voice came through my earpiece. I ignored it, not wanting to talk, mostly because I was holding my breath as I waited for the device to be ready to work.

"Dean, there are more coming!" Slate yelled.

"Come on, come on," I said, and the icon glowed green. I hesitated, seeing the dead female Bhlat on the ground before me, and the door opened once again, laser fire blasting into the room at us. I nearly dropped the device; Slate grunted and ran across the room, shooting a volley of red death on the Bhlat.

Everything slowed for me for a split second. Laser fire inched around the room, Slate's yells turned to slow-motion calls from the movies, and all there was on the moon was this device, and fifty living beings. I pressed the button, and time caught up.

"Thank God," Slate said from twenty meters away. He was on the ground, green in my night vision. The Bhlat were all down, not a breath left in their alien bodies. I found, at that moment, that I wanted to know more about them: everything about their race, but I knew nothing, and I'd killed them without so much as the press of a touchscreen icon.

We'd been told they were evil, and that they would destroy us, but could we trust the hybrids or Delta after all they'd done to us?

"Dean, what the hell is going on down there?" Mary asked again, this time not so cordially.

"Mary, we're okay. It's done."

"What about Mae?" she asked.

I'd nearly forgotten about her. "Slate, are you okay?" I asked, moving to his slouched form.

He got up, dusting his uniform off. "I tripped on something, but no worse for the wear. Just a twisted ankle, and my arm's still tender. We have to find Mae, and quickly."

We entered the hall, stepping over the melted forms of the unarmored Bhlat, Slate hardly noticing them at all.

"I'll go left, you go the way we came," I said, taking

the lead.

Slate's large frame moved quickly down the hall as the sunken corridor lights flared red, alarms still blaring along the way. I tried to not look at the corpses spread around the floor. Some might have been children; most were unarmed.

"Mary, we're searching for Mae. Is her ship still docked?" I asked.

"She's still down there. Do you need assistance?" Mary asked through my earpiece.

We probably did, but the last thing I wanted was the doctor or my injured fiancée to be running around the outpost, looking for our missing hybrid.

"We got this. Whatever happens, don't let that ship get away."

"Affirmative," came the stiff reply.

The outpost had wide corridors, probably enough room for three of the large aliens to walk side by side, and the ceilings were at least ten feet. The sound of a sliding door down the hall caused my heart to race, and I slowly moved toward it, firmly holding my rifle. The door was closed, and I stepped forward, letting it slide open as I moved to the side, trying to catch a glimpse of what was inside. It looked like a classroom of some sort, but I didn't see anyone inside from that quick glance.

This time, I raised the rifle, moving through the entrance, spinning to the left and then to the right, before suddenly getting kicked in the knee as Mae came into view from the near corner of the room. My blaster went off, hitting the ground in a smoldering beam.

"Mae, listen," I tried to say before getting kicked in the stomach. I was down on the ground in an instant, knee aching and breath torn from my lungs.

"No, you listen." She kicked my gun away, stepping

on my hand. It pinned my fingers and palm against the cold hard metal grate floor. "I came here to help you. To tell them you were all gone, dead in the war with the Kraski. This would have bought you a few years. You could have moved to Proxima. But you came here and killed them!"

Anger coursed through me. So she did know them and had left us to meet with them. It all sounded like lies over lies, and if there was a truth left in the story, it was so convoluted and buried, it would be almost impossible to uncover.

"Mae, I believe you," I lied, hoping she would get off my pained hand. Her foot pressure lessened, and my training from Slate took over. I lifted her foot with all my strength, sending her small frame back a yard while I quickly got to my feet.

She wasn't holding a weapon, probably not expecting a fight when she'd landed on the Bhlat outpost. We both eyed my rifle on the ground a few feet away, and when she lunged for it, I made my move. I swung my leg toward her body, connecting to her side, sending her sprawling away. She still managed to grip the barrel of the rifle, and while she tried to turn it around at me, I covered the distance and grabbed the rifle as well. We struggled with each other, her back on the ground, me bent over her.

Her injuries had healed nicely. "We found out your injuries at the base on Earth were fake. How did you do it? Hit yourself with a two-by-four?"

"It was the only way to ensure you guys left. I didn't know where the base and ships were being held, and they would never tell a hybrid. I did it all for your kind. I did it for you." The last words hung in the air as we struggled for the weapon. She tried to kick out, but Slate had taught me how to prevent that when grappling. The wind was starting to lessen from her sails.

"For me?" Realization came over me. "If you lied about Leslie and Terrance, and needed to find the base… then… it was you." I couldn't believe it. I fought in my mind, looking at the face of my close friend Mae, the woman who wore my dead wife's expression as she started to cry. "You killed that guard Clendening and the other one in the garage." Images of Clendening, sticky red blood soaked into his bed, and the bloated face of the woman hanging in the office nearly caused me to vomit on Mae right there.

"I had to. It was the only way for you to focus on them. I knew they were making a move to get off-planet. I knew everything that happened at that damned prison in Long Island."

It all made sense. They just wanted to get to a ship to see if Kareem would take them in, and Mae used it against us, used our hatred of hybrids to fuel their capture, even though they wanted to get caught. They fed off each other, even if the pair hadn't known it.

"You had to kill them in cold blood?" I asked.

"The ends justify the means. Just look around down the hall at all the innocent Bhlat you killed. Or the race of Kraski you ended to protect your own. We've both done terrible things, Dean, but I did them for you."

She stopped struggling then, letting me take the rifle from her. She was right, but I still didn't put those in the same category. I supposed it was a matter of perspective.

Mae looked so small on the floor as I raised the pulse rifle. She was far from helpless.

"You killed those guards to perpetuate our hatred, so we would follow them when they escaped?"

She nodded.

"And then made us think they assaulted you as they escaped? Did you have anything to do with them getting out?"

She nodded again. "They didn't know it was me, though."

"What were you doing here? For real? Why not just tell us you knew them, and that you could help us? Didn't you trust us? Didn't you trust *me*?" I asked. Her eyes welled up with tears.

"You wouldn't have believed my story. I was turned by them years ago. I had so much anger, and nowhere to focus it. The Bhlat didn't ask for much. They offered me a place with them when it was all over, but they really just wanted information. The Kraski were just a nuisance to them, but they were intrigued by their cloning ability, and we hybrids were something of a legend to them. At first, I thought they would dissect me, or throw me in a lab, but they treated me with respect and honor. It was the first time anyone had shown me respect, knowing I was the hybrid of a dying race and a human. The whole mission sparked their interest." Mae slid over, sitting up so her back was against the wall.

"Go on," I said, gun still raised.

"I hated the Kraski."

They had wronged the hybrids, creating them to sacrifice themselves to convince humans to shut down the Deltra Shield, but there had to be more to the story.

"I feel like I'm missing something."

"You are, babycakes," she said, tears falling down her face. The pet name Janine had called me when we first started dating, but seemed to grow away from, hit me like a brick wall. Why had Janine's phrase for me been uttered by Mae?

Looking at her curled up in the dim room, hair in her

face, tears streaming down her cheeks, I suddenly understood. The pulse rifle fell from my hands, clanging on the ground. I knelt before the crying woman, my own eyes watering without control at that point.

"It's you," I said, hardly believing it.

She nodded.

"How?"

I was holding her wet face in my hand. "They were pissed at me for choosing you instead of that beefed-up military guy. They almost killed us both, but I convinced them I was right in choosing you. They let me stay with you that first year. You proposed, and it was so sweet. One day I went for a run, and they picked me up, told me I was being replaced, and that I was now named Mae. No one was to know. I met the other Janine, and they beat me when I wouldn't cooperate by telling them intel on you. I guess they had enough, because they gave her my clothes and sent my replacement back to you."

I slumped to the floor, looking at the real Janine sitting on the floor of an alien outpost so far away from home. The dream from the other day flashed in my mind, and I recalled that day. I remembered how strange Janine had been for a few months after that day, and how I'd let it go because she'd always seemed distant and brooding. Now it all made sense. I married another hybrid, lived with her for years. Watched her die. I had loved that woman too, and I honestly think a part of her had loved me, but Mae was the real one. The woman I'd met at the Boathouse in Central Park so long ago, drinking Scotch with me under the twinkle lights late into the night. Choosing me to help their cause over the other guy. My life would have been a lot simpler without that night. Maybe I'd be dead... maybe everyone would be.

It was too much to take as the alarms around us rang,

red lights flashing from the hall. "How is this possible?" I asked, slumping beside her on the floor.

Could we go back to Earth like this? How would we explain it to the others? How would I explain it to Mary?

"Dean, I'm sorry it all worked out like this. You can't imagine my thoughts when I saw you fly through that door on the vessel ship last year. It was a sign. It gave me renewed hope, and I kept telling myself that you would recognize me, that you would tell me you were in love with me still. But then you were with Mary, and I stepped back," she said. I thought of all the times Mae seemed down, in a dark mood, and it made even more sense.

I held her hand, squeezing her fingers just like I used to do, and she rested her head on my shoulder. I almost laughed at the insanity of it all. The woman I'd fallen in love with that night, so many years ago, wasn't the same woman I'd married and watched die. She was beside me on a remote outpost of an alien race we hardly even knew.

"Do the Bhlat know what happened?" I asked her.

"About the humans? I talked with them right as I got here, but they didn't communicate it out yet, as far as I know. They didn't have time."

"We go to the ship, blast this place to smithereens, go home, and pray they don't come for us."

"I don't think they will. It sounded like they were in the middle of a serious galactic battle out there, a long way away. They have a dozen outposts like this set up to ensure they keep the bloodlines intact, just in case." Mae seemed to know a lot about them. I looked at her, and suddenly found it hard to believe I hadn't known she was really Janine. My Janine.

"Are you ready?" I asked, getting to my feet.

"How is this going to work? Will they take me back?"

She took my hand and got up.

"We'll tell them what you told me. You were going to sacrifice yourself to go to their outpost to tell them there was no point in worrying about the humans. You knew we wouldn't go for it, so when you saw the opportunity, you took it." It seemed like the truth, at least the version she'd given me.

"And what about the other part?" The question came with a look I'd seen many times that first year with Janine. A cute, coy look.

I loved Mary, but this complicated things. Every bit of me knew I was going to marry her, but having my first real love nearby wasn't going to make travelling in close quarters an easy task.

"We tell her. It's only fair," I said. She didn't press me on my feelings, and I was thankful.

"Thank you, Dean."

"For what?"

"Just for being you." She moved to the door, and I was about to transmit to the ship that I had Mae with me, and we were coming back.

Mae took a step through the room's exit and into the hallway, taking the time to turn toward me and give me a small grin. Then she fell to the ground. My brain didn't understand what was happening until I saw the pulse rifle wound through her uniform, blood spilling down the metallic floor grates.

"No!" I yelled, grabbing my rifle from the ground.

"Target down. I repeat, target down." Slate's voice echoed from my earpiece and down the hall.

TWENTY-FOUR

"Nick, get your ass down here, stat," I called into my earpiece as I ran into the hallway. Kneeling at Mae's body, I checked for a pulse, and felt a light heartbeat.

"You okay, Dean?" Slate asked, setting a hand on my shoulder.

I swiped it off with an aggressive elbow. "You son of a bitch. You didn't have to shoot her!"

"What are you talking about? That was our mission. I saw the target and took her down."

I stood up, lifting my head to look up in the soldier's eyes. Grabbing his collar, I pushed him against the wall, which normally would have been impossible, but he seemed to let me.

"It was your mission, not mine! I never asked for any of this. I'm an accountant from a small upstate New York city!" I shoved him a few more times, and he stood there, allowing the barrage of yells and abuse.

Nick came running down the hall, a panicked look showing even through his helmet's face mask. It was one thing to green-beam down somewhere for the first time, but he walked into a place with melted aliens on the floors, a shot hybrid beside us, and me screaming at Slate.

He moved past us, going quickly into trained doctor mode, and opened Mae's uniform up, seeing the gaping wound in her stomach. He checked her pulse and looked up with wide eyes.

"I'm sorry. She's dead," he said, his voice small.

"She had a pulse. Revive her!" I yelled at him now.

He shook his head. "There's nothing I can do for this." His eyes went from me to the deadly wound.

Mary's voice came through my earpiece, and I couldn't even comprehend the words. I was surrounded by death once again, and by all accounts, there was no one to blame but myself.

★ ★

*'T'*m sorry, Dean." Mary sat on the edge of the bunk where I lay curled under the blankets. Two days had passed since the outpost adventure, and I still felt like a mess. Slowly the fog was lifting, and like anything, I knew the pain would eventually dull and pile on top of the rest of my life's memories, both good and bad.

I turned, looking her in the eyes. "Thank you." I had told her everything that transpired between me and Mae. She went on the emotional rollercoaster alongside me, as I talked then, and I was so happy she understood. We shared a bond; we had both married a hybrid and were in very similar mental states about it. Only she had never felt like Bob was truly in love with her, especially after learning the truth of their motives.

"We've downloaded everything from their computer databases that we could. I imagine we'll learn all we ever wanted to know about the Bhlat with it." Mary slid her uniform off and slipped into the bed with me. Her body was cool against my warm, blanket-covered chest.

"All the explosives are in place. We can blast them and erase all the evidence we were here. I don't see how they could track any of this back to us. Clare's good to bring the Kraski ship back?" I asked. We'd discussed blowing it up with the rest of the outpost, and their ships, but decided it was a valuable resource we shouldn't part with if possible.

Mary was face to face with me, her breath sweet and fresh as she spoke. "She is. Slate will go with her."

At the mention of the soldier, I closed my eyes, seeing Mae fall to the ground. I couldn't stop seeing it.

"That's good. Probably for the best," I said. "If we're here, who's setting the explosives off?"

As if on cue, Clare's voice came from the speakers on the wall. "Are you guys coming for the show?"

"Just video-record it. We're busy," Mary said, and we heard the line of communication close with a beep.

"We are?" I asked.

Instead of answering with words, her lips found mine, and soon I saw there were ways to find happiness still in the midst of so much loss.

"*A*nd how is Slate going to fly the ship by himself?" Mary asked Clare. We were standing on the bridge, all in uniform, even though I wished I could be wearing anything but the Earth Defense badge at that moment.

Clare shrugged. "He said he could handle it. I imagine he has some military stims or something. The ship does have somewhat of an autopilot when we're in FTL and not needed to maneuver. Plus, he's really cranky." Her eyes locked with mine for a brief moment before she looked back to Mary.

"What about Nick?" I asked.

"What about me?" the doctor asked back.

"Couldn't you go keep him company? It's only a couple of weeks," I said. As much anger as I felt at Slate for shooting Mae, I couldn't really blame him.

"Let's get through the first wormhole and convince him to take Nick or Clare on board." Mary's idea was a good one.

Mary sat at the helm and communicated over to Slate that we were leaving. Slate was already in the Kraski ship alone, having flown it into space before detonating the explosives below. I looked to the images where the Bhlat outpost once sat, and it was nothing more than rubble and small craters.

The wormhole wasn't far, so we didn't hop in FTL like we had to beat Mae only hours before. Only hours. I couldn't believe it. It felt like a week had passed since we'd approached the outpost. We all sat on the bridge, our task done, but somehow, I couldn't help but feel like we hadn't accomplished much. We'd found out what the hybrids were up to. I learned that Mae was the one to kill those guards in cold blood and realized that Mae was right. There was no coming back for her after that, unless we lied about it, and by doing that, we would have pinned it on Leslie and Terrance, who would never have their voices heard for the hybrids.

I wondered if President Dalhousie would let the hybrids leave. I hoped for their sake she would. They had been through so much. Created to deceive humans, then asked to sacrifice themselves and fly into the sun with vessels full of billions of us. Now we kept them in a cage, pretending everything was normal. It wasn't. If she didn't let them leave, I was going to make it happen.

"We're here," Mary said, slowly flying us to the wormhole.

"Wait, what is that? I asked, seeing a yellow icon appear on the map. It was nothing more than a glowing circle, moving quickly toward us.

"Slate, we have incoming," I said through the ship's comm-link.

"I see that, boss. I don't expect it to be a welcoming party. You guys head into the wormhole and stick to the plan. I'll hold them off." Slate's voice was grim.

"We can't do that. We've already lost one of our own." I wished I could take the words back as soon as I said them.

Mary zoomed on the approaching ship, and it matched the ones parked at the outpost. Probably a Bhlat ship on a supply run. They may have gone home to find everything gone, and now they would be seeking revenge.

"Just do it." Slate's ship veered off from our path to the wormhole as he attempted to take the Kraski ship away and lead the Bhlat with him. We were almost invisible to their eyes, but we didn't know much about their sensors. Since we'd been able to sneak onto their outpost without them knowing, we most likely would be safe hiding in plain sight from them.

"We have to help him!" Clare yelled.

I sat in the captain's chair, my head aching fiercely. We could just leave, go through the wormhole, and destroy it. If Slate survived, it would be a long trip home, but he would eventually make it. Years later.

If he survived.

"Dean, make the call," Mary said, and I was almost surprised they were waiting on me to decide a man's fate. As if I hadn't had enough of that already.

We were survivors. I wouldn't abandon the soldier. If I did, I was no better than our enemies.

"Follow them. We sneak up behind and give them a

show. The Bhlat won't know what hit them." I was done feeling sorry for them, or myself. I just wanted to get my friends home, and away from this new threat.

Nick paled to the right of me as Mary swung us around, racing after the two blinking icons on our map.

We could finally see them in the viewscreen as they darted around, Slate trying to lead them on a wild goose chase away from us.

"Slate, we're on their ass." I stood watching the boxier Bhlat ship fly after the sleek silver ship Slate was racing away in.

"You had your window to leave!" He sounded angry with us.

"Just work with us, and we can be on the other side of that wormhole in time for lunch," Mary said calmly.

I hopped to the console next to Mary and took control of the weapons. We hadn't tested the new ones yet, but Slate had gone over them with us a few times, and I'd done well in the training programs.

"Slate, slow down," Mary said. As soon as he did, yellow fire erupted from the Bhlat ship at him, narrowly missing him.

"They're hostile." I could almost hear his grin.

"You think?" I asked.

"Loop around behind us. I'm going to thrust facing up, and we'll blast the hell out of them." Mary had her Air Force persona on now.

Slate's ship did just that, and we saw him fly over our viewscreen, quickly followed by a firing Bhlat ship. It was my turn. I aimed, letting the computer calculate their trajectory, and then fired the pulse gun. Red beams shot out, one hitting the ship. It kept flying, the small explosion not slowing it.

"I think you angered them," Clare whispered as we

saw their volley of fire increase, and one hit the Kraski ship Slate was trying to maneuver.

"They know I'm not alone now," Slate said. "My shields handled that blast, but I don't think they can handle any more."

Their attention shifted toward our position, and though they couldn't see us, it didn't stop them from firing at will in our direction. Mary swept us away, avoiding the barrage.

"Wait for it," she said, spinning us around the hard-edged enemy ship. They were still firing, nearly hitting our ship. My eyes darted to the viewscreen, where I could see the icon of Slate coming up above them. He blasted a red rain of fire on them just as I shot a combination of the pulse guns and torpedo, Mary racing away to avoid any crossfire.

The Bhlat ship took the barrage, and for a split second, I thought they might have survived it, before they exploded, the flames quickly disappearing in the oxygen-deprived vacuum of space.

"Woohoo!" Nick shouted, jumping from his seat.

"Let's not celebrate too quickly. We need to get the hell out of here in case there's more of them around," I said.

"I agree," we heard from Slate on the comm-link, "and thanks for coming back for me."

"Anytime," I replied.

We made our way back to the wormhole, this time not lingering at it.

"Everyone belted in this time?" Mary asked. When no one answered, she moved us forward.

"Slate, see you on the other side." This from me.

"You got it, boss."

We were off, travelling through the fold once again.

We jostled around hard, but we were expecting it, and the trip didn't feel quite as bad. Moments later, we were through, Slate following closely behind. I breathed a sigh of relief.

"We know what we have to do," Clare said, keying in the locations of the sensors we'd found on the way the other way.

"Targeting," I said, seeing the crosshairs of the pulse gun over the zoomed in wormhole stabilizers. "Slate, let's blast this and get away."

"We have no idea what kind of reaction we're in for by destabilizing this. Best to err on the side of caution." Clare was right.

"Three, two, one." I fired two rounds, one after the other, and was rewarded with tiny twin explosions. Mary engaged the thrusters, and I changed the viewscreen to show the wormhole behind us. Flashes of light sparked inside it, and seconds later, it was gone. No explosion, no cataclysmic event, just vanished from space.

"That was anticlimactic," Mary said, grinning at me.

I got up, set my hands on her shoulders, and leaned down to talk into her ear. "We did it. Let's go home."

Home. A place in disarray, under threat of aliens and ourselves. I suddenly missed Carey very much, wishing the small wiggly dog was with us. Magnus would be taking great care of him, but who knew what happened to them? I couldn't wait to get back and see if there was word on their trip.

Mary leaned back, kissing me quickly.

"Home sounds good."

TWENTY-FIVE

"*W*ho's ready for my galaxy-famous egg skillet?" Nick asked.

"By galaxy-famous, you mean that mix of boxed egg whites and rehydrated potatoes?" Clare threw a sugar cube at him, which he deftly caught.

"Breakfast sounds amazing." Mary was in a good mood, and I found myself being so thankful for her around. Without her, I would be spiraling down an alley of despair. I was so in love with her, and what Mae had said didn't change that. But the fact the real Janine had been with me, ever since finding Mae on that lone vessel last year, had thrown me for a loop. I couldn't believe she was gone… again.

"Wait, if you're here, and I'm here, and…," I said, and it was my turn to take a sugar cube on the head.

"That joke was old last week," Mary said. We had the autopilot on and would be arriving at the first wormhole the next day.

"Do we shut it down?" Nick asked the question we'd been wondering since we started the trip home.

"If we do, the hybrids are going to have a hell of a trip to the planet Leslie and Terrance are on. If we don't, we leave a back door open into our solar system," I said. "My vote is leaving it, and letting the government make the call. They can get back out here to shut it down if they decide to."

"Slate agreed with that. He's a soldier who wants to follow orders, not make decisions. So that leaves us," Mary said.

"I vote leave it." This from Nick.

"Same." Clare poured another coffee and offered the pot to me. I extended my cup, letting her fill it up.

"I guess we are unanimous, the wormhole stays." Mary grabbed a plate of food from Nick, and we all seemed glad to be so close to returning.

So much had happened in the few weeks since we'd left. The universe was huge, and our part in it so small, but I was more thankful for what we had then ever.

"Where will you guys go when we get home?" I asked.

Clare fiddled with her food. "I'm going to go get a fat burger and a beer from this place in Albuquerque. It was open long before the Event, and my dad used to take us there when we'd visit our grandma every summer. I miss them all so much. So I go there, eat a burger, drink a beer, and remember my dad's laughter, and my brother whining about wanting no onions. I wish I could hear him whining about them again."

"I'll go with you. I have a great whining voice," Nick said, his joke cutting the tension at just the right time.

Clare looked at him solemnly, before bursting out in a loud laugh we hadn't heard from her before. Eggs spilled out of her mouth, and a snort or two followed, causing more laughter. Soon we were all red in the face, tears filling our eyes for no reason but happiness.

*E*arth was so close I could almost smell it.

I zoomed in and could finally see the planet in all its beautiful glory.

"Wait. What is that?" Mary asked, pointing to the viewscreen as we raced toward our home. We were all anxious to be back, to set foot on the green grass and take a deep breath of good old American air.

I looked where she was pointing and saw what she meant.

"It looks like a station." My heart jumped in my chest. Had Earth been invaded while we were gone?

"Slate, stay back for a moment. We can hide, but you can't."

"Affirmative, boss," he replied from the comm-link speaker. His icon slowed and pulled away, heading back the way we'd come from. "Be careful."

"Let's come around slowly," I suggested, and Mary nodded along.

The minutes went by slowly, none of us speaking for fear we would jinx something. Maybe if we blinked, the station would be gone, and everything would be back to normal when we landed. Instead, we saw the picture more clearly the nearer we got.

It was a space station of an intricate design. Ships much like ours hovered nearby, their cloaking not activated. No one seemed to be frantic, so it didn't seem like a battle was happening.

"What's happening?" Clare stood at the front of the bridge, touching the viewscreen with her right palm.

"Something tells me they've made some changes," I said.

"In two months?" she retorted.

"What do we do?" Mary asked.

Before I could suggest anything, our radio silence ended. "Identify yourselves, unmarked cloaked ship." The voice was tense, but in English, and not alien. That was a good sign.

"What's going on? Can we speak with Dalhousie?" I asked, trying to add authority to my voice.

"Dalhousie? I repeat, identify yourselves." The voice was getting angrier.

"We're members of the Earth Defense Unit. Dean Parker here."

Silence greeted us from the other end of the comm. Mary looked at me and I just shrugged.

"Did you say Dean Parker? What kind of BS is this?" a different voice asked.

"This isn't bull. I'm Dean Parker, we were sent on a mission by General Heart just before they left. We're back."

"That's impossible," the voice said. "You'd better come and dock. We need to talk. Ask for Chen."

"Do we trust this?" I asked, hoping Mary would have a gut feeling about it.

"What choice do we have? Leave?" she asked. Clare's eyes widened at this.

"Slate, we're going to find out what's happening. It looks like the station is Earth's. You want to join us?" I asked.

"Be right there, boss."

We waited for him to arrive, and we disengaged our cloaking tech. Together we flew toward the large station, and instructions for docking were sent to our consoles. Things had changed here. But how had they done it so fast?

The station's outer ring was circular, and not far off the design of the Deltra one we'd first seen the Bhlat on a few weeks ago. The same type of wheel was spinning, and that meant gravity. In the center of it were three huge uniform sections, channels leading between them. This place was bigger than I'd thought when we first laid eyes on it, at least four times the size of the Deltra station.

Behind, or underneath, depending on your perspective, a large hangar sat, a one-way force field letting us in but maintaining pressure. It was quite the feat. A dozen ships like ours sat there, empty.

"Dean, my gut's telling me something's wrong," Mary whispered in my ear. I glanced at Nick, who was staring out the viewscreen with his jaw dropped just enough to look comical.

"We'll soon find out."

It had been quite some time since we'd used the ramp to walk off the ship, and my legs were anxious to be off the moving vessel. I led the way toward the storage area, hitting the ramp trigger, and it lowered to reveal two men in a uniform not too far from ours. If ours was an Earth Defense uniform, these were the two-point-oh version. Where ours were gray, they wore black, with a new logo featuring a blue planet, *EDU* stitched underneath.

I raised an eyebrow to Mary and she looked down at our uniforms, me feeling a little out of place suddenly.

The two guards were young, one man and one woman. We walked down the metal ramp, and they stood there watching us with wide eyes.

"It *is* you," the brown-haired man said, hardly audible in the large hangar.

"And you're you." I stuck my hand out, shaking both of theirs, one after the other. The rest of our group followed suit, and we learned these two were Haley and Devon.

"The Hero of Earth. I had your poster on my wall,"

Devon said.

Poster? "Wait, what?" I stammered.

Slate's ship settled down across the hangar, and he beamed out of it. Quite the show. His long strides allowed him to cross the distance quickly.

He smiled at the others, the girls hugging the big guy, and Nick gave him a playful punch in the shoulder. He didn't look me in the eyes, but he said, "I'm sorry, boss."

I turned to stand right in front of him. "I don't blame you for anything. Let's see what all this is about."

"General Chen wants to see you. Follow us," Haley said, turning on her heel to walk us away from the hangar.

Nick and Clare walked just behind Mary and me, Slate bringing up the rear. Soon we left through a large doorway and were in a hall with what looked like polished concrete floors and composite walls. Definitely more style to it than the Deltra station we'd seen.

Other uniformed people walked by, some ignoring us, some openly staring. I just smiled at them all, wondering what the hell was going on.

"Right this way," Devon said, his arm suggesting we walk into a room without him.

"Thanks, you two," Mary said to the young guards.

We stepped forward, the doors sliding to the side with a soft hiss. The room we entered was a large office, and an older man sat behind a black marble table in the middle of the space, chairs placed all around with room to seat twenty or so.

He motioned us in, standing up and walking toward us with a big smile across his lined face. "If someone had told me the five of you would be showing up on my doorstep, I'd have bet my life it would never happen. Shows what I know."

"Who are you?" I asked, apparently breaching some

protocol, judging by his surprise at my question.

He looked serious, then started to laugh. "I'm General Chen. William Chen. I suppose you're curious just why we have a station here, and how so much has changed since you left."

"What we don't understand is how you did all of this in such a short period of time," Clare said.

He laughed again. "Yes, I suppose seven years is a quick turnaround to build this, but with the new technology, and the world working together for it, we had it operational in five."

My stomach flipped. The room was suddenly far too warm as my pulse raced. Deep breath, deep breath. Clare flopped onto a chair, her face drooping, tears falling down her face. Slate stood as stone-faced as his namesake, and Mary looked far too calm as well. Nick just seemed confused by it.

"Are you telling us we've been gone for *seven years?*" Nick asked, sliding into the seat beside Clare and putting an arm around her shoulders.

"That's right. We have a lot to discuss. What of the hybrids?" he asked, and finally looked around as if realizing someone was missing. "Mae?"

I shook my head, to which he nodded, understanding what I meant by that.

"Before we get into this, what's happening down there? Are we under any new threats?" Mary took over.

"None we haven't faced before. Watch." He hit a button on the table and a projector lowered, flashing a video on the white wall at the left end of the room. He motioned for us to have a seat; someone came in, bringing waters and coffee. It was like being at a meeting with one of my larger clients. If a bar graph showing projected sales had been brought out on a slideshow, I wouldn't have been surprised.

I took a sip of black coffee while the video started. It was news coverage, dated at the bottom. Within six months of us leaving, and the colony ship with Magnus, Nat, and Carey also gone, the world was in turmoil. China teamed up with the US and other world powers, and they forced a treaty on the rest of the world. Most joined without complaint. Others fought it. Images of the dead in the Middle East flashed on the screen, and I watched, not letting myself look away. In the meantime, a second wave of colonists was sent, about a million in total.

Two years later, the world was in a much better place, though still assaulted by the odd threat or bombing. Eventually, they became less and less, the penalties harsh to anyone not playing their part in world peace. We saw a speech by Dalhousie five years after we left, saying anyone could go to Proxima with the third wave, which would be a whole fleet of vessels if needed. She looked older than she had, tired. Her voice had lost the lift and hope, but her eyes still shone with pride.

The newscast showed us two dozen vessels leaving; over half of Earth's remaining population was heading for Proxima, which they were touting as Eden. Images of Eden overtook the screen and I was leaning so far forward, I nearly slipped off my chair. It was gorgeous. Lush grass covered rolling hills alongside crystal-clear lakes.

Mary reached over and grabbed my hand, squeezing it.

We saw the creation of the station, where exploratory ships docked and new technology was tested in space. It was a massive undertaking, and more than impressive in its vast scope.

A priest was interviewed in one segment, spouting out some new religion. It was a little off-putting, but he appeared to have a lot of support. A camera flew over fields all over the world, showing healthy crops. Stats of world hunger being under one percent crossed the screen. Poverty didn't exist, everyone had access to clean water, and illness was way down.

"This is amazing," Nick said, eyes gleaming as they showed some state-of-the-art hospitals around the world.

"No sign of the Bhlat?" I asked, looking for a reaction from Chen. He sloughed off the question with a wave of his hand, and I didn't like that one bit.

"I still can't believe you're all here."

A mural panned onto the screen, a reporter interviewing people on the anniversary of the Event. People were crying, remembering their losses. The mural was of Magnus, Natalia, Mary, and me. Of course, they'd left out the hybrid that helped us.

Then they talked about losing us on our wild goose chase of Leslie and Terrance. It was surreal to see people speculate on what had happened to us, and then debate on the value of us even going on that journey.

It was a barrage of information for missing seven years, but for the most part, I was impressed with the state of our new world. I was also happy to know the colony was doing well. Seven years. My pup Carey might not even be with us any longer, and if he was, he was an old man. I'd only had him for a year but felt like part of me was intertwined with him. That I lost that time to spend with him was heartbreaking.

"Do we have contact with the colony?" I asked.

"It takes about a month to relay the messages."

I nodded, accepting this as reality.

"What do you think?" Chen asked, a glimmer in his eyes.

"I can't wait to see one of those hospitals! You really

found a way to reverse cancer cells?" Nick was almost dancing in excitement beside the table.

"They did. Once we dug deeper, we found so many things the Kraski didn't even seem to think important any longer," Chen said.

"Is Dalhousie still here?" I asked.

He shook his head slowly, before taking a sip of his coffee. "She left to New Spero, in Proxima, with the last wave of colonists. We have an elected world government. Valerie Naidoo from South Africa is in charge. World President Naidoo, if you will. Speaking of which, she'd like to have a meeting with all of you."

Mary smiled at this, and I appreciated the forward evolution we'd taken. Leading this healing planet would be a lot of work, but they finally had the mindset and resources to do it.

"Now what can you tell me about your adventures?" Chen asked.

I started in on our planned story. Meanwhile, our ship was translating the data we'd found on the Bhlat outpost.

TWENTY-SIX

The wheat fields stretched for miles in the remote South African meeting place. As we'd lowered to the Earth, I couldn't help but feel how different it was on our planet. The air felt cleaner, and even though our technology had vastly improved, there was something that made me feel like we'd stepped back into a simpler time. Food, shelter, happiness for everyone. It was a mantra I could get behind. I looked and made sure Nick had the ring I'd brought along on his finger, turned inward so the green gem wasn't visible. Slate had an earring on him, though I couldn't see it. Clare was staying in the ship.

"Quite the place," Mary said as she landed the ship on a dirt pad. A building stood a short way away, and three Jeeps sat parked beside it. "You sure all this is necessary?"

"Looks like this is a low-key meeting. We're survivors, and we didn't make it this far by being naïve."

Mary rolled her eyes at that. "Well, maybe at first we were a little naïve." My pointer and thumb separated about an inch, and she laughed at this.

"Watch your backs," Slate said, giving us a hard look.

"Don't be so paranoid, we'll be fine," Nick said, clapping him on the shoulder.

The air was warm… dry.

"Greetings, heroes." A woman waved to us from the building's front door. I recognized her from the pictures

Chen had shown us: hair cut short, smooth skin showing a youthful strong woman leading the world.

Mary waved back, and we crossed the space. Guards became visible.

"Beautiful earrings," I said to Mary. "They look as fetching as ever." She laughed it off, never quite agreeing with my over-concern, but still playing along. My own green pendant sat against my chest, cool in the heat.

Before we were in earshot, I tapped my earpiece. "Clare, be ready on my mark. If this goes south, and my instincts are leaning that way, execute the plan."

"Done. I just hope you're wrong," she replied.

I patted my breast pocket, feeling a small circular lump sitting over my heart.

The guards weren't wearing the EDU uniforms we'd seen in the station above Earth. Instead, they were more classic military. They had strange-looking semi-automatics, which I imagined had both bullets and pulse power behind them. I smiled at them and got no expression in return.

"We're so glad to have you here," the World President said, sticking her hand out to shake ours. Mary shook it first and said some pleasantry or another. I didn't quite hear it as I scoped out the area. A tower a few hundred yards away looked to be housing another guard.

When it was my turn to shake, I was surprised by the sweaty palm I found. I just smiled. "It's a real pleasure to meet the woman who controls it all."

"Oh, I don't control much, but I facilitate our leaders, and it's been working well so far. Please, come in." She had a slight accent; probably grew up in a South African private school.

The building was squat and square, most likely built just for this type of off-the-radar clandestine meeting.

The inside was plain, a large room with what appeared to be a couple of offices and bunk rooms at the far end, washrooms to the right.

"Can we get you anything?" she asked, glancing at Mary's ears.

I pointed up. "Chen took good care of us up there."

"Of course. General Chen is nothing but the best we have. He takes great pride in that station, and I don't blame him." She stood straight, poised.

"You wanted to see us?" Mary asked.

"Yes. You're heroes, and Heart sent you away on some mission seven years ago. Everyone on this planet wanted to know what happened to you, and here you are. It's a miracle."

"Look, if you need us to do a press conference or something, I think we're done with that sort of thing," I said.

She waved her hand in a dismissive gesture. "Don't be silly. We just want to know what happened to you."

"Apparently, flying through wormholes that take you thousands of light years away causes some time loss. Who'd have known?" I tried to laugh it off, but her face took a serious tone. "All this time, and no word from these Bhlat, huh? Thank God, because they look like some bad dudes."

This got her attention. "Look?"

"Yeah, they're huge. Big square ships, thick body armor." I puffed up my chest in a display of size, and Slate grinned at me.

Her eyes moved to my chest. "No, we haven't had word from them."

"Really? That's not what Chen tells me."

She gave it away right then. My instincts paid off. "He doesn't know what he's talking about. If they've contacted us, I know nothing of it."

But guards were already coming into the room, pulse rifles held up to their chests.

"Don't make a deal with them. They're not friendly. We have a drive with information from an outpost database. They've mined over one hundred planets, on sixty-three of which they either enslaved or killed entire races. The Kraski were one of the smarter ones, and they got away before the big fight." We'd learned a lot, since we'd told Chen a mostly made-up story of our trip.

"Never mind. Give me the drive, and give me that," she said, pointing to my pocket. If she knew what it was, she had been speaking to them for sure, but how had that information made its way to her already? Unless they had some schematics of a similar weapon on one of the few Deltra ships, or from a turned hybrid. In my mind's eye, I saw someone with Bob's face hanging from chains on a wall as the details were ripped from him at the same time as his skin.

The guards were getting closer, and we backed away. "We aren't here to cause any trouble. Just hear us out. You can't negotiate with them. The facts are there."

"Do you think I got to be the president of Earth by being stupid? I'll make the decision that is best for myself, and for humanity, and if that means cutting a deal with an alien race, then so be it."

"Fine, here it is." I tossed the device at her, and she let it slip from her fingers, the metal circle clanging to the floor.

I tapped my earpiece as the guards raised their rifles. "Clare, now!" I called, and the building shook as our ship hovered over it. Green beams entered the building, lifting the five guards and Naidoo. As Clare flew the ship away, they lifted in the beam, and I saw the guard in the tower looking on in confusion as we ran outside. He didn't know what to do and knew his firing at the ship would be fruitless.

"Dropping them," Clare said in my earpiece. Half a mile away, we saw the beam turn off, and the ship rushed back to us. The ramp was lowering even before the ship stopped, and we jumped the three feet up onto the metal grate, letting it shut once all four of us were inside.

"What a rush!" Nick said.

"I would have preferred to overthrow that woman," Slate said matter-of-factly.

"This isn't our world any longer," I said, feeling it through and through.

"Were they going to kill us?" Nick asked.

I didn't know, but the chances were high. Naidoo might have even used us as bargaining chips in her negotiation.

"It doesn't matter. I'm sorry, guys, but we can't stay here." Mary walked the closed ramp, and into the storage area.

We made our way to the bridge, where Clare greeted us with a big smile. "Oh my God, that was exciting!"

"More like terrifying. We could have died. It was awesome." Nick was turning into a regular adrenaline junkie.

I flipped the viewscreen to show behind us as we raced away through the atmosphere and kept going. No ships followed us that we could see, and I flipped on the cloaking from the console. "Slate, thank God you knew about that jamming signal unit in our supplies." I checked and found the real Delta device where I'd left it on the bridge. The one I'd left down there was comprised of spare parts from the engineering room,

"Yeah, should be a while before they realize why their radio communication isn't working," he laughed.

We bristled with hope and energy, but quickly grew sober at the ramifications. Earth housed just under two billion people, and they were all under a direct threat now.

"What are we going to do?" Clare asked, the jovial moment over.

"We go home," Mary said, holding my hand, "to our new world."

"Set course for New Spero," I said. We'd survived another day.

ABOUT THE AUTHOR

Nathan Hystad is an author from Sherwood Park, Alberta, Canada. When he isn't writing novels, he's running a small publishing company, Woodbridge Press.

Keep up to date with his new releases by signing up for his newsletter at www.nathanhystad.com

Sign up at www.scifiexplorations.com as well for amazing deals and new releases from today's best indie science fiction authors.

Destinational pet LLc

2218 - 2220   18th st NW

Washington D.C 20009

H GR Retail

A member of chainlink

Adviser

Made in the USA
Coppell, TX
27 December 2022